CHOICES & CHANGES

K.L. Belanger

Dreamspinner Press

Published by
Dreamspinner Press
5032 Capital Circle SW
Ste 2, PMB# 279
Tallahassee, FL 32305-7886
USA
http://www.dreamspinnerpress.com/

Choices and Changes
Copyright © 2013 by K.L. Belanger

Cover Art by Aaron Anderson
aaronbydesign55@gmail.com

ISBN: 978-1-62380-345-2
Digital ISBN: 978-1-62380-346-9

Printed in the United States of America
First Edition
February 2013

CHAPTER
ONE

IT WAS only 8:00 a.m. and already it was shaping up to be the worst day of Bo Sanford's life. Oh, not the kind where your girlfriend dumps you and your car gets repossessed and you find out you have a terminal illness all in the same twenty-four-hour period: that would be too easy. This kind of day was almost worse. At least on the truly awful days you might get some sympathy. On this kind of day, everything you touch goes wrong from sunup 'til sundown.

And nobody gives a damn.

It started even before he left his bedroom that morning, when the zipper on his favorite pair of work pants broke and he'd had to fish another pair out of the dirty laundry. When he got to the kitchen, he found he was out of both Froot Loops and Cocoa Puffs, and the milk he'd sworn he'd bought just last weekend turned out to be three days past the expiration date. He broke one of the laces on his steel-toed boot, spent ten minutes looking for his keys and another five hunting for his work gloves, and he couldn't even find his raincoat or an umbrella or even a stupid piece of cardboard to hold over his head and had to sprint through the rainy parking lot before climbing into his beat-up pickup truck.

Not that the cop who pulled him over ten minutes later cared about any of that. Bo knew people from Massachusetts had a reputation for bad driving, but not Bo. He was always careful behind the wheel. Even now when he was running late, he still hadn't been speeding. And he certainly wasn't drunk. He just had a busted taillight. A taillight that shouldn't even be busted because he'd just had the truck inspected two damn days ago.

But busted it was, and so was Bo.

Not just for the light but for failing to wear his glasses while driving.

It wasn't that he didn't know he was supposed to wear the stupid things, but he hated them. They made him look like a geek, or worse, some kind of rainforest bug that all those overeducated "Save the Planet" types were always studying. More to the point, they made the protective glasses he was required to wear on the job site even more uncomfortable.

But there was little he could do about any of it, and after accepting the painfully large ticket and the stern lecture that accompanied it, Bo finally pulled up in front of his best friend and coworker Mac's house and tooted the horn.

Mac came running out, lunch pail—no doubt packed by his mother, whom he still lived with—in hand, the hood of his raincoat pulled up over his curly hair.

"Where the hell have you been?" he demanded as he slammed the door and Bo backed out of the driveway. "If the Boss Man finds out I was late again, he's going to chew my ass down to nothing."

Though technically speaking, Bo was the foreman on this particular job, both men knew Mac wasn't referring to him. He was speaking of Bo's father—Bill "the Boss Man" Sanford—owner and operator of Sanford and Sons Construction, for whom they had both worked since graduating high school. A man who ruled his employees—and his sons—with an iron fist, a lead boot, and one steely eye permanently fixed on the bottom line.

"If you'd get that heap of a car of yours fixed, I wouldn't have to pick you up all the time," Bo retorted, irritably tapping his fingers on the steering wheel as he fumed at a red light.

"Hey, don't talk that way about Bessie," Mac protested, speaking of his 1985 Crown Victoria—a car that spent more time in the repair shop than it did in Mac's mother's garage. "She's a classic."

"Yeah, right. A classic piece of shit."

Bantering back and forth in this way with Mac soothed some of Bo's frazzled nerves, and he had just began to hope that his day might be looking up when he pulled up to the building his crew was currently rehabbing and saw his father's new black Ford F-150 parked next to the trailer they used for an office.

"Shit."

The only time the Boss Man left his cushy downtown office for the less comfortable accommodations on the job site was when there was trouble brewing.

"Damn it! I knew it." Mac jammed his hard hat on his head and hopped out of the truck, saying, "Punch me in, will you?"

Before Bo could respond that doing so under the watchful eye of his father would be next to impossible, Mac was already gone and Bo had no other option but to get out of the truck and continue on with his day and hope things got better.

UNFORTUNATELY, they never did.

No sooner had his father finished reaming him out for being a day and a half behind schedule—even though the old man had been the one who had ordered the wrong size windows in the first place—than the main generator decided to die on them, a problem that took Bo most of the day to resolve. Then one of the nail guns went on the fritz, the molding for the fourth-floor lobby arrived two feet short, and three of his crew members unwisely ordered their lunch from the roach coach that stopped by every day at noon and by two thirty were vomiting up their toenails. Finally, his best framing guy smashed his thumb with a hammer and had to go to the hospital, leaving the fourth-floor work crew one man short and Bo with a ten-page incident report to fill out.

By the time he had finished the paperwork and locked the door to the office, all Bo wanted to do was go home, lie on his couch, and watch some mindless action movie, preferably one in which a great number of things blew up.

The last thing he wanted to do was go to a keg party thrown by a bunch of college kids, most of whom hadn't worked a day in their lives.

"Come on, dude. It'll be fun," Mac said at Bo's apartment that evening, even as Bo tugged his sweaty T-shirt off over his head and tossed it onto his bedroom floor. He wasn't the type to work out, at least not at a gym, but years of work on construction sites had given him a body that generally got the job done.

Both on and off the work site.

Not that any girl had seen it in a while. He'd been so busy with his promotion to foreman and helping his brother Ham remodel his house, he'd had little time or energy for female company. Even the lure of potentially ending his dry spell wasn't enough to make him want to go any farther than his living room tonight.

"Forget it, Mac." Bo shucked his filthy pants and tossed them aside as well.

He knew he should at least toss all the dirty clothes into the same pile, but what did it matter, really? He'd get around to doing his laundry… someday.

If he got desperate enough, he could always stop by Mac's house and raid his closet, seeing as, despite her son's age, Mac's mother still did *his* laundry.

"But it's Friday night."

"So…?"

"So… give me one good reason why I should let you stay home on a Friday night."

"I'll give you four good reasons," Bo said. "I'm sore. I'm tired. I'm in a crappy mood. And I'm staying home."

"That's only three reasons and one lame-ass statement. Besides, you've been home every night this week. It will be good for you to get out for a while. Change the scenery a little."

"I said no, Mac."

After stretching to work the kinks out of his back, Bo stepped into the bathroom and shut the door in his disappointed friend's face. Stripping off his last remaining garment, Bo turned the hot water up as high as it would go, stepped into the tub, and resting his hands on the shower wall, let the water pour over him. The heat felt good against his tired muscles and he stayed in a bit longer than necessary, but when he reappeared, a towel hanging low around his hips, Mac was still there.

Bo hadn't bothered to hope otherwise.

"Think about it," Mac said as if there had been no interruption in the conversation. "We can drink a few beers, pick up a couple of girls, and maybe even end up with a little female company for breakfast. Sounds great, right?"

"Yeah, it does sound great." Dropping the towel, Bo rummaged around for a clean pair of boxers and sniffed a couple of T-shirts. After donning both, he tugged on the rattiest pair of jeans he owned, zipped his fly, then sat on the edge of the unmade bed to put on his socks. "Except that's not what's going to happen."

"What's that supposed to mean?"

"It means that if we go to that party tonight, all that's going to happen is we're going to drink cheap beer, waste our time hitting on girls who look down on us because we swing a hammer for a living, and round out the evening with me driving you home while you puke all over my truck."

"That's only happened twice," Mac pointed out.

"Three times," Bo corrected and rose, crossing to the mirror to comb his hair. He kept it short—less to bother with that way—but it grew quickly and he could tell he was due for a trim. "And that's only because I started carrying an empty bucket in the backseat."

"Well, there, you see? Problem solved."

Bo shot him a look that would have made most other guys back down. But he and Mac had been friends since middle school and it was tough to intimidate someone who had known you when you were four feet tall and had a mouthful of braces and a face full of zits.

"Look at it this way," Mac continued. "Maybe we'll both get lucky and you won't have to drive me home at all."

"If we both get lucky—which would be a miracle—all that's going to change is that I'm going have to get up tomorrow morning—with what will most likely be a massive hangover—and get rid of *my* female company so I can go pick you up and bring you home so your mother doesn't find out you've been lying to her about all those sleepovers you've been having at my house ever since we were seventeen and you were banging Pam Foster on her living room couch while her mother worked nights."

"Now that's a low blow. True! But low." Like a faithful basset hound, Mac retrieved Bo's sneakers from under a chair, trotted back, and handed them to him. "Now put these on and get your ass moving."

Sighing wearily, Bo sat on the edge of the bed again, but rather than put the shoes on, he held them in his big hands. "Seriously, Mac. Don't you ever get tired of this?"

"Tired of what?"

"All of it. Working your ass off all week, then partying it off every weekend? Sucking down weak beer or knocking back killer shots, then rolling around in the sheets with some girl whose name you learn one night and forget the next? Don't you ever want more than that?"

"Dude, we're twenty-five. What more is there?"

"We're not twenty-five yet," Bo said firmly. He didn't usually make a big deal about birthdays, but for some reason this one had him a little freaked out. "I've still got three more months to be twenty-four."

"Twenty-four, twenty-five, what's the diff? We're still young enough to have a life." Catching Bo's glare, Mac sobered as well. "Look, I hear what you're saying, okay? I don't get it. But I hear it. But how do you expect to meet anyone if you never go out?"

"It's not the 'going out' that's the problem," Bo argued. "It's where we go. Frat houses? College parties? Getting snubbed by snobby rich kids? Having to check a girl's ID just to make sure she's legal before you take her home? It's boring. Just once I'd like to go somewhere where I can hear myself think and have a conversation with someone that doesn't include how many shots she can do in an hour without passing out."

"All right. Fine. Next time, we'll visit the old folks' home. But tonight, my friend, tonight is our night." Mac plucked the shoes from Bo's hands, dropped them at his feet, and clapped him on the shoulder. "Tonight—we're young. We're virile. We need to get laid." That teased a small smile out of Bo. "Now quit your bitching, put your shoes on, and let's go already."

Bo only sighed. He'd known from the beginning he was going to cave. He always did. All his life he had taken the easy road, the path of least resistance. So he supposed he shouldn't complain about where it had gotten him.

Even if it was nowhere.

After shoving his feet into his sneakers, he rose, saying, "All right. I'll go. But, I swear, if you puke in my truck again, I'm leaving you on the side of the road somewhere, like an unwanted puppy."

WHEN the two men arrived at the party, the place was already rocking. Literally. In fact, Bo would have sworn the whole house was shaking from the volume of the music coming from inside. And judging from the general condition of the outside, he could only hope the weight of all those people wouldn't bring the whole thing down on top of them. Unlike the Wicked Witch of the East, having a house fall on top of him was not the way Bo wanted to go.

It would be like Michelangelo being crushed beneath a block of marble.

Still… the rain had gone and it was a nice night for so early in March, especially in New England, so a few people were still lingering outside, but instead of joining them, Bo followed Mac in the front door. Just inside, tucked in a little room off the living room, they saw a daybed where it seemed others had tossed their jackets.

Unfortunately, the couple currently sitting on the end of said bed were making out so heavily it seemed clear—at least to Bo—that in a very short while several of those coats would be harboring a few sticky substances.

Bo chose to keep his on as he followed Mac into the fray.

The living room, such as it was, was wall-to-wall people. Even without the neon sign pointing the way, it was easy to find the bar, if you could call a table made out of half a sheet of plywood and a couple of sawhorses a bar. But it did support a huge bowl of punch that looked as lethal as nuclear waste and two half kegs of beer sitting in a pair of pink plastic tubs filled with ice.

Between the kegs was a hand-lettered sign reading "Green cups $2.00/beer—Red cups $20/unlimited refills." Considering the kind of day Bo had had, he chose the twenty-dollar option, and after stuffing the money in the coffee can set there for the purpose, filled his cup to the brim and downed the whole thing in one gulp.

Like medicine.

"Jeez, dude, slow down," Mac said, even as Bo refilled his cup. "We haven't even checked out the action yet."

Bo was tempted to say the only action he wanted to check out was a comfortable chair in a quiet corner, preferably somewhere where no one would throw up on him.

Then he saw her.

Or a glimpse of her, anyway. She was standing in the middle of a group of five or six girls in what passed for the kitchen in this tumbledown wreck. They all seemed to be laughing at something, and even without seeing her full face, Bo could tell she had an amazing smile. Then the crowd shifted a bit and he could see more of her. The strong profile, the shaggy blonde hair, the pink shirt she wore with a matching scarf wrapped casually around her neck. She was beautiful.

Not the type of girl he usually went for. Usually he liked bigger girls, ones with lots of hair and curvy figures, but something about her intrigued him. Maybe it was simply his reaction to her. He'd never felt such an instant attraction to someone before. As if there was no one in the room but her. And when she threw back her head and laughed, Bo felt his heart begin to race.

Like a parched man stumbling toward a promising oasis, he started to cross the room but found his way blocked by several guys intent on reaching the bar. Bo sidestepped, desperate not to lose sight of her, and ended up bumping into yet another guy, spilling beer down his leg.

"Jeez, man, watch where you're going."

"Sorry," Bo said automatically but didn't take his eyes off the girl. He was afraid if he glanced away, even for a second, she would disappear like a mirage.

Another group of guys made their way past, again blocking his view, and Bo jogged to the side, trying to regain sight of her.

"Earth to Bo," he heard Mac say, and realized he'd been calling his name for a while. Bo ignored him, fixated on finding the girl. To his relief, when the way was clear again, she was still there, and he started to move forward.

Mac grabbed his arm. "Hey, what's the matter with you? You look like you've seen a ghost or something."

"It's that girl over there," Bo said reverently.

Mac peered around, trying to see everywhere at once. "What girl? Where?"

"In the kitchen."

Mac stood on his toes and craned his neck, trying to see around the crowd. "Which one is she?"

Bo's mouth was so dry he had to lick his lips to get the words out. "The blonde."

"Dude, they're all blonde."

Really? Bo hadn't noticed. He'd only seen her.

"The one in the pink shirt." Out of the corner of one eye, Bo caught Mac's look of confusion. "The pretty one. With the scarf around her neck."

Bo was finally shaken out of his trance when Mac burst out laughing, and when he turned to look, Mac was all but bent double with mirth.

"What? What's so funny?"

Between spasms, Mac managed, "Dude, that's not a girl. It's a guy."

"What?" Bo turned his head to look at the girl again. "No, it's not."

"Yeah, it is." Still laughing, Mac slapped Bo on the back. "That cop was right, buddy, you really do have to start wearing your glasses. Either that or get your hormones checked. In the meantime, I'm going to get another beer and find some real girls to talk to."

Mac walked off, still laughing, but Bo just stood there, staring. Now that he looked more closely he supposed it could be a guy... maybe. Surrounded as she—or he—was, he couldn't see any details of the body except to note that whoever it was was slightly built, but there was something so essentially graceful about the way the person held him or herself that Bo couldn't believe it wasn't a girl.

Unfortunately, before Bo could make up his mind, the object of his scrutiny turned, and when their eyes met, instantly Bo knew Mac had been right. It was a guy. One with eyes the color of freshly mown grass and a pair of full, curvy lips that might have been carved by a master craftsman. For a timeless moment, the two stared into each other's eyes, and though the connection made Bo uncomfortable, he couldn't seem to look away.

Then the guy touched the arm of the girl standing next to him, as if to excuse himself, and began to walk straight toward Bo.

To his own humiliation, Bo didn't bother to wait or try to explain.

He turned and ran.

CHAPTER
TWO

EVENTUALLY Bo's heart rate returned to normal, but he couldn't seem to shake the feeling of embarrassment. He knew he shouldn't let it get to him. So he'd made a mistake. Big deal. It happened. It was over. Time to move on.

More easily said than done, however.

It was just… for those few brief moments, he'd been so sure he'd seen "the one"—the girl of his dreams—that the disappointment was intense. As was the humiliation. Not to mention a couple of other uncomfortable emotions he was having trouble identifying. So rather than try, he simply pushed them all to the side and concentrated on getting drunk enough not to feel anything at all.

But no matter how much he drank, he couldn't quite get to that point and the frustration was driving him crazy. He wanted to hit something or break something, if only to release the tension, but he knew the momentary relief he would find wouldn't be worth the guilt he'd feel tomorrow.

Still… he knew himself well enough to recognize his own dangerous mood and so he took what he promised himself would be his last beer out onto the deck and settled down on one of the steps to enjoy the relative peace and quiet.

He had almost finished his drink when someone behind him said, "So… is this a solo pity party or can anyone join in?"

When Bo turned and looked up, he saw the source of his foul mood smiling cheerfully down at him. "Oh, great!" he snapped. "This is just friggin' perfect. A crappy end to a crappy day!"

The guy just cocked his head. "Would that be a 'yes' or a 'no'?"

Because he knew the guy had done nothing to deserve his temper, Bo gentled his tone.

"Look, I'm sorry if I gave you the wrong impression earlier, but I'm not into guys, okay? So... thanks but no thanks."

Still sounding pleasant, the guy said, "Well... setting aside for the moment your prejudiced, if correct, assumption that I'm gay, and your arrogant, if understandable, presumption that, being gay, I would necessarily find *you* attractive enough to follow you out here, how about if I just say 'I come in peace.'" He lofted a six-pack. "Bearing gifts."

The guy had guts. Bo had to give him that. After all, Bo had a good six inches and well over eighty pounds on him. Shaking him off would be as easy as swatting a fly. Picking him up and throwing him headfirst off the deck would be even easier.

But Bo didn't do either.

Instead he heard himself say, "Yeah, sure, why the hell not? It's not like this day could get any worse, right?"

"Well... not the most gracious invitation I've ever had, but...."

The guy sat down next to Bo and set the six-pack between them. Then, slipping a bottle opener out of his back pocket, he took a bottle out, popped off the cap, and offered it to Bo.

Bo eyed it, and him, warily. "What is that?"

"Well, it's not a magic potion that's going to put you under my gay spell if that's what you're afraid of. It's just beer." When Bo still hesitated, he said, "Shall I taste it first to prove it's not poisonous?"

Because it was there—and because it felt stupid to make an issue of it—Bo accepted the bottle. But when he checked the label, it wasn't one he recognized.

"Where'd you get this?"

"I brought it with me."

"You bring your own beer to a keg party?"

"Usually." Bo watched as the guy popped the top off his own bottle and then slipped the opener back in his pocket. "Have you tasted the crap they serve at these things?"

Bo had, indeed, tasted it and found himself in complete agreement—it was crap.

"Besides," the guy continued, "I came here tonight with the intention of getting very drunk. Therefore I decided it would be prudent to do so with something that will let me retain at least a bit of my stomach lining. Which counts out pretty much anything that is being served here tonight. Try it," he urged. "There's a money-back guarantee if not completely satisfied."

Since he couldn't think of a reason not to, Bo took a sip. It was good. Really good. Darker and heavier than what he was used to, but with a fuller flavor and a sort of mellow aftertaste. "You're right. This is good. Thanks."

"You're welcome."

Though the guy seemed personable enough, there was still something Bo was confused about. "Tell me something: if you aren't attracted to me, why would you bother coming out here and sharing this with me?"

"I didn't say I wasn't attracted to you, I said I didn't follow you."

"Then why are you here?"

"Actually, I came out looking for a quiet spot in which to wallow in my own self-pity at being stuck at this party. Then I saw you and I thought *now there's somebody who doesn't want to be here almost as much as I don't want to be here*. Which, believe me, is saying something."

"So, what? You decided to share the wealth with the equally unfortunate?"

"What can I say? I'm a sucker for a sad face?"

Still trying to figure this guy out, Bo said, "If you're that miserable here, why don't you just leave?"

"Why don't you?" the guy retorted.

Despite himself, Bo grinned, then gestured with his bottle. "I asked you first."

"Fair enough." Shifting his position so he could lean back against the upper step, the guy said, "I guess it's because I know the friends who dragged me here tonight mean well… even if they are a pain in the ass."

Bo could certainly relate to that. "Why'd they drag you here?"

The guy shrugged again. "You know how it is: still trying to get over a bad breakup… feeling down in the dumps… time to get back in the saddle… that kind of thing. And since tomorrow is Saturday, I couldn't even claim homework as a good excuse to hole up in my cave and lick my wounds in peace."

"You're a student?" Bo asked with surprise. The guy looked older than that.

"Grad student. I'm working on my master's degree in psychology. I don't live on campus, though. I got tired of that scene a long time ago. So what about you? What are you studying?"

Here it comes, Bo thought. "I'm not a student. I'm more of a party crasher. My buddy Mac and I do construction work."

"Construction? You mean like… building buildings?"

"Yeah, sometimes. Mostly we do remodeling. Some restoration work. My crew's rehabbing a building not too far from here. The Howe building? Out on Central Street?"

"Yeah, I know where that is. You're in charge of all that?"

"Well… technically, my old man is, since he owns the company, but I'm pretty much in charge of the day-to-day stuff out at the site."

"Wow! That must be a lot of work. Not to mention a huge responsibility."

Hearing the admiration in his voice, Bo couldn't help but respond. Usually when he told college types what he did for a living, they automatically tuned out.

But this guy seemed genuinely interested.

"It is a lot of responsibility. In fact, it's kind of a pain in the ass. Making sure we get done on time and on budget. Trying to keep everybody safe. It takes time away from doing the hands-on construction work, which is the part I really enjoy."

"Why not do that instead?"

"Like I said, my old man owns the company." Bo took a sip of his beer, trying to wash away the bitter taste in his mouth. "And believe me, when my pop says 'jump', you don't stop and ask questions, you just jump."

"Even if what you really want is to sit down?" the man asked, then shook his head. "Sorry. Occupational hazard: asking probing personal questions. Feel free to tell me to mind my own business."

"No, it's okay." He didn't know why, but Bo found himself sharing something he didn't often talk about. "My grandfather was the one who started the company. Then, when he retired, Pop took over. So when me and my brothers came along, he naturally expected us to go into the business too. Unfortunately, when my oldest brother, Charlie, decided he'd rather go to law school than swing a hammer, the old man threw him out, and the two of them haven't spoken since."

"Well, that sucks!" the guy said matter-of-factly, and Bo found himself laughing.

"Yeah, it does. Especially since the next little Sanford son to come along was my brother, Ham, who, unfortunately, is all thumbs. Honestly, the guy doesn't know an Allen wrench from a socket set. And after about the third time he nailed his foot to the floor with his own nail gun, Pop sent him to school to learn bookkeeping, and now he works in the office. Which sort of leaves son number three—me—holding the bag."

"What would you be doing if you weren't stuck doing that?"

Again, Bo found himself sharing something he rarely talked about. It was a private dream—not one to share with just anyone. "I'd like to get into flipping houses."

The guy shook his head. "Flipping houses? I don't know what that means."

"You know. You go in, buy a fixer-upper, do all the repairs, then sell it for a profit."

"Do the repairs? You mean like plumbing and electrical and all that stuff?"

"Yeah."

"And you can do all that?"

Again, Bo was caught off guard by the admiration in his voice. "Not all of it. You need a license for some of it—plumbing and electrical and things like that—but the rest of it—framing, roofing, putting in the cabinets, those I can do myself."

"Wow. I barely know which end of a hammer to hold."

They were quiet for another minute until the guy said, "So, is that why *you're* here tonight? Scouting out your first fixer-upper?"

Bo snorted. "This place isn't a fixer-upper—it's a tearer-downer and starter-over-again."

"What do you mean?"

"Well, just look at this place." Bo gestured around, mentally tabulating the cost of whipping the house into shape and then concluding it wouldn't be worth the effort. "The roof is sagging, the foundation's cracked, and the kitchen is a complete joke. Not to mention if this deck doesn't manage to fall off the house tonight, it'll be a miracle."

"Ah, I see. You came out here hoping to avoid getting buried under the rubble."

Bo chuckled, charmed in spite of himself. "Actually, I think I was just trying to avoid all human contact. I'm not exactly good company tonight."

"Well, I think you are," he said simply. "But if you'd rather be alone, I could go find someplace else to drink myself into a stupor."

Did he want that? Bo wondered. Ordinarily he would be wishing this guy would leave, but for some reason he didn't. "Naw, you might as well stay. Why drink alone if you don't have to, right?"

The guy raised his bottle and tapped it to Bo's. "To not drinking alone."

They were quiet for a long few moments before the guy said, "I'm Erick, by the way. Erick Stevens."

"Bo Sanford," he said, shaking Erick's proffered hand.

"Bo, huh?" Erick said with a hint of that wonderful smile flirting with his lips. "Would that be spelled B-O-W as in 'bow on a birthday present', or B-E-A-U as in 'a southern belle's gentlemen caller'?"

"Actually, it's spelled B-O."

"Really? As in 'something one gets when one doesn't shower often enough'?"

Maybe it was the five—or had it been six?—beers he'd already consumed, or maybe it was Erick's brand of humor, but instead of brushing aside the question, Bo found himself telling him something he never, *ever*, told anyone. "More like 'someone who doesn't want to admit his name is Beauregard because if someone happened to call him that, he'd have to kick that person's ass'."

"Ah, I see."

"Oh believe me, you don't know the half. My brother, Charlie? His real name is Charleston, and Ham's name is actually Hamilton."

"Colorful," Erick said with another twitch of his lips.

Bo rolled his eyes. "Tell me about it. My mom was obsessed with *Gone with the Wind*."

"Well, then, I guess it's a good thing you weren't a girl, or she might have named you Scarlett."

"She probably would have, come to think of it. As it is, I feel pretty lucky she didn't name me 'Ashley'."

"If she had, you might have spent your whole life being mistaken for a girl."

Bo felt his stomach lurch, but when he flicked a glance in Erick's direction, he didn't see anything amiss. He was just sitting there, calmly drinking his beer, and after taking a deep breath to steady his heart rate, Bo slowly relaxed again. Thankfully, Erick didn't seem to mind sitting in silence, and the two men finished their beers and popped the tops off two more before Bo gathered enough courage to broach the subject that had been eating at him all night.

"Do you remember earlier when you caught me looking at you and you stared back at me?"

"Vividly," Erick said dryly, and it made Bo smile.

"Yeah, I guess it was a little awkward, huh?"

"I'd say it was more intense than awkward, but I know what you mean. So... what about it?"

"I was wondering: why you did you stare at me that way?"

"Why did you stare at me?" Erick countered.

Bo had known Erick would ask and had spent considerable time formulating his answer. "Let's just say I thought you were someone else."

Bo was proud of his nonchalant delivery until Erick laughed. "Yeah, right. Don't you mean some*thing* else?"

As far as Bo was concerned, you could never go wrong playing dumb. "Excuse me?"

"Come on, admit it." Erick coaxed, bumping Bo's shoulder with his. "You were looking at me because you thought I was a girl."

Bo's jaw dropped. "How the hell did you know that?"

Erick grinned. "I didn't. Until now."

Caught in his own trap, Bo hung his head. "Shit." When Erick laughed, Bo couldn't help joining in. "Fine, you caught me. I'm a nearsighted idiot."

"Don't worry about it," Erick soothed. "The truth is, I kind of had it figured out already."

That did surprise Bo. "How come?"

"It happens to me all the time. Ever since I was a kid. People are always mistaking me for a girl. I even got hit on by a couple of lesbians once."

Bo almost spit out the mouthful of beer he'd taken and had to wipe his lips with the back of his hand. "You're kidding, right?"

"Nope! Of course, it was really dark in the bar and they were both seriously drunk at the time, but still—" Erick took a sip of his beer. "—it was pretty humiliating."

Bo didn't know why, but he felt an odd need to comfort Erick. "It must come in handy with other guys. Guys like you, I mean."

"Not as much as you might think." Erick idly flicked at the label on the bottle with his fingernail. "You see, most guys who like their guys to look girly want them to look really girly, and somehow I just don't look good in a skirt. And most other guys go for the big beefy types. Kind of like you." Though Erick's tone had been matter-of-fact, Bo felt himself flush with a complex mixture of emotions. "Unfortunately, I have absolutely no hope of ever looking like you, since I seem to have one of those bodies that the more I work out, the smaller I get. So I pretty much end up SOL."

Bo snorted. "You want to talk about shit outta luck? Try finding out the first girl you've been attracted to in a really long time is actually a guy."

When he heard himself say those words, Bo almost wished this disaster of a house *would* fall down on top of him. But Erick just smiled.

"Kind of like finding out the hottest guy you've seen in a long time isn't gay. Talk about a crappy end to a crappy day."

When Erick smiled that way, his whole face lit up, and Bo couldn't help but smile back. And this time, he tapped his bottle to Erick's. "To the end of a crappy day!"

A few people came and went as the two men slowly finished their second beers.

When they were alone again, Bo felt mellow enough to say, "You know, you never really answered my question."

"What question is that?"

"Why you were staring at me. It's not like you thought I was a girl, right?"

"Definitely not."

"Then why stare?

"That would depend." Leaning forward again, Erick rested his forearms on his thighs and began to roll his bottle between his palms. "Are we talking the cultural answer, the personal answer, or the—for lack of a better word—philosophical answer?"

"I didn't know this was a multiple-choice test," Bo griped, running an agitated hand through his hair. After a moment's thought, he said, "How about we start with the first and work our way down the list?"

"Okay." Erick cleared his throat as if preparing to give a lecture. "From a cultural—or what would probably be more correctly termed a 'subcultural'—perspective, I stared at you because maintaining that kind of intense eye contact is how gay guys communicate… let's call it 'romantic'… interest in each other."

"And you were interested in me? Romantically?" Maybe it was the numbers of beers he'd had, but for some reason, the idea didn't bother Bo the way he'd thought it would.

"Again, that would depend." Erick curved his lips. "Are we talking about before you ran out of there like a scared rabbit or after?"

Rather than be embarrassed, Bo found himself amused. "I guess I did do that, huh?"

"It's okay. That kind of sustained eye contact makes most people uncomfortable. In fact, in some situations, it's actually seen as a sign of aggression. Try locking eyes with a gangbanger or a prison guard sometime and see what it gets you. But most of the time, it's just considered rude."

"But not for gay guys?"

"For gay guys, it's considered an invitation."

"To what?"

"Pretty much anything. Anything from 'buy me a drink, sailor' to 'how about meeting me in the upstairs bathroom for a quick blow job'."

Bo's jaw dropped far enough to smack his knees. "You weren't actually planning on meeting me in the upstairs bathroom, were you?" he blurted, then blushed, but again, Erick only smiled.

"Ah… well… you see… that question would now be moving us down the list into the more personal area of the answer."

Bo hesitated a moment, trying to decide. Maybe he didn't want to know. Face it! In the last five minutes, he'd heard enough to keep him freaked out for a week. Why borrow any more trouble?

He sighed. "If you don't tell me, it's just going to end up driving me crazy. So if you wouldn't mind…."

Once again, Erick rolled the bottle between his hands, and Bo decided it was something Erick did when he was feeling ill at ease. "Let's just say that… at another time… and if, indeed, you had been making an offer like that… which I figured out pretty quickly you weren't… I would most likely have met you any place you wanted me to for pretty much anything you wanted me to do."

Obviously more relaxed now that he'd gotten that out, Erick leaned back, resting his elbows on the step above him. "And while I know that probably doesn't sound like one to you, I have witnesses who can testify that it is, in fact, a rather large compliment, as I am very selective about who I hook up with. Even in what we'll call my wilder days."

Again not sure whether to be pleased or embarrassed, Bo said, "Well, then, thanks for the compliment, I guess, but why would it have to be 'at another time'? Why not tonight? Or would that be getting a little too personal?"

"No, it's okay," Erick said easily, but he sat forward, idly playing with the now empty bottle. "I just recently—or not so recently, depending on who you ask—got out of a really bad relationship. We're talking bad as in Hurricane Katrina bad. And I'm just not ready to get back out there and start looking for a new one right now."

"Not even if it's just for the night?"

"Especially if it's just for the night," Erick said firmly. "Like I said, even in my wilder days, I didn't do a whole lot of that, but I still got tired of it a long time ago. Unfortunately, since this most recent breakup, I am also now sick of all the drama that goes along with having a relationship that lasts for more than one night. So I'm pretty much screwed. Or not. Depending on how you look at it." Erick set his empty bottle back in the six-pack holder and faced Bo directly. "So what about you?"

"What about me?" Bo asked warily.

"What would you have done if I really *had* been a girl? Would you have met me in the upstairs bathroom for a quick blow job?"

Responding to the mischievous grin on Erick's face, Bo said, "You really must be gay. Otherwise you would know that the only girls who make that kind of offer are either A, too drunk to actually deliver the goods; or B, the type who expect you to leave a C-note on the back of the toilet on your way out the door."

"Good to know," Erick affirmed. "Let's just say, for the sake of argument, that I was just a regular girl. What then?"

"Honestly? I don't know," Bo said, surprised at himself. "I would have *wanted* to take you to the upstairs bathroom. Or anywhere else you wanted to go, for that matter. But with the way I've been feeling lately, I don't know if I actually would have done it."

"How come?"

A part of Bo couldn't believe he was actually having this conversation, but something was pushing at him right now, a dissatisfaction he'd only recently become aware he'd been feeling. "I guess it's because I'm starting to get tired of that whole thing too. I want more than just a one-night stand or short-term fling. I want...."

Bo stopped himself just in time and gave a self-conscious laugh, but Erick urged him on, saying, "Go on. Tell me. What do you want?"

Still unable to believe he was saying this stuff out loud, Bo said, "I guess—in a way—I want the exact opposite of what you want. I want some drama in my life. I want passion. I want romance. I want to fall head over heels in love with someone and have her feel exactly the same way about me." Bo blew out a long breath. "And if the guys on my crew could hear me right now, they would rag on me until the end of time. Oh, don't get me wrong, they're all good guys, but the younger ones still want to party their asses off and screw anything that moves, and the older guys are mostly married and settled and have a kid or two. And I'm just... stuck in nowhere land. And just lately... I'm starting to get really scared that maybe I'll never get out."

Bo didn't know what either of them might have said next, because at that moment someone from inside tore open the sliding glass door, bolted for the porch railing, and vomited copiously over the side of the deck. The splattering sound on the blacktop below and the resulting bellow of annoyance had both men sighing heavily.

"Well, on that note," Erick said, "I guess this life raft of sanity in an ocean of chaos is over. I should probably go back inside and find my well-meaning, if annoying, friends."

Bo could tell that Erick wasn't any more eager to go back inside than he was. More importantly, he didn't want this interlude to end.

He was enjoying talking to Erick. He was so completely different from anyone he knew, and yet he was the easiest person to talk to Bo had ever met.

Feeling almost as nervous as when he'd asked Colleen Keenan to the junior prom, he said, "You know... if you wanted... we could both get the hell out of here. Not for anything weird or anything," he said quickly. "I was just thinking we could... I don't know... go get a cup of coffee or something? Maybe talk a little bit more?"

He didn't know what he'd been expecting, but it wasn't the hosanna of a smile Erick gifted him with. "Now that's the best offer I've had in a long time."

As it had earlier, that smile did something strange to Bo's insides, but he decided he didn't want to think about that right now. Rather, he concentrated on logistics. "I don't know about you, but with the way my day has been going, if I try to drive right now, I'm going end up with a DUI on my record. So unless you feel sober enough to get behind the wheel...?"

Erick shook his head.

"Then I think we should probably stick to someplace close enough so we can walk. That is, if there's any place like that around here."

"There's a twenty-four-hour diner around the corner," Erick told him. "We could go there."

"That sounds great."

Even as he said it, Erick's smile faded, and Bo felt his heart sink. "What's wrong?"

"Nothing really. I was just thinking about my friends."

"What about them?"

"Well, I don't know about you, but if I go in there and tell my friends I'm leaving, they're going to assume I'm trying to sneak out and go home, and they're going to insist on coming with me."

Bo thought about telling Mac he was leaving and knew Mac would do the same thing. Or at least put up one hell of an argument.

For another minute, Bo hesitated. Then he asked, "What's your stance on little white lies?"

"Generally speaking, opposed, but under the right circumstances, flexible. Why?"

"Well, I was thinking… if we each told our friends we'd met someone and we're leaving with them, they'd probably be happy enough for us not to ask too many questions. That way we could make our escape without having to completely lie our asses off."

Erick considered a moment. "That could work."

"All right. How about we meet at the diner in, say, half an hour? That should give us both enough time to say our good-byes and get out."

"That sounds perfect." Erick stood and took one step up so they were eye to eye. "I'll see you there."

CHAPTER
THREE

SINCE Mac was thoroughly engaged in trying to talk a pretty brunette into one of the upstairs bedrooms and out of her designer jeans, Bo was able to get away easily and arrived at the diner a good fifteen minutes ahead of schedule.

Not a good thing.

Though he still wasn't anywhere close to sober, the walk had cleared his head enough to have him wondering just exactly what he thought he was doing by meeting Erick here.

The guy was gay, for Pete's sake!

What the hell did he know about gay people? Nothing. In fact, he could probably count the number of gay people he knew on his right hand. Better yet, he could count them on his uncle Joe's right hand.

And *he* was missing two fingers.

Not to mention Erick was not only a college graduate but well on his way to having his master's degree.

While Bo, as far as he could tell, was pretty much going nowhere.

What could a guy like him and a guy like Erick possibly have to talk about?

No… it would probably be best if he just cut his losses and left before Erick showed up. But before he could gather the courage to do it, Erick walked in the door.

For an instant, Bo wished he'd run when he'd had the chance.

Even with the dim lighting in the diner, Bo knew there was no way anyone could mistake Erick for a girl. Yet there was something about him, a kind of innate grace that was almost feminine, that stirred Bo in a way he'd never felt before. It was so unfamiliar he could almost believe there really had been something in that beer they'd shared. How else could he explain the heat presently surging through him?

A heat that had begun in the area of his heart and was rapidly working its way two feet due south.

Okay! Time to hit the road before he made a complete ass of himself.

Before Bo could bolt for the nearest exit, Erick spotted him and smiled. The beauty of it was just as mesmerizing as it had been the first time he'd seen it, and Bo found himself sitting there, watching Erick move toward the table Bo had selected.

With a kind of elegant shrug, Erick stripped off his jacket and draped it over the back of the chair, then, still wearing the pink scarf, slid into the seat across from Bo.

"Hi. Sorry I'm late. I had a little bit of a problem shaking off my friends. They wouldn't let me leave without giving them a few details."

"What did you tell them?"

Erick narrowed his eyes at Bo's harsh, almost accusatory tone, but he said, "Only what we agreed to tell them. 'I met someone and we're going somewhere else to get to know each other better.'"

"Okay." Bo relaxed a bit, but his thumbs and fingers were still tapping out a staccato rhythm on the table, something he had a habit of doing when he was nervous.

Not that Erick could know that, but he must have sensed something was wrong because he said, "You know, Bo, if you've changed your mind about being here, it's okay. We can both say 'it was nice to have met you' and go home and count ourselves lucky to have gotten out of that place in one piece."

It was tempting. Very tempting.

"And there'd be no hard feelings?" Bo asked.

Erick raised one hand. "No hard feelings. I promise."

Bo thought for a moment while he continued to beat his thumbs against the table.

"No. I don't want to do that," he said finally. "It's just… I guess this is all a little weird for me."

"I can certainly understand that."

Bo stopped his nervous fidgeting. "You can?"

"Sure." Erick smiled in a way that made his eyes glow. "I may have only just met you tonight, but it doesn't take a genius to guess this is the first time you've ever gone to a party, had a little too much to drink, and instead of leaving with a girl, you leave with a guy. And not just any guy either, but one who, by his own admission, thinks you're seriously hot. Am I right?"

Bo blushed wildly but couldn't help the grin. "Well, when you put it that way…."

Thankfully, the waitress came by at that moment, giving Bo something else to concentrate on.

"What can I get you boys?" she asked.

With one hand, Erick gestured toward Bo, and for a moment, Bo froze. He wasn't sure what the proper etiquette in a situation like this might be. If Erick had been a girl, he would, naturally, have gestured back and said, "Ladies first," but if he had been with one of his guy friends, the guy probably wouldn't have deferred to him in the first place, so it wouldn't have been an issue.

Already, he could feel a tension headache beginning in the back of his neck.

He was in way... *way*... over his head and they hadn't even ordered yet.

Feeling awkward, he said, "Coffee, I guess. Sweet and light. And a side of fries."

"Sure thing." She turned to Erick. "What about you, honey?"

"Just coffee, please. Black."

"You're not eating?" Bo asked.

"I can't eat this late at night and still fit into my jeans."

Just the thought of the fit of Erick's jeans made Bo shift uncomfortably in his seat, but the waitress said, "Oh, I don't know. It looks to me like you could use a few extra pounds."

"Oh, trust me, any extra weight I gain goes right to my ass."

Bo didn't want to think about that, either, but the waitress laughed as she tore off the slip and stuffed the pad in her apron.

"By the way," she said, "I like that scarf you're wearing. Goes nice with your eyes."

"Thanks," Erick said, smoothing it down.

"Where'd you go to find something like that?"

"I got this one at Filene's Basement at their annual 75 percent off sale."

"Hey, my daughter shops there all the time," she said brightly. "She doesn't have your sense of style, though."

Bo saw her glance from one man to the other as if slightly puzzled. Not that he could blame her. He and Erick must look like a modern day *Beauty and the Beast*.

Or more like Timon and Pumba from *The Lion King*.

And guess which one was the warthog?

"I'll be sure to tell her to be on the lookout for something like that," she went on. "She's about your size and coloring. Gets it from her daddy. Me... I'm lucky if I can eat a piece of pie once a week and still get into my uniform. Even if I am on my feet all the time."

When she walked away to get the coffee, Erick rolled his eyes. "Sorry about that. I seem to have one of those faces that says, 'No, please, tell me your whole life story. I don't mind.'"

Bo just shook his head. This was way more than he could handle. Fashion consultations with the waitress? What next? Hairstyles with the dishwasher?

Would somebody please get him out of here?

Both men stayed quiet until they had their coffee in front of them and the waitress had left again, then Erick said, "So... are you planning on telling me what's bothering you? Or are you planning on shaking the table apart a piece at a time?"

Suddenly aware he'd been tapping again, Bo yanked his hands back and dropped them in his lap. "Sorry. I do that when I'm nervous."

"I figured that out for myself. What I can't figure out is why you're so nervous. You weren't like this at the party."

"I know. But this just feels... different somehow."

Actually, Bo knew exactly why it felt different. The party had simply been a chance encounter. This? This felt like a date. Not that he was going to say that to Erick, but something of the direction of his thoughts must have conveyed itself because Erick said, "Would it help if I told you I have a lot of straight male friends—some of whom I also think are seriously hot—and we go out for coffee all the time, and so far I've managed to avoid making a pass at any of them so it's highly unlikely I'm going to start with you?"

"Honestly? Not really."

"Why not?"

"Because if I was worried you were going make a pass at me, I wouldn't have left the party with you in the first place."

"That sounds reasonable, I guess. Still it's obvious you're worried about something. So what is it?"

"I guess you could say—it's the complete opposite of that."

Erick shook his head. "Okay… now I'm confused."

"Yeah, well, join the club," Bo muttered, and unconsciously his hands crept back to the tabletop and began tapping again.

Erick reached out and put his hand on top of one of Bo's, stopping its motion.

Though it definitely wasn't as soft as a girl's hand, it was small and delicately boned and it gave Bo an odd feeling to see it lying on top of his larger, hairier one.

Erick didn't seem to give it a thought. "Look, Bo, this is nuts! You're obviously upset about something. Why not just tell me what's on your mind so we can talk about it?"

Obviously, Bo still had enough alcohol in his system to loosen his tongue, because he heard himself say, "Okay. You want to know what's on my mind? I'll tell you what's on my mind. What's on my mind is that I can't tell you what's on my mind because as far as I can tell, I've lost my mind."

"How so?" Erick asked neutrally.

"You mean besides the fact that I walked into a party tonight, took one look at a girl, and fell flat on my ass in love with her? I mean… I had us married with three kids before I even blinked for the first time. Then it turns out my dream girl is actually a guy—which should, at the very least, make me feel like I got kicked in the balls— except the minute I lock eyes with the guy, instead of feeling like I got kicked in the balls, I feel like somebody stuck my dick in a light socket and flipped the switch.

"And what's worse, instead of standing there and taking it like a man, I turn tail and run like a Chihuahua being chased by a pit bull."

Erick opened his mouth as if to say something, but Bo just rolled over him.

"Then, while I'm sitting outside trying to figure out how my brain could be so screwed up I would actually be considering going back into that madhouse to try to find that guy again and prove to myself he really *is* a girl who's only *pretending* to be a guy, what happens? The guy comes to find me.

"And instead of being an asshole about the whole thing—which would at least give me an excuse to punch him—he turns out to be somebody I could really like if I didn't have to worry all the time that I was going to do something really stupid like tell him I'm attracted to him even if he is a guy.

"Then I come here and I finally manage to convince myself that, rather than finding myself suddenly 'pinch-hitting for the pink team', I've just been working too hard. That's all. No problem. It's just stress. Except then he comes walking in the door and I get hit with another jolt from that light switch, only this time I can't even run, because if I stand up, he's bound to notice I get a hard-on every time he smiles.

"Now if you don't mind… I have to go throw up."

With that, Bo bolted for the men's room.

SINCE "better" was a relative term, Bo supposed he did feel better once he'd gotten all of that out of his system.

Literally and figuratively.

Even as he splashed cold water on his face, he wished the men's room had a window he could jump out of—a cowardly but expedient solution to the problem at hand. But it was not to be, and after waging a pitched battle with his inner chicken, Bo forced himself to walk back into the dining room and found Erick still sitting at the table.

He wasn't looking in Bo's direction, but Bo could tell he knew he was there. But he didn't turn to look at him until Bo slid back into his seat across from him.

"Sorry about that," Bo muttered.

"It's okay. Do you feel better now?"

"A little, I guess." Because his fingers wanted to tap again, Bo folded his hands in his lap. "I wasn't sure if you'd still be here or not."

"I wasn't sure either. I wasn't sure if you'd want me to be."

"Neither was I." They both remained quiet until Bo finally couldn't take the silence anymore. "Why are you still here?"

"Because now that you've had your say, I want to have mine." Erick glanced away as if trying to avoid eye contact. "After I do, I'm going to leave and you can decide where we go from here."

"Why do I have to be the one to decide?" Bo asked irritably.

"Because while you were otherwise indisposed, I made my choice," Erick said, bringing his gaze back to Bo's. "You're going to have to make yours all on your own."

That sounded fair, Bo supposed. "Okay. So what do you want to say?"

Erick turned his head to look out the window at the parking lot, as if gathering his thoughts, then turned to face Bo again. "First of all, let me say I'm just as freaked out about what's going on here as you are."

Bo snorted. "I doubt that."

"Well, don't, because it's true."

Erick certainly sounded adamant enough, but.... "Then why don't you seem it?"

"Because appearing calm in the midst of a crisis is one of my more highly developed skills. But that doesn't mean that my insides match my outsides. They don't. Right now my insides are just as much of a mess as yours. The only difference is, the fact that I get a hard-on every time you lick your lips doesn't freak me out the way it does you because I'm used to responding to guys that way. But just because I'm comfortable being attracted to you doesn't mean I'm happy about it. I'm distinctly unhappy about it!"

"Why?"

"You mean besides the fact that the last guy I was this attracted to could have given Osama Bin Laden a good name?"

"Yeah, besides that."

"I guess it's because Rule #1 in the *Gay Guy's Handbook to Not Getting Your Heart Broken* is 'don't fall for a straight guy.' Period! That kind of dumbass move leads to nothing but heartache, and believe me, the last thing I need in my life right now is more heartache."

"Why are you still here, then?" Bo demanded. "Why don't you just leave?"

"Because I can't."

"Why not?"

"Because of the third answer to the question."

Bo shook his head. "What the hell are you talking about?"

"Do you remember earlier when you asked why I stared at you and I said there were three answers to that question: the cultural, the personal, and the philosophical?"

"Yeah. So...?"

"So... I'm still here because of the third answer."

As if needing something to do with his hands, Erick reached out and began rolling his now empty coffee cup between his palms.

"I don't have what most people would consider a defined belief system," he said, focusing his eyes on the coffee cup in front of him. "I think Christianity, Buddhism, Islam, fate, karma, destiny, the universe—all of those kinds of things—they all have bits and pieces of truth to them. But the one thing I do believe is: things happen for a reason. That no matter how random something seems, there is a plan.

Somewhere. And when someone just suddenly appears in your life, out of the blue, that person is there for a reason. They're there to teach you something, or to help you to grow in some way, and you need to be open to whatever it is that person is there to do.

"So maybe we met tonight because you're here to teach me something. Like… I don't know… how to fix my leaky kitchen sink, or how to get my damn toaster to stop burning my bagels in the morning. Or maybe it's to help me remember that even broken hearts still have the capacity to feel something, because, believe me, when I got to that party tonight, my heart was pretty much as broken as it could get, and yet I still managed to feel something for you. I'm not entirely sure what that 'something' is, but I do feel it—deep and real and very, very scary."

He looked away for a long moment, and Bo thought he was done but he then turned back. "Then again… maybe I have it all backwards. Maybe it's you who needs to learn something."

"Like what?"

"I have no idea." Now he looked straight into Bo's eyes, and Bo felt the intensity of his gaze all the way to his toes. "I have to believe that you and I met for a reason, because there's no way we can feel this strongly about each other and not have it mean something. And despite the fact that we're obviously physically attracted to each other, it doesn't have to be a romantic thing, either. In fact, it would probably be better if it wasn't. Either way, I'm willing to hang in there until I find out exactly what it is I'm supposed to be doing here. You need to decide if you're willing to do the same."

Without another word, Erick slid out of his seat and stood, but when he reached for his jacket, Bo took hold of his wrist. It was so delicate—almost like a woman's—that he automatically loosened his grip.

Still he held on.

"I don't have to decide anything," he said. "I already have."

Erick didn't pull away, but he didn't relax either, and without conscious thought, Bo began lightly stroking the inside of Erick's wrist with his thumb.

"I don't really believe in much either," Bo said. "And I don't know if I buy into the idea that there's some kind of master plan out there. Much less that we were 'supposed to meet tonight'. What I do believe is, when all else fails, you need to follow your gut, and right now, my gut is telling me not to let you walk out that door."

"Well… that would be fine except sooner or later the management does put an end to that whole 'free refills' thing. Believe me, I know," Erick said, and Bo was pleased that some of the tension had disappeared from his voice. Then he went serious again. "What happens then, Bo? What happens when we both have to leave here and go back to our lives?"

"I don't know," Bo admitted. "Unfortunately, that's one of the drawbacks to the whole 'use your gut' theory. It speaks up loud and clear whenever there's a fork in the road, but then it kind of quiets down again until the next turn comes up."

"Kind of like a gastric GPS?"

Bo smiled at the light teasing. "Something like that." Then he went serious as well. "I don't know where this is going either. And I wish I could promise you I won't break your heart, but I can't. The only thing I do know is that right now, right this minute, this is where I want to be. Here. With you. Everything else is just going to have to be 'wait and see'."

Bo forced himself to let go of Erick's wrist and was relieved when he didn't move away. But he didn't sit down either, and Bo sat on tenterhooks, waiting.

"I guess I can live with that," Erick said finally. "But only if you can promise me one thing."

Instinctively, Bo braced himself. "What?"

"That whatever happens, you won't just leave me hanging. If you decide whatever this is is too much for you to handle, you'll at least tell me. You'll give me a chance to say good-bye before you walk away."

Ordinarily Bo would have said, "Sure, no problem," but somehow this promise felt different. It had a weight to it that Bo wasn't sure he wanted to shoulder.

Then again, this whole night had been like something out of a bizarre dream.

What was one more oddity?

"I promise I won't just walk away. I promise, whatever happens, I'll give us both the chance to say good-bye."

Bo was relieved to see that when Erick sat down again, he was smiling. It was a small smile but it was there, and Bo felt that same stirring deep inside him.

It didn't terrify him the way it had before, but neither was it comfortable. He doubted it ever would be.

But he was making progress.

CHAPTER
FOUR

ONCE they had gotten things out on the table—so to speak—the two men spent the rest of the night at the diner, talking.

Literally. The whole rest of the night. The weirdest part was Bo couldn't even remember exactly what it was they talked about. Not that he had ever found himself at a loss at making conversation. In fact, he prided himself on being able to shoot the bull with pretty much anyone.

With Erick it was different.

They didn't just talk about everyday things. They talked about important things, things that mattered. And even though Erick was much more educated than Bo, he somehow seemed able to talk about subjects Bo knew nothing about in such a way that not only did Bo understand them, he didn't feel foolish or looked down upon for not having known about them in the first place.

And he got Bo talking as well.

About the things he was knowledgeable about—not just construction and tools but other things too. Like cooking, which was one of his lesser-known skills. Erick's genuine interest and obvious admiration made Bo feel a hundred feet tall.

There was more as well. Erick had done a lot in his short life and thus had a million stories to tell about the people he knew, the places he'd been. And he had knack for telling them that made you feel like you were really there with him, sharing the experience. What was more amazing, at least to Bo, was he seemed to like hearing Bo's stories too, about the characters he'd met, the quirks of the men he worked with and their funny superstitions.

Like Jerry Hughes's refusal to work on the thirteenth floor of any building unless everyone on the crew agreed to call it the twelfth-and-a-half floor.

With all the stories going back and forth, the two men laughed a lot. Even Erick's humor was different than the humor of the guys he usually hung with.

It was drier and somehow more refreshing. And stimulating.

The whole night was stimulating enough; Bo hadn't felt the least bit tired. So it was with a great deal of surprise when he realized it was morning. Even as the sun began to brighten the skies, Bo actually felt a whisper of fear that Erick would simply disappear with the dawn. Like the stars in the sky.

Or an angel from heaven.

But he hadn't, and after walking back to their respective cars—and after having exchanged numbers—Bo went home.

Unfortunately, the respite was to be short-lived, as he only managed to fit in two hours of sleep before he was due at Ham's house for work detail. He supposed he could have begged off if he had been willing to admit he'd spent the night with someone. If he'd done that, he would have had to answer a bunch of questions he didn't want to have to answer.

The most important and the least answerable being why he found Erick so much more fascinating... and attractive... than any girl he'd ever met.

Rather than try to explain to others what he couldn't explain to himself, he rolled out of bed, tugged on work clothes, and made his way across town to his brother's house.

When he pulled up in front of the cunning little Cape Cod home—complete with white picket fence—in the quiet neighborhood, he almost changed his mind. Along with Ham's grubby old pickup and his wife Andrea's Impala, Bo saw his old man's truck parked in the driveway.

Perfect! Just what he needed today.

Though Bo's agreement to help his brother fix up the house before the baby came had been made more out of obligation than an actual offer, Bo didn't really mind it. At least with his brother there was the camaraderie of a busman's holiday to ease the burden. And his sister-in-law's obvious gratitude and her willingness to cook them a good meal at the end of the day was a reward worth working for.

When Pop was there, it was a different story.

Oh, not that his father wasn't a good carpenter. He was one of the best. But ever since Bo had officially joined the company, Pop had begun doing less and less actual hands-on work and taken on a more supervisory position.

In other words, he stood on the sidelines criticizing every move his son made.

Digging deep, Bo forced himself to get out of the truck. With a move so ingrained it was automatic, Bo buckled on his tool belt, the weight of it so familiar he barely noticed it, and then hoisted his toolbox out of the bed of the truck.

Before he got to the front door, he could already hear banging coming through the upstairs window. Yet another sign he was late. With his father there, he would be sure to hear about it. He couldn't help but smile when he saw Andrea holding open the door for him, her pregnant belly sticking out just enough for her to look like she'd stuffed a pillow beneath her sunshine-yellow shirt.

"Hey, we were wondering where you'd gotten to," she said, popping up on her toes to give his cheek a kiss. "Come on in. Do you want coffee?"

Bo's stomach churned at the thought. "No, thanks. I think I'm coffee'd out at the moment."

"Really? You don't look it. You look like you've been up all night."

"I was. Pretty much."

"How come?"

"Long story," he told her and, purposely distracting her, rubbed her little basketball of a tummy. "How's my favorite niece doing today?"

"Doing handsprings at the moment."

Andrea Sanford was a pretty woman—in a Midwest farmer's daughter sort of way—with her long auburn hair tied up in a bouncy ponytail and a pair of blue eyes that saw a great deal more than most people gave her credit for.

"With the way she's going at it in there, I think she's going to be a gymnast."

Bo ignored the grumpy sound that came from farther in the kitchen.

Unlike his old man, Bo had been thrilled to discover that, rather than a son to carry on the family name and business, Andrea and Ham's baby was going to be a girl. His first, and so far only, niece.

One he intended to spoil shamelessly at each and every opportunity.

"I guess we'll have to get busy building her a balance beam. Get her started early on that Olympic career of hers."

"That'll be the day," his father grumbled, but Bo ignored that too.

It was easier that way.

Once Bo had managed to squeeze past Andrea and her belly, he put his toolbox out of the way, then bent to greet his brother's dog, Buster, who was presently trying to knock him over. On the few occasions the three brothers managed to get together without their father present, Charlie liked to say Buster was the "inevitable consequence of an increasingly global society."

Which everybody knew was lawyer talk for "just plain mutt."

Mutt or not, he was lovable, and as Bo scratched his ears, Buster wagged his tail ecstatically, over the moon with joy at the unaccustomed attention. Bo was thankful for another few more moments of peace before he straightened and finally looked at his father.

Even in his late sixties, Bill Sanford was still a large man, though most of the muscle he'd had when Bo was a child had gone flaccid, and he had collected quite a bit of fat around his middle. He still had a head of thick white hair and the big, hard hands that Bo clearly remembered having connected with the back of his head on more than one occasion growing up.

"Hey, Pop. I didn't expect to see you here this morning."

"Morning, huh? Why, it's practically noon, boy. Where the hell've you been?"

"I overslept."

"Overslept? I thought you just told Andi you'd been up all night."

Nobody had ever said the Boss Man was slow or hard of hearing.

"I just meant I didn't get to bed until really late."

"You look like something the cat dragged in."

Bo wanted to resent the statement, but since he'd glanced in the mirror before he'd left his apartment and come to the same conclusion, he could hardly argue.

"Yeah, I know. It was a long night."

"Did you get that generator snafu straightened out like I told you to?"

This was another reason why Bo hated when his dad came to these weekend work sessions. Both Bo and his brother had a long-standing agreement to avoid "talking shop" whenever they were together, even if they were sawing and hammering and sanding Sheetrock at the time.

Instead, they joked and teased and generally made things as fun as possible.

When Pop was around, it was impossible to avoid talking about work because to his dad, work was everything. Sanford and Sons Construction consumed every minute of every hour of every day of his dad's life.

And woe to anyone who didn't feel the same.

"I talked to the repair people on Friday afternoon. They said they couldn't get anyone out there until Tuesday morning to fix it."

"You swallowed that?" his pop demanded. "Call 'em back and tell 'em they'd better get there Monday or else."

"I can't call them today. It's Saturday," Bo said through gritted teeth. "Besides, I already rearranged some stuff so it won't matter if the generator's not up and running until Tuesday. We'll still make the schedule on time."

"That's not the point. You've got to know when to push these guys." The old man pointed one sausage-like finger in his son's direction. "You know what your problem is? You haven't got the balls to stand up for yourself. You just let people walk all over you."

Normally, that statement wouldn't have made an impression on Bo. Certainly it wasn't anything he hadn't heard before, but whether from lack of sleep or something else, Bo could feel annoyance begin to churn in his gut.

"If that's how you feel, why'd you put me in charge in the first place?"

"Same reason I tossed you in the lake when you were eight. Sink or swim. That's my motto."

How about "I'm a father who enjoys torturing his children" as a motto? Bo thought, but he only said, "Then why don't you just back off and let me do it?"

"Because it's not your name on the sign, boy, it's mine. Sanford and Sons has a reputation to protect."

Technically, it was Bo's name too, but that was beside the point.

"You don't have to worry. Even without the generator, the project will still come in on time and on budget. I promise."

"It better, or I'll be finding myself a new foreman."

It was on the tip of Bo's tongue to say, "Be my guest," but at that moment, Andrea said, "Pop, would you go up and ask Ham what he wants to do about lunch? I'd go myself but my feet hurt."

Since she'd been bopping around the kitchen since Bo arrived, he highly doubted her feet were the issue, but he had to admire the way she managed the old man. Maybe it was because she was a woman, or maybe it was because she wasn't his son, but as far as Bo could tell, Andrea was the only one in the family who could handle him when he was in a bad mood, which was most of the time.

She all but had the old man wrapped around her little finger.

How else could you explain why, despite a bit of grumbling, the old man got up and lumbered his way out of the room?

Bo blew out a long, slow breath.

"Thanks. I think you just saved my life. Or at least my job."

Unfortunately, when he turned to look at his sister-in-law, she'd folded her arms and wore the face of a woman determined to get to the bottom of something.

Crap! Out of the frying pan and into the fire.

"All right, Beauregard Sanford, what's really going on here?"

Sometimes, he thought, it was smarter to play dumb. "I don't know what you mean."

Ticking them off on her fingers like a laundry list, she said, "You show up late, looking exhausted, and say you've been up all night. Then you say you weren't up all night, you just went to bed late and overslept. Either way, you look like you've spent the last three days locked in a jail cell. Not to mention the fact that I haven't seen you this cranky with Pop since the last time you quit and got talked into coming back."

It was true. Bo had quit the business several times. He'd even gotten fired. More than once. But somehow, once both men cooled down, he had always gotten talked into coming back.

He wasn't proud of it but… there it was.

"So what gives?" she asked.

"I already told you. It was a long night."

"A long night? You look like you've been up *all* night."

Bo blew out another breath and dropped into a chair. Obviously, he wasn't going to make it out of the cheery kitchen without answering a few questions.

"All right. The truth is, I was up all night. When I finally did get home, I crashed, which is why I'm late."

"Do I want to know why you were up all night? Or does it include content that is too adult for an innocent girl's ears? Not to mention the baby's."

The truth or a lie? Bo wondered. He hated lying, especially to the people who meant the most to him, of which Andrea was definitely one. Even if she hadn't been his sister-in-law, he'd have loved her for herself. She could keep a secret too, but he wasn't ready to tell the whole story yet.

He settled on a part of it.

"I met someone at a party last night and we ended up leaving together."

"Okay! That's enough. You can spare us the intimate details. We get the picture."

"No! There. You see? That's the thing." For some reason, Bo felt it important to clarify. "We left together but we didn't do anything. Or not anything like you're thinking, anyway. We went out for coffee and somehow we ended up talking all night."

"Talking?" Andrea said skeptically. "The two of you just talked? All night?"

When Bo nodded, she gave a cute little jump of excitement. "That's great!"

"It is?" Bo asked even as she bent and kissed his cheek.

"Of course. It's the first sign."

"First sign of what?"

"That you've finally met 'the one'." Somehow she got her arms around Bo's thick neck and gave him a squeeze. "Oh, I'm so happy for you, Bo."

"Whoa, whoa, whoa, wait a minute." Bo was starting to feel a little nauseated. "I didn't say that this… person is 'the one'. I mean, aside from a whole lot of other… *stuff*"—stuff he really didn't want to get into right now—"all we've done up to this point is talk."

"I know. That's what makes it so wonderful. I'll bet it was like the two of you were in your own little world the whole time, wasn't it?"

Now that she mentioned it…. "Look… it's a little more complicated than that, okay?"

"Oh, this just gets better and better." Andrea pulled out another chair and perched on the edge of it. "So… tell me all about her. What's she like? Is she nice?"

Before Bo could even think of where to start, he heard a bellow from upstairs.

"Yo, bro! Are you planning on getting any work done today or what?"

Saved again! This time by his brother. Must be his lucky day.

"Look, Andi," he said, calling her by her special nickname, hoping to deflect her annoyance, "please don't say anything to Ham about my meeting someone, okay? I need to think about this whole… *thing*… before I start telling people."

For a second, it looked like she might argue. Then she sighed. "Oh, all right. But you've got to give me something here. A crumb, at least."

Bo thought for a moment. "Do you remember Mom's diamond and emerald earrings? The ones you wore at the wedding?"

"Yeah."

"This person I met has eyes just like that, and every time I look into them, I feel like somebody punched me in the gut."

"Oh, my God, you're in love!"

Before Bo could recover from that pronouncement, his pop called, "Come on, boy, get your ass in gear. We're burning daylight."

Because he was a desperate man, Bo moved quickly enough that he made it all the way to the bottom of the stairs before Andrea called after him.

"Don't think this gets you off the hook forever, Bo Sanford. Sooner or later I'll get all the details out of you."

Bo had every confidence she would.

For the moment, he did as he was told.

He got his ass in gear!

CHAPTER
FIVE

BY THE time Bo showed up at the job site on Monday morning, he was the most exhilarated, the most confused—and the most tired— he'd ever been in his life.

The worst part was, he knew it was his own fault.

The tired part, at least.

After having put in a full day working with his brother on Saturday, he'd known he should have gone home and fallen into bed. He'd meant to. Really. But before he did, he decided to put in a quick call to Erick—just to check in and see how *his* day had gone—and they had ended up talking into the wee hours of the morning.

Again.

It was the same thing on Sunday. Spending all day hanging Sheetrock in the baby's room and then sitting up most of the night talking to Erick, this time over a couple of beers at a bar not far from where Erick lived.

He supposed he shouldn't have been surprised it had taken every ounce of energy he had to roll out of bed and come to work this morning. He felt like he could sleep for a week. Yet every time he tried, something inside him feared that when he woke up, he'd discover it had all been a dream.

It was so damn confusing. And annoying. So annoying that his mood resembled the sky— now turned an ominous dusky gray with an oncoming storm—when he pulled up to the site.

It figured the first person he'd run into would be Mac.

"Aha, so you are still alive," Mac said, walking toward Bo, his curly hair hidden by the yellow hard hat he wore. "I was starting to wonder if I needed to file a missing persons report on you."

Because they knew each other so well, Bo knew Mac was only half kidding, and he couldn't help feeling a twinge of guilt. He supposed he should have responded to at least one of Mac's attempts to get in touch this weekend, but since he hadn't wanted to answer any questions about the "someone" he'd met at the party, he had ignored all of them.

It was time to pay the piper.

"Yeah, hey, look, I'm sorry. I was a little busy this weekend."

"No shit. You look like hell."

"I feel worse. Believe me."

"What'd you do all weekend?"

Bo shrugged. "You know, just… stuff."

"Stuff, huh?" Mac had a broad smile. "Would any of that 'stuff' happen to include a certain girl you left the party with Friday night?"

"Some of it," Bo admitted, sticking to his decision to evade whenever possible and fib whenever required.

Mac waited a beat. "Well…?"

"Well what?"

"Did you spend the weekend with her?"

"Not the whole weekend. I spent most of it out at Ham's place, fixing up the baby's room," Bo said. Then, feeling guilty, he tossed his friend a bone. "We did talk on the phone a lot, and we met up for drinks last night."

Hoping Mac would be satisfied with that, Bo headed for the office trailer, trying to convey the impression he had a lot of work to do. Rather than go away, Mac just followed him like a pesky little brother, intent on getting the details.

"What's she like? Is she smart? Is she sexy? Does she have a great rack?"

Uncommonly annoyed, Bo said, "Yes, yes, and no. Okay?"

"Did you at least get her into bed?"

With one hand on the door to the office, Bo turned toward his friend. "Look, it's not like that, okay? This is different."

"Why? Is she jailbait or something?"

"Of course not. It's just… this person is… special." When Mac opened his mouth again, Bo said, "You know, I'm really not in the mood to talk about this right now, all right? So could you just lay off?"

Bo could tell Mac was hurt and he gentled his tone. "Look, it's not you, okay? I've never felt like this about anybody before, and I don't want to jinx it by…."

"By talking to your best friend about it?" Mac said, still sounding hurt.

"By talking to *anyone* about it," Bo stressed. "I need to figure this out for myself before I share it with anyone else."

Mac's eyes narrowed. "You really are hooked on this chick, aren't you?"

Bo closed his eyes. "Honestly, I don't know what I am." When he opened his eyes again, he saw compassion in his friend's eyes. "As soon as I figure it out, you'll be the first one I tell, okay?"

"Oh, all right," Mac said, sounding dejected. Then he grinned. "Just remember—I've still got that 'thinking that guy was a girl' story to hang over your head. So don't wait too long to fill me in or the rest of the crew may just catch wind of your mistake."

For the first time since he'd met Erick, the thrill that went through Bo's body had nothing to do with excitement and everything to do with something much more unsettling.

Something that felt very close to fear.

THAT feeling only got worse once the dreams started. He supposed he shouldn't be surprised when Erick began appearing in his dreams since his voice was generally the last thing Bo heard before falling asleep. They had taken to calling each other every night after Erick got home from work.

Erick worked at The Java Room on the east side of town, serving up skinny grand mochaccino lattes and other kinds of fancy coffees Bo couldn't keep straight, never mind drink. It was an easy job, Erick told him, and the hours were flexible enough for him to work around his ever-changing class schedule.

Most importantly, it paid enough for him to keep body and soul together.

If just barely.

It was one more way his and Erick's lives were worlds apart, since Bo would rather die than sit in one of those places sipping coffee and discussing politics and the latest book club best seller. But he supposed it took all kinds, and even he could admit his mind could probably use a little expanding.

Practically, what it meant, however, was they couldn't stay on the line for hours anymore because both needed their sleep. Even so, as the week went on, Bo found himself unconsciously waiting for the phone to ring before heading to bed.

So dreaming of Erick was perfectly understandable.

It was the nature of the dreams that was disturbing. The first time he woke up, hot and sweaty and aching, he put it down to having eaten a large Italian sub with extra hot peppers for dinner that night. Not that the heat he'd been feeling had been anywhere near his stomach, but he did feel a little nauseated so he was able to make it work for him. The next dream wasn't so easy to explain, and after waking up with his heart pounding and his sheets dampened, he had to get up and get a drink of water before he stopped shaking.

The next night was the same. And the next.

This was crazy. He was crazy! Never, not once in his whole life, had Bo ever questioned his sexuality. He'd always been attracted to women. Period! So why, suddenly, was he dreaming things he shouldn't be dreaming—and thinking things he shouldn't be thinking—about a guy?

He should end this right now, he told himself. Call Erick up and say, "It's been nice knowing you, buddy, but… adios, amigo," and that would be it. What would make it that much easier was he knew Erick wouldn't blame him for it.

In fact, on some level, he thought Erick was probably expecting it.

Which only made it that much more impossible for Bo to do.

He didn't like to think of himself as a coward, and that was exactly what the idea of running away from his feelings for Erick felt like.

Cowardice!

Still, he had to admit he was a little nervous by the time the next weekend rolled around. They had made tentative plans to get together Friday night, but Bo still wasn't sure how he felt about seeing Erick again. If just hearing his voice gave him sweaty dreams, what would seeing him do?

Cause his Levi's to spontaneously burst into flames?

Unlikely, perhaps, but clearly worrisome. Which was why, when quitting time came, Bo found himself dragging his feet, fussing with things in the office, going over the schedule for the umpteenth time. It let him stall the inevitable and gave him an acceptable reason to avoid the teasing of the crew members who were calling "good night" to each other as, one by one, they headed out.

Just when he thought it was safe, Mac popped his head in the door.

"Hey, Bo, a bunch of us are meeting at The Blue Shamrock for a couple beers, you want in?"

Bo shook his head. "Sorry. I have plans."

"With the 'mystery girl'?"

Inwardly, Bo cringed. Mac had begun calling Erick that earlier in the week, and though Bo felt guilty about it, he hadn't felt up to explaining that this mysterious person he was sort of seeing wasn't, in fact, a girl. Oh, he had thought about it, but when he'd asked Erick's opinion, Erick had encouraged him to wait and see how things panned out. It hadn't been a hard sell. Especially once he discovered the crew had somehow gotten wind of the situation.

He supposed he shouldn't have been surprised. As anyone who has ever worked with a bunch of guys knows, guys gossip more than girls do. But again, they didn't know that Bo's new "lady friend" was actually a guy.

Though he knew someday he would have to come clean, for the moment, he was willing to bow to Erick's greater expertise. "Yeah, we're supposed to be getting together later."

"Why not bring her by The Shamrock? We're all dying to get a look at the girl who has single-handedly managed to bring The Great Bo Sanford to heel."

Bo felt another stab of guilt. "I'll make the suggestion, but...."

"Yeah, I know... *but*. Still, I know the guys would just love to find out what kind of girl could get you so turned around you almost put that window in upside down."

Bo groaned. Jeez, that had been humiliating. He never made those kinds of mistakes. Ever! But even he had to admit his mind hadn't exactly been on his work these days.

So he couldn't really resent the grin on Mac's face.

"How about if I just say I'll see you on Monday?" Bo asked.

"In that case, be good," Mac said by way of good-bye. "And if you can't be good, be sure to name it after me."

That was one thing he wouldn't have to worry about, Bo thought, but it was small comfort. Even if he couldn't get Erick pregnant, the thought of having anything even remotely resembling that kind of… call it "intimate"… contact with him had Bo's heart leaping out of his chest to dance a jig on the desk in front of him. The worst part was, he didn't know if it was dancing for joy or having some kind of weird attack that would have him dropping dead any minute.

The wondering made it jitter even faster as Bo shut off the lights and headed for home.

As THEIR plans for the evening had been definite in intent but vague in detail, Bo was surprised when he approached his apartment building and found Erick sitting on the steps outside reading a book.

For a split second, Bo was annoyed. What if someone saw him out there? What would they think? Then he told himself he was being paranoid. There was nothing odd or unusual about a guy waiting outside his friend's apartment for his friend to get home from work.

It was perfectly normal.

It was all the feelings bubbling up inside him—the joy, the excitement, the anticipation—that weren't exactly normal.

When Erick looked up from his book and their gazes met, Bo felt his irritation dissolve. Normal or not, he felt happier when he was with Erick than he had in a very long time. Despite his misgivings, he wasn't ready to give that up.

As Bo walked toward him, Erick tucked the book he'd been reading into his backpack, stood, and slung the backpack over his shoulder. He was more conventionally dressed today than he had been at any other time they'd seen one another—in a worn University of Massachusetts sweatshirt pushed up to his elbows and a pair of faded jeans—but there was still something innately feminine about him. The way he moved, the way he tilted his head and smiled at Bo before coming down the steps to meet him, the ridiculously long eyelashes that framed his green eyes, they all worked together to give the impression of softness, and for lack of a better word, femaleness.

Which might possibly explain why, even as their gazes caught and held, Bo felt an uncomfortable tightness start in his chest and slowly work its way to his groin.

Obviously, his body wasn't having the same misgivings as his brain. It was already firing on all cylinders and they were only at the starting gate.

Feeling flustered by the surge of what could only be termed lust, the only thing he could come up with to say was, "Hey."

Erick smiled. "Hey. My three o'clock class got cancelled, so I came on over. I hope that's okay."

"Yeah, I guess it's okay but... how did you know where I live?"

"There's this funny little invention they have nowadays called the Internet you can use to find out all kinds of stuff about people."

Erick's eyes crinkled around the edges, a sign Bo already recognized as Erick readjusting his thought processes. "But now that you mention it, I didn't stop to think you might be keeping it a secret on purpose. I'm sorry. I can go and we could get together later. That is... if you still want to."

"No! I mean yeah. I mean, no, I don't want you to go. It's great you're here now. It's just I wasn't ready... I wasn't prepared...." He blew out a breath, trying to gather his scattered wits. "I guess I'm not dealing very well with the unexpected these days, that's all."

It wasn't what he wanted to say... it didn't even come close... but somehow Erick seemed to understand.

"Considering all the unexpected things that have been going on in your life lately, it would be surprising if you weren't feeling a little off."

You can say that again! Bo thought.

"How about if I promise to keep any future spontaneous appearances to a minimum, okay?"

Bo blew out another breath, nodded, and then started leading the way up the steps.

Then he stopped dead.

He'd just thought of something else that wasn't quite prepared for visitors.

"Ahh… look… seeing as I wasn't expecting company, my place is a little bit of a mess right now."

"Don't worry about it," Erick said. "You wouldn't believe what a pig my third roommate was. I had to keep my shoes on all the time just to avoid stepping in the hazardous waste."

Though it sounded bad, Bo had no doubt the pig had nothing on him at the moment, and he tried to remember exactly how long it had been since he'd last shoveled the place out.

Timing it at somewhere between the last poker night he'd hosted and his brother Charlie's birthday—both of which had been more than three months ago—he gave up in despair.

"Maybe we should head out now instead."

"Fine with me, but I would have thought you'd want to change first."

Bo looked down at his clothes. They were covered in mud and sawdust and a bunch of other substances he probably didn't want to identify. Then he gave himself a discreet sniff, which instantly decided the matter for him.

"All right. We'll go in. But I'm warning you, it's a disaster area in there."

"I'm your friend, Bo, not Martha friggin' Stewart," Erick said dryly. "I think I'll live."

"If you say so." Bo took a deep breath and opened the front door to the building. "Here goes."

CHAPTER
SIX

AS HE led Erick through the entryway, Bo bypassed the row of mailboxes and used his key card to unlock the second door. The stairs were straight in front of them, and they climbed up to the second floor and then walked down a carpeted hallway before stopping next to a door that had a small bench sitting in the hall outside of it.

Out of habit, Bo sat, unlaced his work boots and took them off. He stood up again, boots in hand, and unlocked the door. After letting Erick in, he closed the door behind them and set the boots down on a mat that had seen better days.

"You can drop your stuff anywhere," he told him.

Once Erick had dumped his backpack, Bo led the way down the little hallway into the main living area and turned on the overhead light. Thankfully, it wasn't too bad, mostly because there wasn't enough space in the room for much more than the enormous black leather sofa that took up one whole wall and a television the size of Montana that was mounted to the other. The only other furniture in the room—a scarred glass and chrome coffee table—stood between the two and bore a pair of balled-up, holey socks and the remnants of last night's dinner.

A bit untidy, perhaps. But not too bad, all in all.

Bo had left the door to his bedroom open, and even from this distance, he could see the floor was pretty much obscured by dirty clothing—a blessing in disguise since he couldn't remember the last time he'd vacuumed the place. Thankfully, the unmade bed was only partly visible, and the bathroom, which stood off the bedroom, was completely hidden from view.

The kitchen, however, was another matter.

Open as it was to the living area, there was no way to avoid seeing the mess Bo had to admit had gotten way out of hand. Dirty dishes cluttered every inch of the counter, some still retaining leftovers from one meal or another, and the sink was piled high with what was probably every other piece of dishware he owned.

None of which had been washed in the memorable past.

The small round table in the corner—the one Bo wasn't sure why he owned since he never ate there—was littered with piles of newspapers he hardly ever read and bits and pieces of junk mail he'd tossed there for lack of anywhere else to put them. It also held an assortment of cereal boxes, most of which were the sort that usually came with a toy inside.

Not exactly health food, but then he was usually in a rush in the morning.

Dinner was another matter, and as Bo liked to cook, the stove top was usually clean. At the moment, however, it was covered with pots that were still crusted from Wednesday night's spaghetti dinner, and a few dried puddles of sauce dribbled across the cooktop and down the front of the stove.

Even the garbage can by the back door was filled to overflowing and the floor around it splotched with random sticky spots that clung to Bo's socks as he hurried over to tug the bag out of the bin and tie it up. Feeling sheepish, he opened the back door and tossed the bag out onto the little balcony. He turned to face Erick, who was still standing in the living room, looking shell-shocked.

Bo shrugged uncomfortably. "I told you it was kind of a mess."

"Kind of a mess? Bo, this place looks like Haiti after the earthquake. Does your mother know you live like this?"

There was a long, awkward pause.

"My mother died when I was twelve," Bo said quietly.

"Oh, shit." Erick closed his eyes and ran his hand over his mouth as if he could erase the words that had just come out of it. "I'm sorry."

"It's okay."

"No. It's not." Erick opened his eyes and they were filled with apology. "Sometimes I have a really big mouth."

"It's okay, really. You couldn't have known."

"Maybe not, but I did know something was wrong somewhere."

"How?"

"Because you never talk about her. You talk about your father and your brothers all the time, but you've never once mentioned your mother. But I never stopped to think… do you mind if I ask how she died?"

Again there was a pause, but this time it wasn't so much awkward as it was painful.

"She killed herself."

Abruptly, Erick turned his back, but somehow, now that he'd started, Bo didn't want to stop. "Not that anyone in my family actually acknowledges that. The official party line is that she died in a car crash."

"Then how do you know it was intentional?"

"Because no matter how much I might have wanted to believe the official version, eventually I grew up enough to know a single car on an empty highway on a perfectly clear day doesn't just happen to slam itself into a bridge abutment, killing the only passenger, who, coincidently, wasn't wearing her seat belt at the time, unless there's something wrong somewhere." Bo cleared his throat. "So I had a buddy of mine down at the police department pull the case file."

"And?"

"It was all there in black and white. No drugs or alcohol in her system. No evidence of heart attack or stroke. No skid marks. No evidence of foul play. Official cause of death: undetermined. Unofficial: suicide."

Though he didn't turn to face Bo, Erick did ask, "Do you know why she did it? Was she depressed or...?"

"Not that I can remember. I tried asking Pop about it once, but he refused to talk about it, and when I pushed.... Let's just say the fact that I couldn't sit down for a week afterwards convinced me never to ask again."

Erick nodded but he still didn't turn around, and there was something about the set of his shoulders that was somehow... off.

After a moment, Bo walked over to where he was standing, but Erick didn't face him, and when he put a light hand on his arm and tried to turn him, Erick resisted.

"What's the matter?" Bo asked him.

"Nothing."

Bo tried again to turn him around, this time a little more firmly, and again Erick resisted, even taking a step away from him.

The "no trespassing" sign was as clear as daylight.

Not sure what was going on, Bo stopped trying to touch him, but he couldn't help asking, "Erick, what's wrong?"

"Nothing's wrong. I'm just sorry you lost your mother, that's all."

The words were clear enough, but his voice sounded strange. Muffled. Bo was completely at a loss. Then a crazy thought dawned on him.

"Are you crying?" he asked.

"Yes," Erick said shortly.

"Why?"

"I told you: I'm sorry you lost your mother. Now, could you please just give me a minute here?"

Bo was seriously confused. "Why would you cry about my mother? It's not like you knew her or anything."

"I know that."

"Then why are you crying?"

"Because that's what I do, okay?" Erick said, his patience clearly strained. "I cry. I cry over everything. I cry over Save the Children commercials. I cry over Hallmark cards. I cry at every damn thing. Now, why don't you just go take your shower or something and leave me alone?"

Rather than head for the bathroom, Bo took another step toward Erick, but Erick countered it, taking a step away. Bo tried to go around him, and again, Erick turned away—as if they were involved in some kind of macabre dance ritual.

Losing patience, Bo put a hand on his shoulder to hold him still, and when Erick tried to jerk away, he tightened his grip and gave him a little shake.

"Stop it," he commanded.

"I'm trying, you jerk!"

Now Bo could actually hear the tears in Erick's voice.

"No, I mean stop trying to hide from me. I don't care if you cry. Actually, I think it's kind of sweet."

Erick rounded on him. "Oh yeah? Well, try being the only seventh-grade boy who cries when the class hamster dies and see how sweet it is then. Talk about being the class clown, and not in a good way."

Because he didn't know what else to do, Bo went with his gut and put his arms around Erick, pulling him into a hug. To his credit, Erick didn't resist, but he didn't relax either.

Hoping to ease some of the tension, Bo said, "You know, even though my apartment may look like it, I'm not in seventh grade anymore. Which means I'm not going to tease you for crying. Especially about something like this. It is sad someone would do that to herself. Not to mention what it did to all of us."

"But that's just it," Erick said tightly. "This is *your* sorrow, not mine. So I'm the one who should be comforting you, not the other way around."

"I don't need comforting. I got over what she did a long time ago."

Erick let out a sound that might have been a laugh. "Yeah, well, I've got about $40,000 in student loans that say no one ever gets over losing their mother. Especially like that."

"Okay. So I didn't get over it," Bo admitted. "I have learned to live with it, though. And I'm sorry I hit you with it so bluntly. I guess I could have put it a little more tactfully."

"It doesn't matter," Erick said, and his voice sounded more normal, at least to Bo's ears. "Sooner or later this would have happened. But in defense of gay men everywhere, I do feel I have to tell you this whole 'crying at everything' thing isn't a gay thing, it's a me thing. And I'm sorry I got defensive about it. It's just… you can't believe how much shit I put up with over the years."

Maybe Bo couldn't know. But he could imagine.

"I'm sure it must have been tough—then. But I'll bet it will come in handy with your patients someday, having that kind of empathy."

"Oddly enough, I don't do it when I'm in a clinical situation. Which is good. Because when I'm working, I'm there to help the person, not blubber all over them. I still can't seem to control it when it involves someone I care about personally."

A surge of warmth that had nothing to do with lust flooded through Bo.

"I care about you too. So why don't you just shut up for a minute and let me do what *I* do when *I* care about someone?"

"Which is…?"

"I hold them when they cry. It's not a straight thing, it's a me thing," he teased. "So work with me, okay?"

This time Erick's laugh sounded genuine. "Well, if you really feel like you have to, I guess I can live with it."

Erick finally relaxed in Bo's arms, and Bo found it was nice being close to him this way, not that he hadn't hugged guys before. He had, on occasion. He'd hugged his brothers, Mac, and even some of his other friends at one time or another.

But "holding" is different from "hugging."

And holding a guy, Bo was finding, was different from holding a girl. There wasn't any softness to Erick's frame to counterbalance his own hard strength, no curves that fit in and around Bo's body the way a woman's would. All the same, Erick fit nicely. He even rested his head on Bo's chest in the same way a girl would—snuggling his cheek in the little cove beneath his collarbone that his first girlfriend used to call "the nook"—as if it had been put there especially for her comfort and convenience.

When he instinctively smoothed his hand over Erick's hair, Erick gave the same kind of sigh of contentment Bo's first girlfriend had.

As the holding went on, it became something more than comfort—for both of them. Something more like… need. That is, if the hard ridge of flesh that was currently pressing against Bo's thigh was any indication. Bo supposed he wouldn't have minded it so much if he hadn't known Erick was feeling the same kind of pressure somewhere in the area of his belly.

More than a little embarrassed, Bo dropped his arms and stepped back.

Erick didn't resist or even comment and there was a short and—to Bo's mind anyway—awkward pause before Bo jerked a thumb in the direction of the bedroom.

"I guess I'd better go take that shower now. I probably reek."

Now Erick smiled, just a bit. "Actually, you smell kind of sexy, but that is a gay thing, so I doubt the people at the pizza place are going to agree with me."

Oddly enough, rather than embarrass him further, the comment made Bo laugh.

"I guess I'd better get going. We wouldn't want to gross out the masses."

"Yeah, I guess you'd better." Erick gave him a little shove to get him moving. "If you find yourself needing your back scrubbed, give me a holler."

As Erick was already headed toward the kitchen as he said it, Bo told himself he had been only kidding, but when he finally got into the shower, he decided not to take any chances.

He turned the faucet all the way to cold.

ODDLY enough, though he was only in the shower long enough to get his body clean and his hormones under control—which, in retrospect, was probably longer than his usual postwork showers—when he opened the door to his bedroom, it looked like an army of house elves had been hard at work. Every piece of dirty clothing had magically disappeared, to the point that he could actually see the floor.

And yes, it did need a good vacuuming.

Not only that, but his king-sized bed was not only unmade, it had been completely stripped—the deep blue comforter folded neatly on the end of it, with two pillowcase-less pillows plumped on top of it.

A quick peek around the room confirmed the rest of his things were still in place, more or less. Except for the stray glassware and plates that had been there. They were gone and so was all the trash. Thankfully, when he checked his dresser drawers, he found there were still enough clothes in them for him to make it out of the room with his modesty intact.

But just barely.

The jeans were especially bad, as they were uncomfortably tight and deeply worn in several awkward places. They also had a number of holes in them to go along with the tattered hems. The T-shirt was in better shape but it, too, was tight and had shrunk enough to leave a small strip of tanned skin showing between it and the waistband of his jeans.

When he got to the living room, it looked the same as it had when he'd left it except for the now clean coffee table and a pair of giant trash bags, filled almost to bursting, that had been plopped beside the front door.

It was when he got to the door of the kitchen that he stopped dead in his tracks.

He could actually see the counters, and the stove top was not only devoid of pots and pans but clean. The table had been cleared as well except for a short stack of mail piled in the center. A mountain of newspapers sat by the back door, neatly tied with string, and the assortment of cereal boxes that had decorated the table were now neatly lined up on top of the refrigerator.

Even the dishes were gone. All of them!

Considering how briefly he'd been indisposed, Bo would have thought it was the dishes that were filling the bags by the front door except there were still a few standing next to the sink. Ones Erick was drying with... well... he wasn't quite sure what the piece of material was. It might have been a T-shirt at one time.

Now it was just a rag.

"What the hell happened in here?" Bo demanded.

"It's called cleaning," Erick said, reaching up to put some glasses away. "You should try it sometime."

Once he was done putting the rest of the dishes away, Erick turned, and after looking Bo up and down, he grinned and wiggled his eyebrows. "Nice outfit."

Bo wasn't sure he trusted the glint in Erick's eye.

"What's that supposed to mean?"

"It means we're going to have to be careful where we go tonight. If the two of us happen to wander anywhere near a gay bar, the guys are going to come swarming out in droves and drag you in off the street. As it is, no matter where we go, I'm going to have to beat the competition off with a stick."

Blushing fiercely, Bo said, "I would apologize, but somehow, while I was showering, the rest of my wardrobe seems to have disappeared."

"Don't worry, we'll find it. When we do, that little number is going in the 'only wear when I'm around' category."

As if literally throwing in the towel, Erick tossed the rag he'd been using into the now empty trash can at the end of the counter.

"For the moment, beggars can't be choosers." He pushed off the counter and headed for the living room. "Come on. Let's go."

"Where are we going?" Bo asked.

"You did mention something about pizza, right?"

"Yeah."

"Well, then?"

Telling himself it was laziness rather than fear of running into any kind of awkward situation that prompted the idea, Bo said, "Now that the place is cleaned up, wouldn't you rather order in?"

"This place isn't cleaned up, it's simply been removed from the board of health hit list—temporarily. So… after you feed me, we're going to find a Laundromat. Then, assuming your wardrobe doesn't dissolve when it comes into contact with soap and water, we will come back here and finish the job. But not before we hit the hardware store for a box of cleaning supplies, a pair of rubber gloves, and a hazmat suit, because I'm not touching anything in that refrigerator without any and all of the above."

After moving to the front door, Erick grabbed one of the two big bags, lifted Bo's ring of keys off a hook on the wall—one that hadn't been there when they'd first arrived—and tossed them to him.

"Oh, and even without having inspected the area for myself, I'm telling you right now, judging from the rest of this pigsty—that bathroom in there—is all yours."

Bo shrugged. He'd only just showered in there. How bad could it be?

He thought again. Maybe they'd better make that two hazmat suits.

CHAPTER
SEVEN

AFTER that first weekend, things settled down into a predictable—if not always comfortable—routine. More to keep up appearances than from any real desire, Bo went back to meeting with the guys after work for a beer now and then. It wasn't a major sacrifice. Erick was usually working or studying at that time, anyway, and while it didn't keep the questions from coming, it did keep the teasing to a minimum.

Even Mac backed off. A little. Oh, he still continued to harass Bo about the "mystery girl" at each and every opportunity—to the point that, on several occasions, Bo had threatened to punch him if he didn't stop—but he had put up with enough of Mac's teasing over the years not to let it get to him.

Too much.

Even with all that going on around them, Bo and Erick still managed a quick phone call every night. They chatted about their respective days or what they were doing at the time or what they might decide to do that weekend. Little things like that.

But the weekends... the weekends were a different story.

Those were spent together. Especially now that Ham's house was finished. They didn't do anything earth-shattering. They mostly hung out, spending time at Bo's place—now that it was habitable again—or having coffee or a beer in places that were off the beaten track. Places where they were unlikely to run into anyone either of them knew. They even ventured farther afield now and again, taking trips into Boston or up to New Hampshire, exploring the hamlets and villages of New England even as they explored one another's lives.

However, as the weeks went on, Bo slowly came to the realization that despite their hours of conversation, he knew very little about Erick.

Oh, Erick could and did spend hours talking about other people, his friends or his various field study cases—with no names mentioned, of course. Still his greatest gift seemed to be his ability to draw other people out, to get them talking about themselves, to the point they never even noticed he volunteered almost nothing about himself.

But Bo noticed, and the more he thought about it, the more it bothered him.

Finally, one beautiful day in April—a day he knew Erick got out of class early—he decided to take matters into his own hands. He called the crew together at noon and announced he was letting them all go home early. With pay!

Why the hell not? They were on schedule—more or less—and he was confident they would make the June 1 deadline.

Why not goof off a little?

Besides, if he was going to be forced into being the boss, he might as well take advantage of the situation and give himself, and everyone else, a break now and then.

Unfortunately, it took him longer than he thought to get across town and he was just pulling up to Erick's building when he spotted Erick heading down the sidewalk.

Already smiling, Bo parked, got out, and waited for Erick to notice him.

Once he did, he came to a dead stop. "What are you doing here?"

The harshness of his tone made Bo's smile fade. "I let the crew go early so I could come over and surprise you."

Erick's face didn't change by as much as an eyelash. "You shouldn't have done that."

His tone put Bo's back up. "Why not? Afraid I'll get fired for playing hooky?"

"No. I just don't think you should have stopped by without warning me you were coming."

Trying for a bit of humor, Bo asked, "Why? Do you have a boyfriend I don't know about waiting for you upstairs?"

"No."

"Then what's the problem?"

In his usual blunt fashion, Erick said, "I don't want you to see where I live."

"Well, it can't possibly be worse than my place was the first time *you* saw it, right?" Bo teased, but Erick didn't respond in kind.

"Not in the same way, no. But I still don't want you to see it."

Now Bo was getting annoyed. "There's a lot you don't want me to see, isn't there?"

"What does that mean?"

"It means you know just about everything there is to know about me—every stupid mistake I've ever made, every disastrous date I've ever been on. You even know about the time when I was four and I ran out to meet the ice cream truck stark naked. And I don't know anything about you."

"That's not true."

"It's true enough. I want to know why." There was a long, *long* pause; then Bo said, "Look, I know we haven't exactly defined what it is we have going on here, but at the very least, I like to think we're friends. And in my book, friends know stuff about each other. I want to know more about you. Is that such a crime?"

Finally, there was a hint of a smile. "No, it's not a crime."

"Then are you going to let me in or not?"

He was asking about more than simply entering the apartment and he was pretty sure both of them knew it.

"All right," Erick said with a sigh. "Don't say I didn't warn you."

As he had often dropped Erick off at the door, Bo had already seen for himself the building he lived in was old and not well maintained, but when Erick opened the front door, he was surprised at how small and dingy the entryway was.

He also noted there were only two mailboxes hanging on the wall, neither of which was labeled "Erick Stevens."

To the left of the entryway was a door that obviously led into one of the apartments, but rather than enter it, Erick led the way up a narrow set of stairs to the second floor. Straight ahead of them was a cramped bathroom with a small sink and tiny shower stall, and on either side of the landing was a door.

Because it was what he did, Bo knew neither door was a proper entryway door. Rather, they were hollow-core closet doors.

A building code violation of major proportions.

Bo expected Erick would open the door on the right, as it was the only one with a lock set. Instead he opened the one on the left. Surprisingly, rather than leading into an apartment, it opened onto another set of stairs that, if possible, was even smaller and narrower than the last.

"Watch your head," Erick told him, and Bo had to duck before he could enter the stairwell.

When they got to the top, there was a door. It was of the same quality as the one below, only this one boasted a better lock and an obviously new deadbolt.

After turning the lock, Erick opened the door and gestured Bo inside.

"Here we are. Home sweet home."

After they both got in, Erick turned and locked the door behind him. Bo would have told him not to bother, since any twelve-year-old with a stout pair of boots could simply kick the door off its hinges if he wanted to get in, but he was too shocked by what he saw to say much of anything.

This wasn't an apartment, it was an attic!

Or at least it had been before somebody had Sheetrocked the ceiling. They had also covered the long walls with paneling up to the roofline so that while the edges of the room did slope a bit, you could stand up straight in most of it. But it was still just one, small, narrow room with a window at either end. There wasn't even a bathroom, and Bo had to assume the one they had passed on the second floor was the one Erick used.

That wasn't the only thing wrong with the place, either.

Though it was clean and almost fanatically tidy, the furnishings were… sparse, to say the least. At one end, beneath one of the windows, a full-sized box spring and mattress sat on the floor, covered with a bedspread folded neatly over the pillows. It reminded Bo of the spread his grandmother had once had, only this one had stripes rather than flowers. Still, it was old and had been washed so many times it was faded and the nap was worn smooth in spots. Sitting beside the bed was an upended orange crate that obviously served as a nightstand with a clock sitting on top beside an open book.

All along the back wall—on either side of a beat-up desk—there were short bookshelves built out of several lengths of pine board and a bunch of cinder blocks. The ones at the end nearest the bed held a couple of baskets stacked with neatly folded clothing while on the other side there was a fairly large collection of books and a small boom box with a stack of CDs sitting beside it.

A brown couch that could only have come from a trash heap somewhere slouched in the middle of the room and had been turned to separate "the living room" from "the kitchen."

Or what the landlord probably called "the kitchen." Bo would have called it "pathetic" but even that word didn't cover it. The whole thing consisted of one cheap cupboard hung on the wall with a tiny sink and a smidgen of countertop sitting below it. Next to it sat a tiny refrigerator and a set of shelves someone had made, again, with pieces of wood supported by cinder blocks.

Sandwiched between the cinder blocks at about knee height was one long piece of wood that served as a shelf for storage of pots and pans and dishes, while the upper piece, covered in cheap contact paper, held a small coffeemaker, a toaster oven, and a single hot plate.

That was it.

"Judas Priest," Bo said under his breath.

While Bo had been otherwise occupied, Erick had crossed the room, put his backpack next to the desk, and extracted his laptop. Setting the computer on top of the desk, he turned, and leaning back against the desk, faced Bo directly.

"Now do you see why I don't encourage visitors?"

Bo was still too stunned to think clearly, never mind be tactful. "Is this place even a legal apartment?"

"I doubt it. But it gets the job done."

"What job?"

"It keeps the rain off and gives me a place to store my stuff that doesn't consist of a shopping cart or a cardboard box."

"Not by much it doesn't. Why do you live here?"

"Because it's cheap, and after paying for tuition, books, gas for my car, and food, there isn't much left over for the niceties. What little there is left, I'd rather use to spend time with my friends than pay for a place I pretty much use only to sleep."

Bo thought guiltily of all the beers he and Erick had drunk and the pizzas they'd split. "If things are that tough, why not live in a dorm on campus? They must be better than this place."

"In some ways they are, but they're also more expensive, and while I could use some of my financial aid to help pay for it, I already have enough in student loans—not to mention some medical bills I've managed to rack up—to keep me in debt until I'm well past retirement age. Besides, I'm tired of living with roommates. Not to mention the other guys in the dorm, most of whom are okay but some of whom were starting to become a problem."

"You mean the ones who hate gays?" Bo asked, but Erick shook his head.

"No, those types I can deal with. It's the bicurious ones who really drove me crazy."

"Bicurious? I don't even know what that means."

"It means just what it sounds like. People who are curious about what things are like on the other side of the fence. Either because they think they might be gay or bisexual and want to find out for sure, or because they're pretty sure they aren't gay or bisexual, but figure, 'What the hell? Why not try it out?' Either way, it's a little hard on the ego to hook up with someone and find out that, rather than actually liking you, they were using you as a lab rat to experiment with their sexuality."

Something must have shown on Bo's face, some of the helplessness he was feeling, because Erick said, "Look, Bo, this is my choice, okay? With the degree I have now, I could get a job if I wanted to. I could move to a better place, finish my degree at night. I don't want to. I'm tired of being a student. I just want to get all of this done and over with so I can start living my life. So, until then… this is it for me."

Bo couldn't quite believe what he was hearing.

"Isn't there anyone who could help you? Like your parents?"

When Erick looked away, Bo felt the familiar frustration begin.

"What's the matter? Too personal a question for you?" When Erick didn't respond, he pressed. "Look, I know we haven't known each other long, but I'm supposed to be your friend. And the time we spend together isn't a therapy session where you, as the counselor, get to ask all the questions and I, as the patient, have to answer them. Communication is supposed to go both ways or it's not really communication at all. It's just background noise."

"You're right." Bo was surprised Erick agreed so readily. He thought it would be a much harder sell. "Things should go both ways. Then again… it's the same as you coming over here and seeing this place. You have every right to ask the questions, but you're the one who's going to have to deal with it if you don't like the answers."

"Whatever the answers are, I can deal with them. I just want to know."

"All right. What do you want to know?"

There were a thousand things Bo wanted to know about Erick, but he decided to start with the most pertinent question at the moment.

"Why can't your parents help you pay for grad school?"

Though Erick's stance was rigid, his voice remained cool and even. "My parents can't help me because, in the strictest sense of the word, I don't have any parents. I do have a mother and a father, obviously, but they were never married. At least to each other."

"So they weren't married, so what? Your dad must have paid child support or something like that, right? Can't he help you now?"

"My dad—if you want to call him that—isn't in a position to help anyone right now because he's busy serving seven to ten years in prison for his second count of armed robbery."

As if he'd been punched in the gut, Bo huffed out a breath, but Erick ignored him. "That's assuming the guy my mother said was my father really is my father. Which, with my mother, could go either way. She has what we'll call 'issues' when it comes to telling the truth."

Feeling sick to his stomach, Bo said, "So she has issues. She's still your mother. Can't she help you now?"

"She could, I guess, if I was willing to ask."

"Why aren't you?"

"Because she's worked hard enough already," Erick said, and Bo heard a slight softening in his voice. "See, she was only sixteen when I was born. And although her parents helped out enough in the early years to make sure she graduated from high school, after that, they kind of washed their hands of both of us. To give credit where credit is due, I have to say she did a pretty decent job of taking care of things, most of the time. She worked two jobs, sometimes three, trying to keep a roof over our heads, put food on the table. It was tough, but she did it.

"But even from the time I was little, I knew she wasn't really interested in being a mother. Much less a parent. All she wanted to do was put in her time until I got old enough for her to get her life back. I think the way she saw it, she'd made one little mistake and spent the next fifteen years paying for it."

"The next *fifteen* years?" Bo asked. "What happened after that?"

"Nothing horrible, if that's what you're thinking. She just met a guy. A pretty nice guy actually. Larry, his name is. Larry the cable guy, if you can believe that one, since he really was at our house fixing the cable when they met. After he moved in, things got a lot easier for her. She didn't have to do it all on her own anymore."

"Forget about her… what about you?"

"Oh, I was still around, but I was pretty much self-sufficient by that time. I'd had jobs practically from the time I could walk— delivering papers, mowing lawns, that kind of stuff—so by the time Larry showed up, I was already paying most of my own way—buying my own clothes and school supplies and things. After he moved in, I started spending most of my free time at the library, which was a good thing because I was able to get enough in scholarships to cover almost all of my first year of college. Plus it got me out of the house, which was also a good thing."

"How come?"

"Let's just say Larry and I didn't always see eye to eye on things, especially when it came to discipline. See… I had gotten pretty used to doing whatever the hell I wanted, and I didn't appreciate him trying to boss me around. On the other hand, he didn't appreciate having to share my mother's time and attention with a mouthy teenager—especially a gay one. So we pretty much stayed out of each other's way until I graduated from high school and left for college.

"Two weeks later, the two of them packed up, moved to Texas, and I haven't seen either of them since."

"Ever?"

"Nope. We exchange birthday cards, and she usually sends me something for Christmas. I call her on Mother's Day when I remember, but for all intents and purposes, we stay out of each other's lives."

Not quite ready to give up, Bo asked, "What about your grandparents? You said they helped out when you were little. Couldn't they do anything for you now?"

Erick's eyes changed in a way Bo had never seen before: they went as hard as emeralds, and just as cold.

"I tried contacting them once, when I was really desperate. They didn't want to have anything to do with me. You see, my mother's father is an elder in his church, and having had a sixteen-year-old daughter who got pregnant out of wedlock had been a major embarrassment to them. So you can imagine how they felt when they found out their only grandson was gay. Not a pretty scene, as you can imagine. After a few harsh words on both sides, I was very politely shown the door and told never to come back."

Feeling sick, Bo moved to the sofa and sat down. Leaning forward, he propped his elbows on his knees and dropped his forehead onto the heels of his hands.

"I don't believe what I'm hearing," he said, then lifted his head abruptly. "I didn't mean that the way it sounded. I *do* believe you. I just meant…."

"I know what you meant," Erick said, sounding more like his usual self. "The whole thing sounds like a really bad country and western song, doesn't it?"

When Bo didn't respond, he said, "Look, Bo, I didn't tell you all of that to upset you or to make you feel bad. My life is what it is. The only thing pitying me is going to do is piss me off."

"Pitying you? Is that what you're afraid of? That I'm going to pity you?"

"Don't you?"

"Hell, no! I admire you."

"Admire me?" The genuine shock in Erick's voice would have made Bo smile if he hadn't been battling so many other emotions. "For what?"

"How about we start with surviving? For becoming such a great person in spite of it all? But mostly, for not going around whining about it all the time."

Bo got up and crossed to where Erick stood, then put his hands on Erick's shoulders, commanding his attention.

"Do you have any idea how many people I know who haven't had it nearly as tough as you have and still spend all their time whining about how unfair their lives have been? Plenty. But not you. You just go out and do what has to be done. You know what you want and you're not afraid to work your ass off to get it. I find that absolutely amazing. I find *you* amazing."

"Yeah, well, don't be too impressed," Erick said, but even as he did, tears came into his eyes. "There's still a lot you don't know about me."

"Maybe so, but I can't think of anything you could tell me that would change the way I see you."

When one of the tears spilled over, Bo reached out and brushed it away with his thumb, cupping Erick's cheek in his palm. There was a long moment of silence as they looked at each other. Erick's cheek didn't feel soft—not in the same way a girl's would—but it was smooth and warm and Bo felt something pulling at him, a need that had him drawing closer.

Even as he leaned in, Erick put a hand on his chest, subtly pushing him away.

"I can think of a dozen things right off the top my head, but I think you've seen enough of my dirty laundry for one day."

By the tone of his voice, Bo could tell Erick was trying to break the sexual tension that had risen between them and he was about to call him on it when Erick said, "You were right when you said communication should go both ways. I guess I'm just not used to talking about myself. I promise I'll try harder, okay?" Then he smiled. "And for the record, I think you're pretty amazing too. Most construction guys I know would be afraid to even walk into a place like this. Not without a hard hat, anyway."

Though he was still annoyed, Bo couldn't help smiling back.

"It's not so bad. Besides, if it's held up this long, I figure it will hold up a little bit longer. Still, I can't help thinking that a skylight in the roof would help brighten the place up."

Erick laughed, as he'd intended. "I'll be sure to mention that to the landlord, but somehow I doubt he'll go for it."

"I could get the window for him at cost and I wouldn't charge him for the labor."

"Now *that* he might go for."

"You could also try telling him it would make things a lot cooler up here, especially in the summer. It must get hot as hell in here in June because it's only April and already it's hot enough to bake a cake."

"It is a little warm at the moment." Erick seemed to consider for a minute. "You know... now that you've seen the seamier side of things, I could show you the upstairs terrace, if you'd like."

"There's an upstairs to this place?"

"Of a sort. How are you about dealing with heights?"

"I spent almost an entire summer doing roofing when I was sixteen."

"That'll do," Erick said. "Come on."

CHAPTER
EIGHT

GRABBING a pair of towels from one of the shelves on his way by, Erick led the way to the bed. Then, to Bo's surprise, he crawled onto it, shoved open the window, and lifted out the screen. He threw one leg over the sill, ducked through the window, and stepped out onto a tiny fire escape. With a bit of squeezing, Bo was able to follow, and he watched as Erick lifted one foot up onto the rusty railing and, grabbing hold of the edge of the roof for leverage, hauled himself up and climbed onto the roof.

Again, Bo followed, and after he'd gotten up, he followed Erick across a short portion of the roof to a flat area that backed up against a spot where the roof was more steeply pitched, as if the two sections had been added at different times.

After laying out the towels side by side, Erick sat down on one and leaned back against the roof. Bo did likewise and found that the angle of the roof was perfect for resting against, like sitting in a lawn chair on a summer day. Because they were on the east side of the roof, facing away from the afternoon sun, it was shady up here and the two sat there enjoying the fresh air for a few moments.

"What do you think?" Erick asked after a bit.

"Not too bad," Bo admitted. "A little hard to get to, but... otherwise it's great."

"I love it up here. When I look out over the city this way, I feel like the king of all I survey." Erick's voice held a smile, as if amused at his own fancies. "It's even better at night."

"You come up here at night?"

"All the time. Especially when it's hot. Once the shingles cool off, it's a nice place to sit. Maybe catch a breeze. Sometimes I even bring a blanket and sleep up here."

Bo knew he was just being overprotective, but.... "Are you crazy? What if you roll over wrong? One minute you're sleeping and the next you're flatter than my old man's first try at baking a cake."

Erick laughed. "I thought you said you weren't afraid of heights."

"I'm not. I'm just not crazy about the idea of falling off them."

"I guess I can't argue with that. But you can relax. I don't do it very often and I'm not a restless sleeper. Mostly I come up here for the view." Erick tipped his head back and looked up at the sky. "Sometimes, when I was little and my mom was in a good mood— which wasn't very often—we would go for a walk after she picked me up at school and we'd end up lying down in the grass and looking up at the sky, trying to find pictures in the clouds. Like that one there." He pointed at a bunch of fluffy clouds. "If you look at it sideways, it kind of looks like a dragon with smoke coming out of its nose."

To Bo, it looked like a bunch of cotton balls mounded together, but he was more interested in listening to Erick talk than looking at the sky. Whether it was because of what he'd shared earlier or what Bo had said about communication, he didn't know, but for some reason, Erick seemed willing to talk about himself right now.

Bo was more than content to just listen.

"At night," he went on, "I like to come up here and look at the stars. They're not as bright here in the city, but I still love looking at them. I know it makes some people feel small and insignificant when they do that. They see all that space out there and think, 'I'm just a tiny speck of dust floating around in a great big cosmos, nothing special. Here one minute and gone the next.' Kind of depressing if you think about it that way."

"Is that how it makes *you* feel? Depressed?"

"In a way, I guess, but it makes me feel good too. Like there's a whole big universe out there and I get to be part of it, even if I am just a tiny speck of dust. I like knowing I'm part of something bigger than myself and my own problems. Keeps things in perspective." He turned his head so they were face to face. "I figure, even when my life's a mess, it's still small potatoes compared with whatever's going on out there, right? So why bitch about something that's really not such a big deal after all?"

"I don't know," Bo murmured but, again, he wasn't really thinking about what Erick was saying as much as he was thinking about Erick.

He cared about him so much. He was so wise and strong, yet his gentleness touched places inside Bo's heart he hadn't even known were there. Everything inside him yearned to be closer to him.

Almost of its own volition, Bo's hand came up, and he brushed the side of his index finger across Erick's cheek. "I've never known anyone like you before."

Very gently, Erick put his fingers on Bo's arm and nudged his hand away.

"Everybody says that," he teased. "I know it's probably just a polite way of saying, 'You're a real weirdo, Stevens,' but I appreciate the sentiment."

Erick turned to face the city again, and the two men sat there for a few long moments before Bo gathered up the courage to say, "Could I ask you something?"

"Haven't you heard enough for one day?"

When Bo didn't answer, Erick sighed. "Sure. Go ahead."

"Do you remember when you were talking earlier about those guys at school? The 'bicurious' ones?"

"Yeah."

Bo had to take a deep, fortifying breath before he could ask, "Is that why you think I'm with you right now? I don't mean now as in *right this minute* now. I just meant, in general. Do you think I'm spending time with you because I'm unsure of my sexuality or because I'm curious about what it would be like to be with a guy?"

"I don't know. Is that why *you* think you're spending time with me?"

Bo knew that kind of answer was a psychologist's trick, turning the question back on the one who asked it, but he answered anyway.

"Sometimes, I guess. Not that I was unsure of my sexuality before I met you. Up until then, I was 100 percent convinced I was straight. Now I'm not so sure. It's like... how can I be completely straight and still be so attracted to you?"

"I don't know. But I can imagine how wondering about it would tend to make you feel unsure of yourself."

Bo didn't think "unsure" was exactly the word he would use. More like "shaken to the core of his being," but for the moment, "unsure" would have to do.

"The funny thing is, though," Bo continued, "knowing I can be so attracted to a guy hasn't made me curious about what it would be like to be with one, or at least not with just any guy. What I *am* curious about is what it would be like to be with you. But I don't know if that's the same thing or not."

"It's not the same thing," Erick told him, surprising him. He hadn't really expected to get an answer to his question. "You're not spending time with me so you can figure out where you stand sexuality-wise, you're spending time with me because you like me and you enjoy my company. Just like I enjoy yours. The sexual attraction thing is just a side issue. A major one, but still a side issue."

Erick pulled up one knee and rested his arm on it. "In fact, if you want to talk about admiring people, I guess I'd have to say I admire you for not turning tail and running when you realized you *were* attracted to me."

"I tried that, remember?" Bo said dryly. "It didn't work so well."

"You could have made it work. Even after we spent that night at the coffee shop. You could have told yourself it was the beer talking—or me using my gay wiles to seduce you—called me up to say the good-bye you promised me and tossed my number in the trash. Instead you decided to keep seeing me, to see where this thing would go. That's not curiosity, Bo. It's courage."

"If you know it's not just curiosity, then why won't you let me kiss you?"

Lifting his other knee, Erick sat up and wrapped his arms around his legs, closing in on himself like a turtle being poked with a stick. But now that Bo had finally worked up the courage to have this conversation, he wasn't going to give up until he had the answers he needed.

"I know you know I want to," Bo said. "I know you know I would have done it downstairs if you hadn't pushed me away. And again just now. You knew I wanted to kiss you but you pushed me away. Why? Don't you want to kiss me?"

"Of course I do. I want it like I've never wanted anything in my whole life."

"Then why won't you?" When Erick didn't answer, Bo pushed, saying, "Is it that whole 'never fall for a straight guy' thing?"

Erick laughed but there was little real humor in it. "Well... it would be if I had any brains at all. Unfortunately, I'm starting to think when it comes to this kind of thing, I'm the dumbest guy in town."

"How come?"

"Well, no offense intended, but I don't exactly have the greatest track record in this area. See... I have this really bad habit of falling for all the wrong guys." Erick turned to look at Bo directly. "It's too late for me to avoid falling for you, Bo. I already have. Big-time!"

"And you're afraid I'm going to break your heart."

It wasn't a question, but Erick answered it anyway.

"I *know* you're going to break my heart. One way or another. I knew it going into this, and I made my choice. That's not why I've been holding back."

Bo leaned forward and wrapped his arms around his legs as well, unconsciously mirroring Erick's pose. "Then why have you been holding back?"

Erick turned his head and waited for Bo to do the same, so they were eye to eye.

"Because I can handle getting my heart broken, when it comes to that, and I can handle having missed out on sharing anything other than friendship with you, if I have to. What I can't handle is sharing something more than friendship with you—even if it is just a kiss— then having you wake up one morning and regret having done it. I know that may sound cowardly to you, but I honestly don't know if I could survive knowing you were out there somewhere and the only thing you felt when you thought about me was regret about having gotten involved with me in the first place."

"Ah, correct me if I'm wrong," Bo said, "but I'm pretty sure I'm already involved with you."

"You're right. You are. But for the moment, that involvement is friendship. Friends who are attracted to each other, sure, but still friends. And even though we've never talked about it, I'd be willing to bet you've had other friendships like that. Girls you wanted something to happen with but nothing ever did, and you survived, right?"

Despite wishing otherwise, Bo had to admit Erick had a point. He had had friendships like that. Plenty of them. But still....

"I want more than that."

"I want more too," Erick admitted. "But wanting and having are two different things. And if we act on this attraction we feel for each other, I think you and I both know it's not going to stop at kissing."

Bo felt his insides quiver. "What makes you say that?"

"Oh, come on, Bo," Erick chided. "We can't even hug each other good-bye without getting a hard-on. Hell, I've got a hard-on now and all we're doing is talking about kissing, and unless you happen to be carrying a hammer in your pocket, I'd say you feel the same way."

Bo would like to have argued, but the evidence spoke for itself.

"And while I'm pretty much okay with there being more than friendship between us," Erick continued, "I have a hunch you're more than a little... let's call it... *unnerved* at the prospect of fucking another guy."

Bo knew Erick had said it that way on purpose to shock him and he wished he could say it hadn't worked. But he couldn't. Not with the image Erick had planted in his brain. But he wasn't going to let that stop him from making an important point.

"First of all, let me say I don't 'fuck' anyone. As far as I'm concerned, 'fucking' is what happens between two people who don't give a shit about each other—they just want to get off. I got over that kind of thing a long time ago. Second of all, you're right. I do know it won't stop with kissing and I am unnerved by the idea," he admitted. "The problem is, that's not all I am."

Erick's eyebrows came together in the way they did when he was feeling perplexed, and if the subject they were discussing hadn't been so serious, it would have made Bo smile.

"What do you mean?" Erick asked.

"If I was just unnerved, I wouldn't be pushing this so hard. But I'm not. I'm also turned on."

Bo could tell by the shock in Erick's eyes that the shoe was now on the other foot and he couldn't help but feel vindicated. "I want you, Erick. More than I've ever wanted anyone in my life. In fact, just thinking about making love with you gets me hot enough to melt the chrome off a trailer hitch. And it's *that* feeling that's been holding me back. But it's not anymore."

"Why not?"

"Because the more I thought about it, the more I realized as scared as I am about what might happen between us, what scares me more is what might happen to me if I *don't* do this. That if I let fear keep me from taking this relationship to the next level, I'm going to regret it for the rest of my life. So if what you're afraid of is my regretting becoming more than friends with you, don't be. Because I can promise you the only regret I'll ever have is knowing that, when push came to shove, so to speak, I wasn't brave enough to see this thing through when I had the chance."

There was a pause that seemed to go on forever. Then Erick asked in a low voice, "Are you sure this is what you want?"

"Yeah, I'm sure."

"Really sure?" Erick pressed. "Because this is one of those lines, Bo, that once you cross it, you can't ever go back. Even if you're never with another guy for the rest of your life, you'll always have this in your past. I can promise you there are girls out there who aren't going to understand that, much less be willing to accept it. So if you do this, it means you can never go back to being who and what you were before."

Erick's doom-mongering was starting to irritate Bo. "Don't you think I know all that?" he demanded. "Don't you think I've tried to talk myself out of feeling this way? Well, I have. About a million times. Like it or not, I want you. Which—in case you missed it— means I'm already not who or what I thought I was. So whether I ever get to kiss you or not, it's not going to matter. I'm still going to have to find a way to deal with who and what I am. And I will. I'm not sure exactly how, right now, but I *will* deal with it.

"What I can't deal with is knowing I took a pass on something that could have been really good because I was too scared to step up to the plate and go for it."

Bo couldn't have described exactly what it was about Erick's eyes that changed, but something did. They went warmer somehow, more luminous. "All right, then. Let's go for it."

For a second, Bo just blinked at him. "You mean it?"

"Of course I mean it," Erick said, smiling. "You don't think I'd joke about something as important as this, do you?"

"No."

Erick leaned a little closer. "Then how about you come on over here and kiss me before either one of us loses our nerve?"

Bo had to lick his lips before he could say, "Okay."

Conscious of the solemnity of the moment, Bo slowly leaned in and ever so gently pressed his lips to Erick's. They were softer than he'd expected, yielding beneath his like a pillow yields to the head that rests on it.

After that first, brief contact, he backed off and looked into Erick's eyes. They were soft and, not surprisingly, a little damp.

Bo lifted his hand and rubbed Erick's cheek with the backs of his fingers. "Are you okay?"

"Shouldn't I be asking you that question?"

"I'm more than okay." Absently, Bo ran a finger over Erick's lower lip. "In fact, right now, I'm the happiest guy in the world."

"You mean the second happiest."

Rather than debate the point, Bo leaned in to kiss him again.

This time the kiss was longer and deeper, and Bo felt Erick's response in the way he opened his mouth slightly, giving him greater access. Pressed mouth to mouth, Bo turned toward Erick, bracing himself on one arm as he slid his other hand behind Erick's neck, directing the movement of his head.

When he did, Erick gave a little hum of pleasure, as if he was sampling a particularly tasty morsel. Bo broke off, smiling. "What?"

"Nothing. I just had you figured for a 'go for the gusto', no-holds-barred kind of kisser, that's all."

Bo grinned. "I have my moments. This isn't one of them."

"Then by all means, please, keep going."

This time when they kissed, Erick slid his arms around Bo, holding him close as their mouths mated. As smoothly as if they had done it a thousand times before, Erick lay back against the roof, drawing Bo toward him, accepting, even welcoming, his weight as Bo turned and rested on him, sliding one arm under Erick's neck, cushioning him from the hard roof.

Even as Erick tangled his fingers in Bo's hair, Bo ran the tip of his tongue over Erick's lips, teasing them, begging for admittance. When Erick accepted, Bo groaned as their tongues began a dance of their own.

Flirting, teasing, tasting one another until both were breathing heavily.

Though Bo's body was demanding more, his heart had no desire to rush this important first step. They were in their own little kingdom at the top of the world and suddenly everything he'd ever wanted seemed within reach.

There was no need to hurry.

They had all the time they needed.

CHAPTER
NINE

OVER the next few weeks, Bo and Erick's newly defined relationship continued to move slowly despite the ache of desire each stirred in the other. But neither man wanted to rush through these first few stages. Instead they savored the small intimacies they were now allowed to share.

They touched frequently, brushing a hand across a shoulder while making dinner at Bo's apartment or exchanging a quick caress as they squeezed by one another in the tight quarters of Erick's place. They held hands in the car or while walking on the wooded hiking trails Erick introduced Bo to, places that were still unpopulated enough to allow them the privacy they needed. They spent long hours lying on Bo's couch together, snuggled up like spoons in a drawer, while watching movies or a sporting event.

And they kissed. A lot!

In fact, they kissed every chance they got.

The more they kissed, the more Bo wanted to. Already he was more addicted to Erick's kisses than to the whole bags of Doritos he used to put away in one sitting, and it was getting worse. Though they both were obviously turned on during those kissing sessions, neither man tried to take things further. It was almost like when Bo had been dating his first girlfriend, Becky Fisher, back in the seventh grade.

Except he and Becky had been able to hold hands in public without people staring.

But even with society's blessing and the encouragement of his eager, yet equally inexperienced buddies, it had taken Bo several weeks to get up the nerve to kiss Becky and another solid month for him to attempt to ease his way to second base.

A move Becky immediately rejected before breaking up with him.

But it wasn't fear of rejection that kept Bo from trying to move things along with Erick. He just wanted to savor this time. He loved the anticipation of it almost as much as he loved lying against Erick and feeling his erection pressing against him—proof Erick's excitement matched his own.

The time they spent together—the talking and the kissing and all the rest—made the weekends fly by.

Not so the workweeks. Oh, the project was still on schedule, and though running a bit tight, the budget was in good shape too. Still Bo found himself spending so much of his time on the administrative part of the job—filling out paperwork and forms and keeping in touch with the various city and state bureaucracies, not to mention reassuring the anxious clients—that he almost never got to swing a hammer or cut a board anymore.

The lack was frustrating to say the least.

It was the supervisory part of the job that was really making him crazy, though. The guys he worked with, his crew, were all friends of his. But friend or no, as the foreman, he still had to evaluate their work and take action when that work was done sloppily or took too long.

Something he hated doing.

"Mike, look, I know it's a pain in the ass."

It was late Tuesday afternoon. The sun was shining outside, it was almost quitting time, and Bo hated the thought of having to redo something that had already been checked off the punch list, but the work had to get done.

And it had to get done right.

"We can't just leave the joints in the molding looking like that," Bo told Mike, a guy he'd bowled with, grabbed more than few beers with, and worked with for over two years. "You've got to miter the cuts so the corners meet up perfectly."

"So they're a little off. So what? We'll just fill 'em in with wood putty, that's all," Mike said. "Slap a little paint on it and no one will notice the difference."

Bo hated having to argue over something so simple. "We can't do that. The clients hired us so it would get done right. Otherwise they'd have done it themselves and covered up their own mistakes with putty. We're supposed to be better than that. That's what they pay us for. That's what we pay *you* for. So I need you to take it all down, see what you can salvage, get me an estimate on how much more molding we're going to need, and start putting it back up again. Only this time, take your time and do it right, okay?"

Bo pretended not to hear Mike's opinion on that idea—it was easier that way—and started back to the office trailer to finish the report his old man expected to receive at the end of every work day. He'd started it at ten that morning and hadn't even gotten halfway through. If he hurried, he might get it done before quitting time.

Alas, he only made it to the second floor.

"Hey, Al!" he cried at one of the crew who was about to turn on a table saw. "What the hell are you doing?"

Al looked at him like he had two heads. "I'm sawing a board."

"Where's the guard for the saw? Not to mention your safety glasses?"

The older man straightened, his paunch of a belly bulging over his tool belt. "You know I can't see what I'm doing with those stupid things on, and the friggin' guard just gets in the way. It's a shortcut. Quit your worrying."

Because he knew Al had been doing this kind of work since Bo had been in diapers, he dug down deep for his patience. "Look, I know you know what you're doing, but I can't let you take the safety guards off the equipment like that. If an inspector happens to come by and sees this kind of thing going on, we're gonna get slapped with a safety violation. Not to mention a whopping fine. It'll be my ass the Boss Man will kick from here to the middle of next week. So like it or not, you've got to use the safety equipment."

"You know... your old man wasn't nearly as tight-assed about this kind of stuff as you are," Al said irritably. "He let us get the job done without all this hassle."

As far as Bo was concerned, his old man's ass was tight enough to turn charcoal into diamonds, but that was beside the point.

"Things are different now. They're a lot stricter about safety these days. Even though I agree with you about the glasses, I still can't let you work without them. So either put the guard on the saw and the glasses on your face, or I'll have to move you to another part of the project. One that doesn't require all the safety gear."

"Like what? Going around nitpicking at everybody who's doing the real work?" Al sneered. "Or maybe you'll just have me pushing a broom and picking up everybody else's mess."

It was an obvious attempt to remind Bo that picking up the waste boards and the shingles around the site and sweeping the floors had been his first job with the company when he'd been scarcely fifteen. It had been a dirty, demeaning, irritating job that was about as glamorous as cleaning out the Porta-Potties. Not anything anyone would choose as a career path, but Bo's old man had believed in having his children learn the business from the ground up.

"I don't want to do that," Bo told him honestly. "You're one of the best I've got. But I will if I have to."

Bo could only pray to whatever higher power there might be that Al wouldn't make him have to follow through with the threat. If he did, he would get chewed out by his old man for having harassed a reliable worker over what the old man would probably term "a bunch of piddly shit."

Just as he'd be raked over the coals if they did happen to get slapped with an OSHA violation, and would most likely be expected to pay the fine out of his own pocket.

It was a no-win situation.

Thankfully, Al—though grumbling in a way Bo pretended to ignore—went to get the guard for the saw and his glasses, and Bo decided it would be better for him to get out of the way before Al got back.

Just one more item to add to his daily report.

Once again, Bo tried to make it to the trailer, but as he got to the ground floor the walkie-talkie on his belt crackled. "Yo, Bo?"

Pulling the unit off his belt, he pressed the button. "Bo here. Go ahead."

"Man, I think you'd better get up here quick. O'Malley's not doing so hot."

The panic in Mac's voice had Bo spinning around and heading back up the stairs. "Where are you guys?"

"Fourth floor. East corner."

"What's going on?"

"I don't know. One minute he was bitching that the chili dogs he'd had for lunch were giving him heartburn, and the next he just keeled over."

Bo took the stairs two at a time and when he got to the fourth floor, he saw a knot of guys standing around.

"Everybody back off," he ordered as he pushed his way through the crowd and found Sean O'Malley lying on the floor. He was a big guy—not so much tall as wide—easily carrying sixty excess pounds on his five-foot-eight frame. But from his position, it was clear somebody had tried to move some of the debris out of the way and stretched him out on his back.

His eyes were closed and he was sweaty and pasty-looking.

Bo dropped to his knees on one side of the man and saw Mac kneeling on the other, his expression worried, his eyes panicked.

"I don't know what happened," Mac said. "Like I said, one minute he was bitching, the next he just grabbed his chest and fell over. We tried waking him up but he's out cold."

He was more than out cold and Bo knew it. In the time since he'd gotten there, the guy had gone from pasty to sheet white and his lips and fingertips were starting to take on a blue tinge.

"Did anybody call 911 yet?" he asked.

"I got 'em on the line now," one of the guys said, but Bo wasn't sure which one.

He reached out and put two fingers on O'Malley's neck, praying to feel a pulse. There wasn't one.

"Shit!"

Bo put his ear to O'Malley's chest, and when he still didn't hear anything, he moved into position to start CPR.

"Tell whoever's on the phone he's not breathing and he doesn't have a pulse," he said. "So they better get here ASAP. Baker!"

"Yeah, Bo?" one of the younger men said.

"Run down to the trailer and bring me the resuscitation kit."

"The wha'?"

"It's a white metal box with a red cross on it hanging on the wall to the right of the door. Get it down and bring it up here," Bo said as he felt for O'Malley's sternum and started doing chest compressions.

"Hey, Bo, the lady on the phone wants to know if anybody here knows CPR."

Bo might have rolled his eyes if they hadn't been focused like lasers on O'Malley's face. "Tell her yes and it's already been started. Then stay on the line in case they need anything else. Stokes?"

"Yeah?"

"Go down and wait for the ambulance, then show them the way up here. Tell them to hurry. Fitz, get to the freight elevator and make sure it's on the ground floor waiting for them when they get here. Sparks, you're in charge of the rest. Get everybody out of the building, then keep 'em out of the way so when the paramedics get here they've got room to work. Now go!"

Out of the corner of his eye, Bo saw the older man start to move people along. When Mac started to get up as well, Bo said, "No. You stay. I need you here."

What little color Mac had left drained from his face. "Okay. What do I do?"

"I want you to call O'Malley's wife, tell her what's going on, and get her down here. Now."

"How am supposed to call her? I don't know her number."

Bo wanted to smack Mac upside the head but at the moment both his hands were busy.

"Try his cell phone. It's probably in his pocket." Bo continued what he was doing, praying in his head as he worked. "Otherwise I'll have to go down to the trailer and get it out of the filing cabinet."

"I can do that," Mac said, obviously not wanting to be left there alone.

"No, you can't. It's in the drawer with the confidential files and it's locked." When Mac didn't move, Bo barked, "Just look for the damn cell phone, will ya?"

Mac rifled through the man's pockets as Bo continued working over him. "Got it," Mac said and moved off to make the call.

Bo tried to think of what else he could or should be doing right now but he couldn't think of anything offhand.

He was too busy trying to save the guy's life.

CHAPTER
TEN

UNFORTUNATELY, it didn't work.

Despite the CPR being started so quickly, despite the amazingly prompt arrival of the paramedics with all their expertise and equipment, and despite the crisp orders by the doctors on the other end of the radio—none of it did any good.

In the end, the man was—in official terms—DOS: "Dead on scene."

From what Bo had gathered from the police and other officials roaming around, O'Malley had probably been dead before he'd even hit the floor. Of course, they couldn't be sure without an autopsy, but from what Bo and the others had described, it seemed likely the man had suffered a massive coronary—a heart attack.

For Sean O'Malley, it was over.

He was dead.

One by one, everyone else went home.

Long after all the other guys had left, Bo sat in his office. He still couldn't believe it. It had been your average, ordinary working day. Nothing special. Then suddenly someone you'd known half your life, someone to whom you'd said "hello" just that morning, was gone. Just like that.

He knew he should go home too. There was nothing to be done here. At least not now. Tomorrow, he knew, would be different.

Tomorrow the circus would begin. Whenever there was an accident or injury on the job site, the officials from OSHA would come crawling out of the woodwork and begin to swarm over the place like ants on an anthill, looking for anything that might have caused the problem or anything that should have been done to prevent it.

Far worse, at least from Bo's point of view, was that his father was sure to be there as well. He needed to be. As the owner of the company, he would have to give a statement, go over what happened and what had been done and discuss the whys and wherefores. And, most likely, call into question everything Bo had done before, during, and after the incident.

Then there would be the crew to deal with. Losing one of their own like that was bound to be tough on everybody. Tempers would likely be short and the mood somber. There would be questions to answer, as well. What would the arrangements be for his funeral? Was there anything they could they do for his family?

Of lesser importance yet still a factor, would they still be able to make their contract deadline on time? Even after OSHA finished its investigation, it would likely be weeks before things settled down again.

And now they were one worker short.

Imagining it all was giving Bo an ache in his head to match the one in his heart, and he knew he was going to need a good night's sleep if he was going to be able to deal with any of it. He couldn't seem to get moving.

There was a little knock on the door to the trailer.

"Oh, for God's sake," Bo said wearily.

He thought everyone had already left and had been thankful for it. He wasn't sure he was up to dealing with anyone right now.

"Come in."

To his surprise, rather than a member of the crew, it was Erick who stepped inside. "I got your voice mail," he said. "I'm sorry I didn't pick up when you called, I was in class. I'm sorry about your friend."

There had been nothing accusatory in Erick's statement, yet Bo found himself feeling defensive. "There was nothing I could do. He wasn't doing anything heavy or risky. He wasn't even handling any tools. He was just standing there sanding a chair rail and all of a sudden he dropped dead. How can somebody do that? Just up and die like that?"

"I don't know. But people do."

"If he knew he was sick...?"

"He may not have known. Certainly, you didn't. If you had, you might have been able to do something, but then again, maybe not. Sometimes things just happen, Bo."

"He was only thirty-seven."

"That's really young," Erick acknowledged. "Did he have a family?"

Bo had to swallow the lump in his throat. "A wife and two kids."

"I'm sorry," Erick said again and held out his hand.

Bo pushed himself out of the chair, went to him, and wrapped his arms around him, pulling him close. Erick held him tightly, and Bo felt something around the area of his heart begin ease.

He had been so sure he wanted to be alone but.... "I'm glad you're here. I know you're supposed to be at work right now."

"Right now, I'm exactly where I'm supposed to be," Erick said. "So don't worry about it, okay?"

Bo was too grateful to argue with him.

"Would you... would you come home with me tonight? Not for anything... you know... physical... or anything. You could even sleep on the couch if you want. I just don't want to be alone."

"Of course I will." Erick backed off so he could look into Bo's face. "And I'll sleep wherever you want me to sleep. I'm here for you. However you need me, okay?"

"I need you to be there, that's all."

"Then let's go."

BO WAS exhausted so they took Erick's car and made the drive mostly in silence. Bo could only be grateful. He'd talked so much today—to the EMTs, the crew, O'Malley's wife—he felt talked out.

As soon as they parked, Bo suddenly remembered something. "Oh, shit!"

"What?"

"I left my damn keys in my truck."

"You leave your keys in your truck?" Erick asked, incredulous.

"Mostly, yeah."

"Why?"

"Because somebody at the site is always going out for something and it's easier to leave them there than have somebody have to come find me every time they have to make a run."

When Erick went to turn the car back on, Bo asked, "What are you doing?"

"Going back to get your keys. You need them to get in, don't you?"

"Thankfully, no. Come on."

They climbed out of the car and when they got inside the entryway, Bo rang one of the other tenant's buzzers.

There was a long, *long* moment of silence before a small, quavering voice said, "Yes?"

"It's Bo, Mrs. Peters. I forgot my key again."

There was a girlish giggle, and then the voice said, "All right. But that's two more weeks of trash pickup you owe me."

"I know. Just leave it out as usual." Bo pulled open the door when it unlocked. "Thanks again."

"You're welcome."

When the two men stepped inside Erick asked, "What was all that about?"

"That was my own personal savior, Mrs. Peters." As if preparing to scale a mountain, Bo began to pull himself up the stairs. "She lives two doors down from me and she's ninety if she's a day, but she's still sharp as a tack. Mentally, that is. Physically it takes her all day just to cross her living room. Never mind go out. So she's pretty much always home and she doesn't sleep much. Except for what she calls her 'cat naps'. We've got a deal going. She lets me in whenever I forget my keys and I take her trash down to the dumpster for her. I'd do it for her anyway, but this way she feels like she's paying her own way, which I guess is important to her. Plus she thinks it's hysterical that I lose my keys so much. She thinks I need a wife to take care of me."

"You need somebody to take care of you, that's for sure. You must forget your keys a lot if you've got a system going."

"I forget them all the time. I think I've tried every system there is for keeping track of them and they still go missing on me. It's like they're possessed or something."

By this time the two men were at the door to Bo's apartment, and Erick was about to ask how he was going to get in without a key when Bo lifted up one end of the bench outside his apartment. Lying hidden beneath one of the legs was a key.

"Are you crazy?" Erick asked, horrified. "You can't just leave a key outside your door. What if somebody found it?"

"No one has so far." Bo unlocked the door, then, holding it open with his foot, he bent and put the key back before gesturing Erick inside.

"Come on in."

When they got to the living room, Bo all but collapsed on the couch. He closed his eyes and dropped his head back against the cushions.

"Shit! What a day."

Because Bo had obviously forgotten them, Erick sat on the coffee table in front of him and lifted Bo's foot up, unlaced his work boot, and removed it. He did the same to the other one and took them to their place by the door.

When he got back, Bo was right where he'd left him, his eyes still closed.

"Are you hungry?" Erick asked. "I could make you a sandwich or something."

The thought of food was nauseating. "No, thanks. I'm just tired."

"Why don't you go to bed, then?"

Now Bo opened his eyes and looked directly at Erick. "Would you come with me? Just to sleep next to me?"

"Of course." He held out his hand. "Come on."

The two men went to the bedroom, and standing back to back, they stripped down to their T-shirts and boxers and then got in on either side of the bed. It was an odd feeling for Bo. He hadn't shared his bed with anyone—even for a night—in a long time, and it felt strange to be doing so now.

Erick didn't give him a chance to feel awkward or uncomfortable. He slid close to Bo's side and snuggled up against him, resting his head on Bo's chest and placing a hand over Bo's heart.

Somehow it felt natural for Bo to put his arm around him in return and hold him close, putting his hand over the one resting on his chest.

They lay there for a long time, but though his body was weary, Bo's mind was still running in circles thinking about the day, playing it over and over in his head and worrying about everything he would have to do tomorrow.

He couldn't seem to shut it down enough to fall asleep.

Finally, not wanting to disturb Erick if he was sleeping, he whispered, "Are you still awake?"

"You must be joking," Erick drawled. "The gears in your head are grinding so loud I'll bet everyone in this entire building is still awake."

Bo huffed out a short laugh, surprised he actually felt amused. "Since no one is sleeping anyway, do you think you and I could talk for a while?"

"Sure. What do you want to talk about?"

"Anything. I don't care. Just so long as it has nothing to do with work or what happened today. Right now I want to think about something completely different."

There was a short period of silence in which Erick seemed to be thinking. Then he said, "Okay, how about this? Why don't you tell me where, when, and with whom you first had sex?"

Bo laughed again. "Why would you care about that?"

"I don't, really. But I am curious."

"Oh, you are, huh?"

"On a purely academic level, of course," Erick teased. "I've even been thinking about doing a research study on the mating rituals of heterosexual teenage boys. You could be my first interview subject. If you're willing to share, that is."

"What about you? Are you going to tell me the same thing about you?"

"I will if you want me to. But I have to warn you, I was very precocious in this area, and I was never, ever attracted to girls."

"So the only sex you've ever had has been with guys?"

"Yup. I guess in a way that makes you and me sort of even, huh? Both nonvirgin virgins."

"I guess it does." He waited a beat. "I can live with that if you can. Who goes first?"

"I asked the question, so I think you should answer it."

"You would."

It was funny. Bo wouldn't have thought he'd be embarrassed to talk about this subject with Erick. Certainly he'd never had any problem talking to any of his other friends. Still, he found he had to clear his throat before he could say, "The 'where' was in the back of my old man's Chevy 4x4. He used to let me take it off-roading sometimes, and I had found a great make-out spot over by Shepherd's Pond."

"In the back of a pickup, huh?" Erick said. "Sounds pretty uncomfortable to me."

"I thought about trying to find a mattress to put in it, but I couldn't figure where to get ahold of one—much less a way to get it in and out of the truck without anyone finding out about it. So instead, I brought along a couple of sleeping bags and I kind of laid them out, one on top of the other, you know? Like a bed?"

"That was… resourceful," Erick said cheekily. "How old were you?"

"Sixteen and a half."

"And the name of the lucky girl would be…?

"Christina Donovan. She was a year behind me in school, and we'd been together about three months. Two months and twenty-nine days of which I spent trying to talk her into going all the way with me."

"Why? You know that's not what I meant," Erick scolded when Bo laughed. "I meant why did it take so long? Was it a hard sell? So to speak?"

"No. Not really. It's not like she hadn't done it before."

"How do you know?"

"Because the guy she had with been with before me bragged about it all over school. So much so I kind of felt sorry for her. She didn't seem all that upset about it, though. In fact, I think she was almost proud of it, like she was so much more mature than all the other girls who hadn't done it yet. Of course, when she asked me if *I* had ever done it, I lied through my teeth."

"How come?"

"I couldn't let her think I didn't know what the hell I was doing. It would have been bad for my rep. As it was, I was so excited when she said yes I almost threw up."

"Talk about a mood killer. So how was it? Generally speaking, that is," Erick added quickly. "I don't really want to hear all the gory details, if you don't mind."

Bo grinned in the dark. "You mean you're not interested in the way her alabaster breasts glistened in the moonlight?"

"Not in the slightest. I would, however, be interested in the way your gorgeous ass glistened in the moonlight, but since you don't have eyes in the back of your head, I guess we can't discuss that. So how about you stop putting weird images in my head and just answer the question?"

"Oh, sure, you're thinking about my naked ass and *I'm* the one with the weird images in my head." Because Bo was still holding his hand, the best Erick could do was use his knee to bump Bo in retaliation. It made Bo grin.

"As for how it was, honestly? It was great! Even better than I thought it would be. Until she started talking about what kind of wedding dress she wanted to wear and how many kids we were going to have and what we should name them and whether we should get a dog or a cat or one of each." Remembering it had Bo laughing and shaking his head. "Man, it was so… surreal, you know? There I was, ready to climb up onto the roof of the truck and beat on my chest like Tarzan, then hopefully climb back down for round two. Meanwhile, she's trying to get me to decide whether we should buy a house ready-made or just rent an apartment while I built us one."

Bo actually shuddered. "It was like I'd gone to bed with Malibu Barbie and woke up with Chatty Cathy."

"I see." Erick's attempt at solemnity was belied by the fact that he was shaking with suppressed laughter. "How long did it take you to break up with her?"

"I didn't. She broke up with me. And it only took two days."

"Really?" Erick said, sounding a bit surprised. "How'd you pull that off?"

"I told her that rather than have a big, fancy church wedding, I wanted to dress up like Elvis and get married in Vegas. She dumped me like yesterday's lunch."

Apparently unable to contain it anymore, Erick laughed out loud. "That was pretty quick thinking for a horny sixteen-and-a half-year-old boy."

"Hey, desperate times call for desperate measures, my friend."

Now both men laughed, and then they were silent for a few minutes until Bo asked, "So, how about you? What was your first time like?"

"My first time was with a guy named Steven Bishop. I had just turned fourteen and was a freshman and he was eighteen and a senior."

"Wow, big age difference."

"Oh, trust me, that was the least of our problems," Erick said dryly.

"What do you mean?"

Erick took a second or two to readjust his position, cuddling closer and stretching his arm across Bo's chest, as if settling into story-telling mode.

"First of all, what you need to understand is that I grew up in a very small town in which everybody knew everything about everybody else. Or at least they thought they did."

"Meaning?"

"Meaning that even though *I* knew I was gay practically from kindergarten, there was no way I was going to let anyone at school know it."

"How come?"

"Because it would have given them one more excuse to pick on me. As it was, I used to get picked on by everybody."

"How come?"

"Oh, I don't know. Maybe it was because I was short and skinny and looked even more like a girl then than I do now," Erick teased. "Which meant that even though they didn't *know* I was gay, they all pretty much *assumed* I was gay. But even then I knew if any of them ever found out for sure, they'd do more than just pick on me: they'd beat me to death and dump my body in the woods somewhere. All that changed when I got to high school."

"How so?"

"For one thing, I went from a middle school of about four hundred to a regional high school of about four thousand, which made it a lot easier to escape my tormentors and blend into the crowd. Even better, the school I went to had a very strong—very vocal—gay presence. Talk about whirling my way out of Kansas and landing smack dab in the middle of Oz. It was amazing.... They even had a club called the Gay/Straight Alliance, and when I finally got up the guts to go to a meeting, I felt like I'd died and gone to heaven. Everybody there was just like me."

"Short, skinny, and girly-looking?" Bo teased.

Again, Erick bumped him with his knee. "I meant gay. Or at least, gay-friendly. That's where I met Steven. He was the president of the club, and not only was he the first openly gay guy I'd ever met, but he was also a bad boy of major proportions. This guy didn't care what people thought of him. He would do anything or say anything to anyone at any time with no apologies and absolutely no regrets, which, I have to admit, was a major part of his appeal."

"Tell me something: What is it about bad boys that people find so attractive?" Bo complained. "Seriously, why do that to yourself? Get together with someone you know is going to treat you like shit?"

"I don't know. Why do straight guys go for gorgeous women with only one working brain cell? I think it has something to do with hormones short-circuiting the connections in the cerebral cortex."

When Erick shifted, Bo lifted his arm until he settled again, then put his arm back around him.

"Anyway," Erick continued, "the good news was, because Steven didn't care if he got in trouble—and because he was rumored to have killed a guy, even though I'm pretty sure he was the one who started the rumor—people tended to want to stay on his good side. Which meant only the really brave or really stupid would risk pissing him off by picking on any members of the club. Which was another reason I stopped getting picked on every time I turned around."

"Gee. Sounds like a good guy to have around."

"Well, yes and no. See... while Steven did have some good qualities, he also had some major faults. The first one being, not only would he say anything or do anything, he would also screw anything that had a pulse. Any guy, anyway. Especially if he knew it was that guy's first time. I think he got off on being the one to pop a guy's cherry. Which meant that for him, every September became hunting season and the incoming freshmen—including yours truly—were the prey."

"You mean he went out of his way to seduce virgins?"

"Yup."

"That's awful," Bo said, slightly sickened at the thought.

"Not really. I mean, yeah it was, a little," Erick admitted. "But to be fair, he was good at it, despite his reputation as a badass. He was gentle and patient, and since he took a good deal of pride in being known as a superior fuck, he made sure whoever he was with was more than satisfied with the encounter. Unfortunately, what he neglected to tell those guys—again including yours truly—was that's all it was to him. An encounter. He had no interest in having a relationship with anyone. In fact, he didn't even believe in relationships. He was of the opinion that, as a gender, men weren't supposed to be monogamous. Especially gay men. So he'd happily sleep with anyone… *once*. Twice, maybe, if that person was lucky or particularly good. But that was it. No commitments. No strings. Just 'thanks for the good time and on to the next piece of meat'."

Bo didn't know why, but for some reason, that made him feel sad.

"Were you sorry you did it?"

"Not really," Erick said after a moment. "Like I said, he was gentle about it, and frankly, I was relieved to have it over with. I was ecstatic I could finally admit who and what I was. Of course, being me, I couldn't just say 'thanks for the memories' and go off into the sunset. No! That would be too sane. I had to go and fall in love with the guy. Not the smartest move I ever made, believe me. In fact, it was probably one of the dumbest things I've ever done."

It really bothered Bo when Erick got down on himself that way. "Why? It sounds to me like he went out of his way to make you fall for him."

"He did."

"How is it your fault you fell for him?"

"The problem wasn't so much that I fell for him as it was that, even after I knew it was hopeless—and believe me, he made it perfectly clear it was hopeless—I still couldn't let it go. I figured if I held in there long enough…." Erick laughed a bit and shook his head. "Typical me. Always trying to hold on to a star even when I know the only thing it's going to get me is a nasty sunburn."

"At least you cared about the guy," Bo said, determined not to give up. "Not that I didn't care about Christina. I did. A little. Mostly what I cared about was being able to tell my friends I'd finally gotten laid."

"At least you were smart enough to cut your losses when you found out you two weren't on the same page," Erick countered. "Me? I spent the next year and a half of my life mooning over a guy who probably forgot me two seconds after he got out of bed with me."

Erick shifted again, and almost unconsciously, Bo shifted with him, subtly drawing him closer.

"The one thing he *did* teach me—besides the obvious, that is— was that I didn't want to be like him," Erick continued. "I wanted a relationship. Which knowledge, I suppose, has helped me avoid a certain amount of heartache. So I guess I can't complain too much that he gave me my first taste of it."

The two men were silent for a long time while Bo thought over the things Erick had said. It had all been so long ago, he couldn't imagine how any of it could be relevant now, but something about the story bothered him. Something that niggled at the far edges of his brain, as if there was a deeper meaning he was missing. Determinedly, he put it away. He had enough to worry about right now.

"Now that we've both bared our souls," he said, "what do we talk about next?"

"I asked the first question," Erick answered. "It's your turn."

Bo thought for a moment. "Okay. When, where, and under what circumstances did you get drunk for the first time?"

Erick laughed. Then he answered.

CHAPTER
ELEVEN

THOUGH he didn't get as much sleep as he would have liked, Bo had eventually slept. But he still had Erick drop him off at the site early. He wanted to be there before everybody started to arrive. Unfortunately, Mac's car, "Bessie," was already in the parking lot when they drove in, and though Bo didn't see him anywhere, he skipped the good-bye kiss he'd been planning on giving Erick and got out.

As Erick drove away, Bo looked around but he still didn't see Mac anywhere.

He walked over to his truck, looking for his keys, but they weren't on the seat where he'd left them. "Damn it."

Now was definitely not the time for them to go missing. If he'd lost them for good, there was going to be hell to pay.

Then he noticed the light was on in the trailer. A little bewildered, he walked over to it, and when he tried the door, it was unlocked.

When he stepped in, Mac was standing behind the desk, looking down at the papers strewn there.

"What the hell are you doing?" Bo demanded. "Do you know how much trouble I'd be in if the old man showed up and found you in here while I wasn't on-site? He'd crawl up my ass so far, I'd have to use a tractor to pull him out again."

"I thought you were on-site," Mac said, defending himself. "Your truck was here. But when I tried the trailer door, it was locked. So I got the keys out of your truck and came in to wait for you."

"Mac, you can't just come in here like that."

"Why not? Afraid I'll walk off with your stapler or something?"

"Of course not. But there's a lot of confidential stuff in here—personnel records, financial information—stuff I could get in a lot of trouble if anyone sees who isn't supposed to."

"You mean like this stuff here?"

Mac lifted up a file and spun it across the desk so Bo could see what it was.

Shit! He'd been so distracted when Erick showed up, he'd forgotten to tidy up before he'd left.

"Since when are you planning on buying a house?" Mac demanded.

"I'm not." Exactly! "I was just… you know… crunching some numbers, that's all."

"Numbers for what?"

Bo really didn't want to get into this right now. The old man could get here any second and it was going to be a horrible day as it was. But Mac was his friend. His best friend. He supposed he did owe him an explanation.

"You know I've been thinking about getting into flipping houses someday. We've talked about it lots of times."

"Yeah, we've talked about it. But I didn't know you were serious."

"I'm not, really," Bo said. "It's more like a dream."

Mac flicked open one of the files.

"Fact sheets about a duplex for sale on Oak Street. Another for a single family on Cedar Hill. Estimates on purchase price. Remodeling costs. Plumbers' names. Electricians. Comparisons on hardwood versus carpet. Estimated profits. Looks like more than 'a dream' to me. It looks like a plan. Tell me something: were you ever going to fill me in on any of this?"

"Of course I was."

"When?"

Honestly? Bo didn't really have a good answer to that. "When I had it all figured out, I guess. I still have a job to do here, remember? I'm committed. After the project is done, and if I decided to go ahead with it, I would've told you."

"I'm not so sure about that."

"What's that supposed to mean?"

Rather than answer, Mac asked, "Where were you last night?"

Bo's stomach jittered. "What has that got to do with anything?"

"Just answer the question."

"All right, fine. I was at home."

"How'd you get there? Your truck was here."

Carefully, Bo said, "After everything that happened, I didn't feel like driving. So I had someone pick me up."

"Who? Who picked you up? Was it 'mystery girl'?" Bo didn't answer. "Did she spend the night with you too?"

Bo nearly winced at the pronoun. "Yeah, we spent the night together. So...."

"So... you two seem to be spending an awful lot of time together these days."

"I know. We've gotten really... close."

"So I've noticed. Yet you still haven't told us anything about her. Or let any of us meet her. What's the matter? Aren't your friends good enough for her?"

Guilt had Bo snapping, "Don't be an ass."

"From where I'm standing, I'm not the one being an ass. You are."

"What's that supposed to mean?"

"It means you've changed, Bo. Ever since you met this girl, you've changed. You don't hang out with us on the weekends anymore. You never work with us. That is, unless you're strutting around telling us we're doing it wrong. Other than that, all you do is sit here in the office and push papers all day."

"And I hate it," Bo cried. "You know that. That's why I'm crunching those numbers. So I can the hell get out of here."

"I don't think so. I think there's more going on here than wanting to get out from under your old man's thumb."

"Like what?"

"I think this girl you're so hooked on has been screwing with your head along with the rest of your body parts."

"You don't know what you're talking about."

"Yes, I do. I've been thinking about it a lot. What I think is: the reason you're keeping this girl all to yourself is because she's one of those rich college kids you were always so down on, the ones who think being a construction worker isn't good enough. And I think you think if you owned your own business, if you were the *real* boss instead of a stand-in for your old man, it would impress her. So instead of breaking it off with her, like you should, you're trying to live up to what she wants you to be."

Bo tried not to let his annoyance show, but some of it leaked through. "You're wrong. All the way wrong. *I'm* the one who's trying to live up to be what I think I should be. I'm sick of doing everything because somebody else thinks I should. This is my life, and if I want to live it different from the way it is now, it's none of anybody else's goddamn business."

"So... what? You're going to cruise on out of here and none of your old friends get to come along for the ride?"

Bo could hear the hurt in Mac's voice and he softened his. "Of course not. Mac, you're my best friend. You always have been. You always will be. It's just that things are really... complicated right now."

"Too complicated for a working stiff like me to understand, right?" Mac skirted the desk and made his way toward the door. "How about if I leave you to your new life and your new friends? And when you finally manage to uncomplicate things enough to explain them to me, you can just let me know."

"Mac, please, don't do this," Bo pleaded, but Mac brushed by him and left.

Bo would have gone after him, tried to reason with him, but through the open door Bo saw his old man's truck pull up. Better he got his own "confidential files" away before anyone else found them. So instead of going with his gut and hightailing it after Mac, Bo went to the desk and started clearing the decks.

It was going to be a long day.

IT WAS a long week.

Ending it by having to go to a funeral only made it that much worse. It was hard watching Sean's wife, his daughters, his parents, and his friends, all those people grieving for a man whose life was over too soon.

What made it harder was there didn't seem to be any clear explanation as to why it had happened. Yes, the man had been overweight, but not nearly as much as some of the other guys. He hadn't smoked or drank or used other recreational chemicals. There wasn't even a history of heart disease in his family. There had been no warning signs. No nothing.

Nothing but an early death, a flower-covered coffin, and a bunch of mourners standing around in the rain.

There certainly were a lot of them, that was for sure, the crew included. Every last one of them. Including Mac. Thankfully, he seemed to have gotten over the worst of his mad, but there was a coolness between them that added to the pain of the day. To top it all off, his old man was there as well. It made perfect sense. As the owner of the company and the one who'd hired Sean back when he was twenty, the old man had known him better than anyone else on the crew.

Certainly he'd known him longer.

It was harder than Bo would have thought it would be to see his father so upset, even if he had been a thorn in Bo's side all week. Thankfully, the OSHA inspectors had finished their job and their conclusions, coupled with the results of the autopsy, had resulted in an official determination that Sanford and Sons Construction had no culpability for Sean O'Malley's death.

But that didn't mean Bo didn't feel guilty. The man had died on his watch, and every time he thought about the red eyes of his widow, it was like a knife stabbing him in the heart.

He hadn't been able to see Erick at all since that first night, either.

Nor had they been able to talk on the phone much. The crew was one man short so Bo had to take on some of the construction work to keep on schedule, which would have been great if he hadn't had to spend hours every night sitting in the office catching up on the paperwork that got neglected during the day.

The strain was beginning to wear on him.

Because it was expected of him—once the funeral and the internment and the reception back at O'Malley's house were over— Bo went to The Blue Shamrock with the rest of the crew for a drink. Or two. Or three. It was their way of saying good-bye to one of their own. Not to have shown up would have been an unpardonable sin.

Still, it was the last place Bo wanted to be.

He'd already heard all the stories and hashed over the details and he just wanted to go somewhere quiet and peaceful, somewhere he didn't have to talk or think or do, somewhere he could be. So as soon as he decently could, he paid his tab, left a hundred-dollar bill on the bar to pay for a round of drinks in Sean's memory, and left.

As he'd had a couple of beers, he knew he probably shouldn't drive, but there was something rising inside him, a desperate need that was trying to push its way out of him. So, even though it was late, he got in the truck and drove to Erick's place.

He parked his truck on the street and ran through the rain into the building, then climbed the stairs until he got to Erick's door and knocked.

After a few moments, Erick's voice, sounding heavy and deep demanded, "Who is it?"

"It's me. Bo."

Bo thought it was strange that, rather than just open the door, Erick left the chain on and peeked out, making sure it was him before closing the door and taking the chain off. Then he opened the door, saying, "Hey! What are you doing here? I thought you were out with the crew."

"I was." Erick had obviously been either in bed or on his way there, because he was dressed in only a T-shirt and a pair of boxers. "I'm sorry. It's late. I should go."

"Don't be ridiculous. Come on in." When Bo didn't move, Erick reached out and tugged him inside before closing the door behind him. "I didn't expect to see you until tomorrow night at least."

"I know. I should have waited. Or at least called."

"Don't worry about it."

Now that he was inside, Bo didn't know quite what to do. So he stood there, dripping water everywhere, until Erick helped him out of his coat and laid it over a chair to dry.

"You look nice," he said, and Bo glanced down at himself.

He had long ago discarded the suit jacket and tie he'd worn to the funeral, but he was still in the dress shirt and trousers.

"But your hair is soaked."

"It's raining," Bo said.

He knew it was inane but it was the best he could come up with because whatever it was that had drawn him here was growing stronger. An animal caged too long, fighting for its freedom.

"Well, at least let me get you a towel so you can dry off a little bit." Erick left Bo standing in the middle of the room. "Do you want something to warm you up? A cup of coffee or hot chocolate or anything?"

"No, thanks," Bo said, still struggling with the need inside him.

He fought it hard, but it was a losing battle, and when Erick came back, Bo removed the towel from his hands and tossed it aside and, taking Erick's face in his hands, pulled him into a fierce kiss.

Here, at last, was the heat to warm the heart that had felt cold and dead all week. Here was the easing for the ache that was burning a hole inside him.

The animal within rattled the bars of the cage, demanding release.

With what was his last drop of control, Bo broke off the kiss. "If you want me to go, you need to say so. Now."

Erick's eyes searched his for a long moment. Then he smiled. "You don't have to go. You can stay here. With me."

"I don't just want to sleep beside you tonight," Bo said, wanting to be sure Erick understood. "I want to be with you. I need to be. I need to feel alive again."

"I know."

This time it was Bo who searched Erick's eyes, but all he found there was acceptance.

"It's okay, Bo, really." Erick rose on his toes so his lips were barely touching Bo's and whispered, "I want to be with you too."

This time when they kissed, Bo was thrilled when Erick not only accepted the demand of the kiss but returned it—heat for heat, bite for bite. When Bo used his tongue to demand entrance, Erick opened for him and allowed him to drink as deeply as he wanted. It wasn't enough. Bo needed more. He needed to feel flesh beneath his fingers, so he shoved his hands under Erick's T-shirt, pushing it up and out of the way.

In response, Erick raised his arms over his head and let Bo pull the shirt the rest of the way off. Then Erick quickly lowered his arms and began tugging the tails of Bo's dress shirt out of his trousers. Once they were free, he began unbuttoning the shirt, but rather than help him, Bo undid the buttons on his cuffs as he toed off his wet shoes.

Though they were both off balance, they somehow managed to strip the shirt and the undershirt beneath it off Bo, and then they were standing skin to skin. But even as they kissed and groped, Bo couldn't get enough of the feel of Erick's skin beneath his work-roughened hands. He wasn't soft, like a girl, but sleek and smooth, a sharp contrast to the slight roughness of his cheeks. Enjoying the novelty of it, Bo kissed his way down Erick's throat, thrilling at the rough feel, the salty flavor. When he finally reached the spot where Erick's neck met his shoulder, Bo moaned, and without thinking, sank his teeth into the tendon there, making Erick moan in response.

Erick tipped his head to give Bo better access, even as he began unbuckling Bo's belt. Once he had, he unhooked the closure to Bo's trousers and dragged down the zipper, then slid his hands around back and down, running them over Bo's ass. When the trousers fell to the floor, Bo stepped out of them and slid one leg between Erick's. In response, Erick raised on his toes again so their erections rubbed together through the sweat-dampened cloth of their shorts.

The feel of Erick's body against his was making Bo crazy. Erick moved his hands to the front and began to run them over the huge erection tenting the thin fabric of Bo's shorts. It was more than Bo could take, and without stopping to think, he bent down, scooped an arm under Erick's legs, and carried him across the small room, dropping him onto the bed and then all but falling down on top of him.

There was too much need—a need that had been building for far too long—for them to take their time, but Bo did freeze for a moment when he first felt Erick close his hand over his naked shaft. The strength of his grip felt strange, and yet it was like coming home. Then Erick began to move his hand, sliding up and down in a rhythm that threatened to throw Bo over the edge.

Desperate to return the pleasure, Bo reached into Erick's shorts and fumbled until he found Erick's cock as well. Stroking firmly, kissing wildly, the two rolled over the bed, neither solely dominant, neither wholly passive, but both simply frantic with need as, with single-minded intensity, they drove one another up and over the first peak.

For Bo, it was like being launched into orbit, then bursting into a thousand tiny fragments of pleasure that went spinning out of control.

The intensity of it was beyond anything he had ever felt before, and when he finally came back to himself, dazed and panting, he rolled to his back and just tried to breathe. Though the painful pressure that had been building seemed to have been relieved, something inside him still yearned. Unsure of what to do, he lay there as he watched Erick get out of bed and go back to pick up the towel that had been tossed aside earlier. He brought it back with him, shutting off lights as he came, until only one small light in the kitchen lit the room. Still silent, he walked to the side of the bed and dropped his boxers. Using the towel, he cleaned himself up a bit.

Then he climbed onto the bed and tugged Bo's boxers down his legs and off. He cleaned Bo off as well before tossing the towel aside.

Like a mythical creature rising out of the depths of the seas, Erick rose up and stretched out on top of Bo.

Grasping Bo's hands in his, he lifted them over Bo's head and leaned down for another kiss. And they started all over again.

THIS time they took their time—time to touch and caress, time to kiss and taste. Rather than missing the soft curves of a woman, Bo found the feel of Erick's hard body rubbing against his unbearably exciting.

True, he was slim and delicate, yet there was a tensile strength to him, like a filament of fine wire, able to bend and twist without breaking.

To have that agile body moving over his was both a pleasure and a gift.

For that's what Erick gave to him: a gift. The gift of comfort and forgetfulness as he ran his hands over Bo's nakedness, smoothing them over Bo's wide shoulders and down to his biceps, kneading and rubbing before coming back to massage his shoulders again. Erick moved his hands lower to caress Bo's chest even as he sent his mouth following the same path his hands had just taken. Erick slid his tongue over hard muscle, lingering for a moment at the soft spot on Bo's inner elbow, giving Bo shivers, before licking his way back up. Now Erick moved his hands even lower, running gentle fingertips over Bo's cock while he used his talented tongue to search out Bo's nipple. When it found it, Bo couldn't help the groan that escaped his lips. Never would he have imagined he would be so sensitive there. But each flick of Erick's tongue caused jolts of heat to run through Bo until he felt as if he was being burned alive. But he didn't care.

He didn't care about anything but that the burning go on.

Erick moved his mouth lower and lower, and when he finally closed his mouth over the head of Bo's cock, Bo fisted his hands in the sheets beneath him, trying to find some purchase in the swirling current. But the pleasure was too great and he let himself be pulled along by it, losing himself in the swirling tongue that nimbly licked over the tip of him and the moist tightness that surrounded him as he was sucked deep into Erick's throat—into the swirling vortex of a kind of pleasure he had never known.

The heat of it scorched him down to his soul, and when he came, he wondered if his heart's blood was pouring out of him even as his release did.

Staggered by the pleasure, weary from the struggle, Bo tumbled into sleep.

Finally at peace.

CHAPTER
TWELVE

WHEN Bo woke just before dawn, Erick was still sleeping.

It was probably for the best, Bo reasoned, because he honestly didn't know what to say to him. He had no excuse for what he'd done last night and each explanation he tried to come up with sounded worse than the one before until he finally decided maybe it would be better if he didn't bother trying to explain at all.

Better if he left Erick the way he'd found him.

Alone.

He tried to be as quiet as possible, but as soon as Bo tried to undo the chain on the door, a dry voice came from behind him.

"Is that really how you're planning on handling this? Sneaking out of here in your sock feet?"

Pressing his forehead against the door, Bo muttered a heartfelt, "Shit."

When Bo turned toward where Erick was still lying on the bed, Erick was propped up on one elbow, the sheets barely pulled up to his waist, leaving his bare chest still visible.

How Bo could still want him this much after the night before, he didn't know. All he knew was that he did. "No. I guess not."

"Well, good, because that would be downright rude, especially before I've had my morning coffee. So how about putting on a pot while I take a quick trip downstairs? Then we can talk."

With no modesty whatsoever, Erick got out of bed, searched around for his boxers, then pulled them on. He crossed the room and gave Bo a casual kiss as he walked by on his way out the door and down to the bathroom.

Bo gave a heavy sigh. What else could he do? He zipped up his trousers and put on a pot of coffee.

BECAUSE there really wasn't anyplace more comfortable to sit, they drank their coffee in bed, sitting propped up against the pillows. Bo felt like he was waiting for a lightning bolt to drop out of heaven and strike him dead, but Erick didn't say anything until he had finished his coffee.

Then he took Bo's empty cup from his limp hands and, bending over the side of the bed, put both on the floor. He readjusted the pillows so he could lie on his side propped up on one elbow, facing Bo.

Patting the place beside him, he waited until Bo made the same adjustment before saying, "Okay. So… how about you try explaining to me what you thought you were doing by trying to sneak out of here this morning?"

Bo couldn't look into Erick's eyes so he focused on the bed between them and on the elegant hand resting there. "I don't know. I guess I thought you might not want me to be here when you woke up."

"Why not?"

"Because of what I did last night."

"Which part of last night? The part where you got behind the wheel and drove over here after having what I'm guessing was at least three beers—which, by the way, you *are* in trouble for," he said mildly. "Or the part where you dripped water all over my highly expensive floors? Or the part where you did your Rhett Butler impersonation by picking me up and carrying me to bed—which, by the way, I found incredibly sexy." Erick reached up and brushed a gentle hand over Bo's hair. "Or the part where you said you didn't just want to sleep beside me, you wanted to be with me?"

"How about the part where I used you?" Bo said bitterly.

"You didn't use me, Bo."

"The hell I didn't." Bo sat up and ran agitated fingers through his hair. "I come storming over here in the middle of the night, half in the bag. I yank all your clothes off, scoop you off your feet, toss you on the bed, and jump you like some horny teenager with his first girlfriend."

Erick grinned hugely. "If you change 'girlfriend' to a 'boyfriend', you've got my very first wet dream come true."

Bo pressed the heels of his hands to his forehead, hard. "This isn't funny, Erick."

"No, you're right, it's not." Erick sat up as well and put his hands on the back of Bo's neck, rubbing gently. "Because the truth is, I should have been the one to put the brakes on last night, not you. Instead I took advantage of the situation, and you, and I'm sorry for that."

Bo turned and stared at him blankly. "What the hell are you talking about?"

"You were drunk, Bo. And you were hurting. And instead of comforting you, like I should have, I let things get out of hand... so to speak."

Bo shook his head, confused. "I was the one who wanted them to get out of hand. In fact, I distinctly remember insisting they get out of hand."

"Maybe so, but I doubt you would have *let* them get out of hand if you hadn't been so drunk."

"I wasn't drunk," Bo said firmly. "Buzzed maybe, but not drunk." Then he shrugged a bit shamefacedly. "Besides, I've wanted to let things get out of hand for weeks now. I just didn't know how to tell you."

"Well, you know... you could have just said so," Erick said. "I do speak English, after all. Not to mention some eighth-grade Spanish, a little bit of sign language, and two painfully dreary semesters' worth of Latin."

Bo snorted. "Yeah, right. Like I'm going to know how to say 'I want you naked and in bed' in Latin."

"I'll be sure to look that up for you for next time. The point is, you could have told me how you were feeling."

"I was working my way up to it. But, I don't know, somehow last night something snapped and I finally let go. And even though I didn't know I was going to do it until I actually did it, I'm not sorry I did."

"Are you sure?"

Bo saw Erick's gaze searching his carefully, scanning for any hint of remorse, and knew he wouldn't find any.

"Yeah, I'm sure. The only thing I'm sorry for is that I didn't give you a choice."

"I had a choice."

"Not much of one."

"Sure I did." When Bo didn't say anything, Erick asked, "Tell me something: what would you have done if I had said no?"

Perplexed, Bo shook his head. "What?"

"What would you have done if I said, 'I don't want you here, Bo. Take your drunken, horny self out of here and go home'? What would you have done? Would you have stayed anyway? Would you still have picked me up and thrown me on the bed? Would you have forced me to do what we did together?"

"Of course not," Bo snapped, insulted.

"Well, in that case, we can assume I didn't, at any point in time, say anything even resembling the word no. In fact, I distinctly remember saying a big fat 'yes'. And at least a couple of 'oh, yeah, babys'. And one really big, loud—"

Blushing fiercely, Bo said, "What's your point?"

"My point is, just because you surprised me doesn't mean I didn't have a choice or that I didn't enjoy it. I did. And I sincerely hope you did too."

"I did," Bo admitted a bit shamefacedly. "I just don't understand why I needed you so much last night. Like I said, I've wanted to do more with you for a while. But last night, all of a sudden, it was like I had to have you or I was gonna…."

"Die?" Erick asked gently when Bo didn't go on. "Under the circumstances, I'd say what you were feeling was perfectly normal. In fact, now that I think about it, I probably shouldn't have been as surprised as I was you would show up here like that."

"Why not?"

"Because lots of people crave sex after they've been involved in a death. Not just for the comfort or the release of tension but as an affirmation of life. You said it yourself: you needed to feel alive. At its most basic, elemental level, that's what sex is. Life. It creates life. Literally. Which is why some people consider anything other than unprotected vaginal intercourse between a man and a woman a perversion—because it doesn't have that potential for creating life. That doesn't mean it doesn't have its uses."

Erick put both arms around Bo and rested his head against his shoulder. "You didn't use me, Bo—you needed me. That's not the same thing. And you certainly didn't take anything from me. Believe me, I'd know."

Still feeling a little guilty, Bo nevertheless let Erick pull him back until he lay against the pillows, Erick's arms wrapped around him.

"I want you to listen to me, okay?" Erick said. "Everything I gave you last night was just that. A gift. For both of us."

"Then I guess I should say 'thanks for the present'," Bo told him. "I think I should tell you, it wasn't just the sex I needed. I needed *you*. I needed you because I was scared and somehow I knew if I could just get to you, you'd take care of me. That everything would be okay."

"Well, I can't promise you everything is going to be okay, but I can promise I will take care of you. Whenever you need me, I'll be here for you," Erick said, holding him tightly. "However, professional curiosity begs that I ask. What were you so scared of? Was it dying yourself?"

"Not exactly." Bo wrapped one hand around Erick's forearm, rubbing it lightly. "I guess it was all the 'somedays' that got to me."

"I don't understand."

Bo tried to think of a way to explain something he hadn't quite figured out for himself. "I didn't really know O'Malley very well. I mean, I knew him for years at work, but I didn't really know him as a person. After listening to everyone talk at the viewing and the funeral, I learned a lot about him. Did you know he wanted to be an architect? He even went to college for it. Before he could finish, his girlfriend got pregnant and he had to drop out. Once they got married, he took a job working for my old man. But he always meant to go back and finish his degree. Someday. That's the word I kept hearing: someday. Someday he was going to put an addition on his house. Someday he was going to take his kids to Disney World. Someday he'd buy his wife the engagement ring he hadn't been able to back then. Someday he would stop swinging a hammer for somebody else and be his own boss. Then, just like that, he ran out of 'somedays'."

"We all run out of them sooner or later, Bo. Nobody lives forever."

"I know. I can't even say he had a bad life. He had a great life. He had a wife he loved, two beautiful daughters, a home, friends. But somehow I kept coming back to all those 'somedays'. All those things he didn't do because he thought he'd have time to do them later. It scared me. I don't want that to be me, Erick. I don't want to be wherever I'm gonna be while my funeral is going on and have to listen to all the people who knew me best talk about all the things I was going to do 'someday' but somehow never managed to get my act together enough to actually do them."

Erick was quiet for a moment, as if choosing his words carefully.

"I hear what you're saying. Lately you've been feeling like you're at a point in your life where you need to make some changes, but you're not sure what those changes should be or how to go about making them. So I can understand why thinking about running out of time would scare you. But I know you, Bo. You're not the type of person who's going to sit around forever waiting for something to magically come along and make everything better. Sooner or later, you'll figure out what you want to do and you'll do it."

Very gently, Erick wiped away the tears Bo hadn't been aware he'd shed.

"In the meantime, what you have to remember is, when it comes right down to it, 'someday' doesn't really exist. Because the only day we ever *really* have is today. So as long as you're spending today in a way that fulfills you—that makes you happy—that's all that really matters."

Bo hadn't thought of it that way but he supposed it made sense. It made him feel better too. "Then I guess I'm okay, because right this minute, I'm exactly where I want to be."

Erick leaned in and kissed him lightly. "So am I." He raised his arms and stretched mightily. "However, I think we're both going to have to make a slight alteration in our location and adjourn to the kitchen, because I'm starving."

For the first time in days, Bo felt the same way. "So am I."

"This is your lucky day. You landed on the doorstep of someone who is not only awesome in bed and gives out free psychological counseling, but who also happens to make the world's best scrambled eggs. After all, I can't exactly let you starve to death, right? What self-respecting carpenter would want to be caught dead in a place like this?"

"Not me, that's for sure." Bo wiped his cheeks with the back of his hand, appreciating Erick's effort to lighten the mood. "Even around this place, someone might start to notice the stench. After a month or two. Maybe."

Erick grabbed one of the pillows and hit Bo in the face with it. Then he got out of bed. As he stood there, the early-morning sun shining on his blond hair, turning his eyes a sparkling green, Bo's heart began to beat faster. There was something about Erick's odd mixture of feminine softness and masculine strength that sent his libido running wild.

Something must have shown on his face, because Erick cocked his head in that way he had when he was puzzled. "What?"

"Nothing. I was just thinking: before we eat those eggs, there is one more thing you could help me out with."

"What's that?"

"Well… you see… there's this thing I've recently come to the conclusion I really want to learn to do someday, and since you said all we really have is today, I was thinking maybe I'd better have my first lesson now."

It was obvious from the way the fit of Erick's boxers began to change that some of Bo's message had gotten across but his expression and tone remained bland.

"May I ask exactly what it is you want to learn to do?"

"I want to learn to give a really superior blow job."

"Oh really? And you think I'd be able to teach you that?"

"Oh, I know you can. I've seen your work, remember? If there's anything I know, it's how to recognize an expert when I see one."

With that, Bo inserted the tips of two fingers into the elastic on Erick's boxers and yanked him forward. When he fell onto the bed,

Bo tugged and pulled and generally manhandled Erick until he was lying under Bo, smiling up at him.

"I admit I am a complete novice at this," Bo said as he held Erick's face cupped in his big hands, "but I think you'll find I'm an excellent student. Once I put my mind to something, that is."

"It's not your mind you're going to need," Erick said dryly, but when Bo lowered his head to kiss him, Erick stopped him, his expression going serious.

"You don't have to do this, Bo. Not if you're not ready. I didn't do what I did last night expecting some kind of payback."

"I know that." Bo bent his head, kissing him lightly on the lips. Then on his chin. Then on the small depression at the base of his throat. "And I guess I won't know if I'm ready until I get where I'm going." Slowly, Bo began to kiss his way down the center of Erick's body.

"In that case… I can tell you that you're definitely headed in the right direction."

Bo didn't bother trying to answer.

He was busy with other things at the moment.

CHAPTER
THIRTEEN

OVER the next several weeks, Bo wasn't able to put nearly as much time and energy into his relationship with Erick as he wanted, what with the project deadline bearing down on him. But even with the continuing generator problems and the smaller crew and all the other little headaches that went along with a project of this size, by the day before his twenty-fifth birthday, the whole thing was finished.

Precisely on budget and not only on time, but with two days to spare.

Bo could hardly believe it. It had been a major pain in his ass for what felt like forever. Still… knowing he'd done it—that he'd accomplished what he'd set out to do and done it well—had Bo feeling on top of the world.

Even the old man couldn't find too much to gripe about, though he certainly tried. Bo was too happy to let it get to him. The job was done, the crew had been given two days off, and he had major plans for his birthday, starting tonight.

For once, all was right with his world.

"Thank you again, gentlemen, for a job well done," Michael Howe said as he shook Bo's hand again. "We're incredibly pleased with how it all turned out."

"That's what we're here for," Bo told him.

K.L. Belanger

The four men had been in Bo's father's downtown office signing the final paperwork since two o'clock and now, closer to four o'clock, the clients were finally leaving.

"Thank you, Mr. Sanford," Stanley Howe said, also shaking Bo's hand. "You do good work."

"Thank you, sir," Bo said, and feeling magnanimous now that everything was signed, sealed, and delivered, he added, "It's been a pleasure doing business with you."

Once the two men left, Bo and his father were alone in the office, and as was his habit, his father broke out the cigars. Bo hated this part of the ritual—sitting in the chair across from his father's seat behind the desk, puffing on smelly cigars and talking over the newly completed project—but even that couldn't ruin his mood today.

He had a date with Erick tonight. Their first real date. The kind where you dressed up nice and went to someplace fancy to sip wine, engage in quiet conversation, and, in general, behave like adults. Afterward, they were having a sleepover at his place.

One for which he also had major plans.

He could hardly wait.

As soon as he could, Bo snuffed out his cigar and got to his feet, saying, "Look, Pop. I've got to get going. I've got a date tonight and I have some things to do to get ready for it." He took a deep breath and forced himself to say the words he'd promised himself he'd say. "I'd like to stop by here on my way out to the job site Monday. There's something I'd like to talk to you about."

"Monday?" his dad said gruffly. "Forget Monday. I need you here Friday morning, boy. Nine o'clock sharp! We got work to do."

Bo was annoyed. In his dad's mind, there was always work to do.

"What can we possibly have to do that can't wait 'til Monday? I already gave my crew two days off, remember?"

"Yeah, I remember. What a bunch of mealy-mouthed crap that was," the old man grumbled. "You could have given them tomorrow off if you really wanted to—a national holiday for your birthday or something—and still have gotten them all back to work on Friday."

"Working on what? We've already pulled all the permits we need and the materials are already out at the site. Besides, they worked their asses off on this one. They deserve a break," Bo said for what felt like the millionth time. "We've got until August to finish the rehab on this one. What's the big rush?"

"Time is money, boy. But what's done is done, I guess. The point is, you're not going to be joining the crew on the rehab just yet. I'm putting Joe Sparks on as temporary foreman."

This was something new.

"How come?" Bo asked.

"I've decided to put in a bid on a new construction project in Waltham and I want you to head it up. From start to finish. That's why I need you here Friday, to start putting the proposal together. Once we get it submitted, you can take over on Second Street while we wait to see if we've got the job. When we do, you can move your crew on over to the new project, and if Joe works out okay, he can finish up the rehab with Stevie Clark's old crew."

Had he had his wits about him, Bo might have questioned why his father would even consider pulling a crew midproject when everyone knew it was a stupid maneuver that generally added weeks to the timeline. But he couldn't seem to get the words out.

Maybe it was because somewhere along the line, he had stumbled into a deep, dark hole he hadn't even known was there.

"We've never talked about this," he said shakily. "We've never talked about anything like this."

"I'm telling you now."

Bo didn't know why he was surprised. It was the same as it always had been, with his father calling the shots and Bo falling into line. Not this time. This time, Bo was determined not to be such a pushover. "You should have talked to me about it before you went ahead and made the decision for me."

"Why? What's the difference?"

"The difference is, if you had talked to me, I would have told you I don't want to head up a project like that. Putting in bids, writing up proposals—that's not what I do."

"It is now, 'cause that's how you learn—from the ground up."

Bo didn't know how many times he'd heard that phrase over his lifetime. All he knew was, this time, instead of annoying him, it terrified him.

"I don't need to learn that kind of stuff. That's not who I am. I'm a carpenter, not a contractor. I like to build things."

"And you're good at it," his father said, and Bo blinked in surprise. It was a rare day, indeed, when his father gave anyone a compliment. As Bo was trying to assimilate that, his old man went on. "But knowing *how* to build things is just the beginning. Learning how to get people to *pay* you to build things is something else. You can't take over the company until you know how to do that."

"Take over the company?"

If there had been any spit left in his mouth, Bo might have shouted the question. But there wasn't. Not a drop. So it came out as a whisper.

"Of course. Why else would I have put you in charge on the last project?"

Bo wasn't sure he knew the answer to that, but frankly, that wasn't the point. "I figured Ham would be the one taking over. He's the one who's good at all that stuff—paperwork and writing bids and coordinating schedules. I'm lousy at that kind of thing."

"I know you are, which is why you need the practice."

"Why would I need the practice if Ham's already good at it?"

"Because you're the one I want running this place someday," his old man said, surprising Bo again. "Ham may have the brains to do it, but like you said, you're the carpenter. That's what this place needs:

someone in charge who knows what's what. Ham can still do all the housekeeping if you like, paperwork and all that other piddly shit, but you're the one who's going to be running the place when I'm gone. So you damn well better learn how."

Bo was so shocked, he wasn't sure what to do. He'd had no idea his father had been planning on anything like this. He certainly hadn't planned on having a conversation about his future today. Especially as he hadn't yet figured out how he was going to broach the subject of his own plans on Monday. He was caught in an unforeseen trap, and there was only one way out he could see.

"I really wish you had told me all this sooner, Pop," he said gently.

"Why?"

"Because then I would have told you running the company isn't what I want to do with my life."

Bo's father's thick eyebrows came together. "What the hell are you talking about?"

God, he didn't want to do this. Not now. Not like this.

He had no choice.

"I've decided I want to do something different with my life. So as of Monday, I'm giving my two-week notice."

At that moment, Bo's father did the one thing Bo never would have guessed he would do: he laughed. "Your two-week notice." He waggled his cigar at his son. "Now that's a good one."

"I'm not kidding, Pop. I'm leaving the company."

Finally some of Bo's seriousness seemed to get through. "Oh yeah? To do what?"

"Start my own business. Flipping houses, to start with. Maybe branch out a little bit later. Own some rental properties."

When the Boss Man narrowed his eyes the way he did right then, he looked exactly like a badger skulking in his den. It wasn't a comfortable simile. "Boy, you must be crazy. Where are you gonna get the money to do something like that?"

"I have some money put away, and I've already talked to a couple banks about financing the rest."

"Oh, you have, huh?" The scorn in his father's voice grated like sandpaper. "Who the hell do you think you are, anyway? Some bigwig wheeler-dealer? Head up one project and suddenly you've got to be bigger and better than your old man? Who put you up to all this bullshit? That fancy-pants lawyer brother of yours?"

Bo had no intention of being drawn into an argument. Especially one he couldn't win. "This has nothing to do with anyone but me. And maybe a little bit of Grandpa."

"What's he got to do with anything?"

"You always told us how proud you were that he started with nothing. But with hard work and good old-fashioned know-how, he managed to build this company from the ground up."

"So?"

"So, that's what I want to do. Build my own company."

"*This* is your company." Bo's father banged his fist on the desk for emphasis. "And your heritage. More than that, it's your goddamn responsibility. Sanford and Sons needs you to keep it going so there'll be something left to leave to your sons someday, and to their sons after them. That's the way it's always been and that's how it's going to stay."

It was the same old song and dance. Nothing mattered but the company.

"You don't need me for that," Bo said, trying to remain calm and in control when what he really wanted to do was smash his fist through a wall. "Ham can keep it going, and I can still help out when he needs me."

"*I* need you. Here! And here's where you'll by God stay."

Bo felt the pressure of his father's gaze like a weight on his chest, pressing down on him, trying to squeeze him into a mold he no longer fit, but he fought against it.

"No. I have a right to decide my own life."

"It's not just your life you'll be affecting, boy. There are a lot of other people who are depending on you. Like that crew you're so fond of."

Suddenly Bo got a very bad feeling in the pit of his stomach.

"What's that supposed to mean?

"It means if you walk out that door, you'll be taking your entire crew with you."

Bo felt like he'd been punched in the gut. "You mean you'd let them all go just like that?"

"Yup."

Bo couldn't believe what he was hearing. "But why?"

"They're your crew. That means they're your responsibility. That's what it means to be the boss."

"You know I'd never be able to afford to hire them all to start off," Bo cried. "Those guys depend on us for a paycheck."

"As of now they depend on us. If you leave, they'll be depending on *you*. You want to let 'em all down? Be my guest. But if you go, they go."

"You can't fire them all," Bo challenged. "You need them to finish that rehab."

Bo's father leaned forward, like a cheetah closing in on his prey. "Let me tell you something, boy. As long as it's my ass sitting in this chair, I can do whatever the hell I please. If I want to fire that crew of yours and go out and hire myself a new one, there's nothing anyone can do to stop me. So either you stay on or they all go. It's your choice."

His choice. Right! No, it was the same as it had always been.

There was no choice.

"You know, you really are a heartless bastard," Bo said bitterly, but his father seemed unimpressed.

"Like I said, that's what it means to be the boss."

At that, his father picked up a file and opened it as if nothing untoward had been said. "Enjoy your birthday. And don't forget. Friday morning. Nine o'clock sharp!"

Since there was nothing more he could say, Bo left his father's office.

He had a knot in his stomach the size of the building they'd just completed.

CHAPTER
FOURTEEN

BO TRIED to put it out of his mind. He really did. But it was hard to enjoy getting ready for his big night out while his leg was caught in the jaws of a giant bear trap. He'd known all his life his father could be a hard man when he wanted to be, but he'd never anticipated he would pull something like this. Bo had no idea what to do about it.

For the moment, he did his best to push it aside and just enjoy his surroundings. And the company he was with.

The restaurant he had picked was one of the fanciest in town—The Garlic Bistro out on Commonwealth Avenue. Neither Bo nor Erick had ever been there before, and as they were led through the dining room to the little table in a quiet corner he'd requested, Bo was already questioning his decision to come here now. Not just because it was expensive enough to have his wallet screaming in agony but because, even in his suit and tie, he felt like a water buffalo visiting the White House.

Erick, of course, looked like he'd been born there. Sitting across the table from Bo, studying the menu, he looked amazing—sexy and conservative all at the same time. He was wearing the same scarf he'd had on when they had first met, only this time it was coupled with a light-gray turtleneck sweater and a pair of fitted trousers that hugged him like a glove.

Though Bo had never considered himself the jealous type, he found it bothered him when their waiter's recitation of that night's specials included several soulful glances in Erick's direction.

Erick only had eyes for Bo, and the way those eyes glowed like jewels in the flickering light from the candle on the table had Bo needing several minutes to choose between cavatappi and linguine to go with his chicken piccata.

"You know," Erick said after they had ordered and the waiter had reluctantly left, "we didn't have to go anywhere so fancy. There are a million places in town that won't cost you a week's wages for a bowl of pasta and a little Parmesan cheese."

Bo almost winced. The last thing he wanted to think about was wages. Or work. Or anything like that. He only wanted to think about Erick right now.

"I wanted to do something really special for my birthday. It is my twenty-fifth, after all. Isn't that's supposed to be some kind of a milestone or something?"

"In that case, shouldn't I be the one taking *you* out?" Erick asked.

As they had been over this ground before, Bo reached across the table and took Erick's hand. "I'm counting on you to give me my present later, when we're all alone."

"Oh, really?" Erick leaned across the table toward Bo. "And just exactly what is it you want me to give you?"

Forcing back a rush of lust at the seductive tone of Erick's voice, Bo rubbed his rough thumb across Erick's fingers.

"Well… I was really hoping it would be something we could give each other. Like maybe we could finally…."

"Bo?"

The feminine voice had Bo jerking back in surprise, and when he looked over Erick's left shoulder, he saw his sister-in-law, Andrea, waddling toward them—her enormous pregnant belly leading the way—and his brother Ham trailing behind.

"Oh, shit," Bo said under his breath, but before he could even warn Erick what was about to befall them, Andrea said, "I told you it was him," and she made a beeline for them.

Awkwardly, Bo got to his feet in time to catch his sister-in-law, who enveloped him in a huge hug. "Hey, what are you guys doing here?" he asked.

Andrea backed off and looked up at him, beaming. "Oh, we figured it would be our last chance to get out before the baby comes, so we decided to splurge. We were on our way out when I spotted you. I'm so glad I did. I wasn't sure we'd get by to see you tomorrow. So, happy birthday. One day early."

"Thanks."

"Yeah, happy birthday," his brother said, giving him a brief hug. Then he stepped back and demanded, "Say, what the hell happened between you and Pop today?"

"Ham." Andrea rolled her eyes, but Ham just kept going.

"All I did was ask him what you were doing for your birthday and he just about bit my head off. Said you had a date or something, but you'd 'by God be at work Friday or there'd be hell to pay'. What're you two fighting about now?"

Even if the alternative was being found naked in bed with Erick, this would be the last thing Bo wanted to do right now. "If you don't mind, I'd really rather not talk about it, okay?"

"Why? Did you do something asinine? Like quit again?"

"Not exactly."

"Then what?"

"Ham, please. Now's not the time, all right?" Andrea told him. "Besides, we're being awfully rude to Bo's date." Andrea turned to face Erick. "I'm sorry we barged in like this. I'm... oh!" Bo closed his eyes at the startled surprise in her voice. "I'm sorry," she said, sounding flustered. "For a minute, I thought you were... ah...."

"That I was a woman," Erick said smoothly, and when Bo opened his eyes again, he saw Erick rising to his feet and taking Andrea's hand as if nothing at all was wrong with this picture. "A perfectly understandable mistake. I'm Erick, by the way. I'm a friend of Bo's."

After shaking Andrea's hand, he exchanged handshakes with Ham as well.

"It's nice to finally meet you both," he told them. "I've heard a lot about you."

"Really?" Andrea said, and Bo wanted to wince at her tone. That "I'm going to get to the bottom of this, so help me God" tone that made the hair at the back of his neck stand on end. "That's funny. I knew Bo had met someone new recently, but I hadn't heard your name come up. In fact, I don't remember hearing any names being mentioned, at all." She turned to Ham. "Don't you find that strange, honey?"

Oh, jeez..., Bo thought, but his brother rescued him, saying, "Why would that be strange? I don't tell Bo about every guy I meet."

"We've only recently become friends," Erick said, as if still trying to save the situation, and though Bo wanted to commend him for the attempt, he knew it was hopeless.

Andrea was like an emotional seismograph. She could pick up even the tiniest hint of movement beneath her feet. Right now they were on very shaky ground.

"Is that so?" Andrea said, still probing. "Tell me, how did you two meet?"

Bo wanted to warn Erick to be careful but there was no way to do so gracefully.

"We met at an incredibly boring party and just starting talking," Erick said.

"Talking." Andrea raised her eyebrows and turned smoothly to Bo. "As in 'talking all night' talking?"

Just like that, he was busted!

"Yeah," Bo said, trying not to blush and failing miserably.

"And you've been friends ever since?"

"Uh-huh."

"Then you must be very *good* friends by now," Andrea said, more sweetly still.

Bo made one last-ditch effort to delay the inevitable. "You know how it goes sometimes."

"No. I have no idea how it goes. Why don't you try explaining it to me?"

Andrea was so obviously enjoying watching him squirm that Bo wanted to hold it against her, but somehow he didn't have the heart to.

"You know… you start out as friends… and then, things kind of go from one thing to the next and… before you know it you're… ahh… really *close* friends."

"Ah, I see," Andrea said. "How incredibly interesting."

"What?" Ham demanded, glancing from his smirking wife to his obviously discomfited brother. "What's so interesting about being good friends with some guy you met at a party?"

Erick covered a laugh with a cough. "Sorry."

When Erick glanced toward Andrea, Bo saw the two of them exchange knowing smiles and he barely stifled a groan. He should have known. With that one look, the two of them had bonded like glue.

"Well, you know…," Andrea said to her husband. "Just that Bo would turn out to be such close friends with another man."

"Why is that interesting?" Ham asked.

This time Erick didn't bother to hide the smirk.

"Tell me something," Erick said to Andrea. "Are all the Sanford men this…?"

"Dense?" Andrea supplied. "I'm afraid so."

"You've got your hands full."

Andrea smiled serenely. "Yes. Yes I do."

"All right, what the hell is going on here?" Ham demanded. "I feel like we're playing blind man's bluff and I'm the blind man. And how come you're here having dinner with a friend, anyway? I thought you told Pop you had a date."

"I did, I mean *I do*," Bo said.

"Where is she?"

Andrea shook her head and sighed in exasperation. "Sweetheart, what Bo is trying to say is…."

"Erick *is* my date," Bo blurted. "We're sort of… together."

Once the words were out, Bo expected something spectacular to happen, like the rotation of the earth to suddenly come to an abrupt halt. But nothing did. There were no fireworks, no thunderbolts from heaven.

There was just Andrea grinning and his brother standing there with a confused look on his face. Then, all of a sudden, it seemed comprehension hit his brother and he turned to his wife, saying, "Judas Priest, was there something in the water at home?"

"Okay!" Andrea said brightly. "On that note, we're leaving." She turned to Erick. "Erick, it's been very educational meeting you."

"Yeah, you too," Erick said with a smile and nodded toward Ham, who still looked a little shell-shocked. "Good luck."

"Thanks. You too." Andrea turned to Bo and, reaching up, gave him another hug. "Bo, have a wonderful birthday." She took his face in her hands. "Listen to me… we love you. Whatever makes you happy makes us happy, okay?"

Bo let out a big sigh. "Okay, Andi. Thanks."

She gave him a kiss, and when she let him go, Bo turned and faced his brother. To his great relief, Ham held out his hand to him. "I gotta say, bro, I don't get it, but… whatever."

Ham's resigned look wasn't exactly encouraging, but Bo took his words to mean all would be well, eventually, and he let out a relieved breath.

When he retook his seat, he found himself still feeling a little bit shaky.

"Well." He blew out another breath. "That was awkward."

"To say the least," Erick said, but he was smiling. "Are you okay?"

"I think so." Briefly, he scanned back and forth as if searching his mental databases, then he suddenly looked up. "Oh shit! You don't think they'll say anything to my pop, do you?" Before Erick could say anything, Bo shook his head. "No. Andi wouldn't do that to me." He closed his eyes and sighed. "Christ, what a mess."

When he felt Erick's hand cover his own, he opened his eyes and looked into a pair of troubled green ones. "I'm sorry," Erick said. "I can't imagine this is how you pictured having your family find out about us."

The sympathy in Erick's eyes soothed some of Bo's nerves, and he squeezed his hand. "It's okay. If it had to be anybody, it's probably best that it was them, but… I'm thinking I might need something a little stronger than wine here."

"You're probably right." Erick raised his hand to call over the waiter. "Oh, and just for future reference, you might want to work on your approach to the whole big-announcement thing."

"What do you mean?"

"I mean that bull-in-the-china-shop method you've got going might have worked with your brother and sister-in-law, but I can assure you it isn't going to fly so well with everyone else."

"I don't know what you mean."

Erick shook his head wearily. "How about we talk about it after we have that drink?"

THE two talked it over for a little while, then agreed to put aside their chance meeting and enjoy the rest of their meal. It was—as they had been assured by their server it would be—delicious, and the two of them lingered over it and followed it up with both dessert and coffee. It was quite late by the time they got back to Bo's apartment, but when Bo parked the truck and turned off the engine, Erick reached out a hand and stopped him before he opened the door.

"Bo, before we go in, I need to talk to you about something."

There were a few lights on in the parking lot but when Bo turned to look at him, Erick's face was hidden in shadow, and he could hear the seriousness of his voice.

"What is it? What's wrong?"

"Nothing's wrong, exactly. I need to ask you to do something for me, that's all."

"Sure. Anything."

Erick laughed a bit. "You might want to wait to say that until after you hear what it is."

"It doesn't matter what it is. Whatever it is, I'll do it."

"All right. I need you *not* to ask me the question I think you're planning on asking me when we get inside."

Bo shook his head, perplexed. "I don't understand."

"I know I might be wrong about this but… from the sense I got earlier, I have a pretty good idea that when we get inside, you're planning on asking me if I'd be willing to make love with you tonight. And I need to ask you, please, not to ask."

Bo was confused. He had, indeed, been planning on asking that very thing—had been planning on it for days, actually. He had been hoping to be with Erick completely. A celebration not only of his birthday but of the new life he was trying to build for himself.

Naturally he had expected that Erick would say yes. So he supposed it made sense he was a little taken aback by this new development.

"Why don't you want me to ask?"

"Because I don't want to have to say no."

"Why?"

"Because I don't want to disappoint you or hurt you or let you down in any way. Especially tonight."

Bo gave a huff of annoyance. "You know that's not what I meant. Why would you have to say no?"

"Because I'm not ready for that yet."

"Why not? I thought…."

Embarrassment had Bo's voice trailing off, but Erick must have misinterpreted because he snapped, "You thought what? That I'd jump at the chance to be fucked by a stud like you?"

Bo felt like he'd been punched in the gut. "No! I didn't think that, at all. I just thought…." He shook his head and turned to look out the driver's side window. "I don't know what I was thinking."

"Hey," Erick said quietly, but Bo didn't respond. Erick slid across the seat and cupped Bo's chin in his hand, turning him to face him. There were tears in Erick's eyes. "I'm sorry, Bo. That was completely out of line. I know that's not what you were thinking."

"Then why'd you say it?" Bo asked, still feeling hurt.

Gently Erick ran the backs of his fingers along Bo's jawline. "I guess it's because I'd rather pick a fight with you than explain why I'm not ready."

"You don't owe me an explanation."

"Maybe I wouldn't have before, but I do now." Erick dropped his hand and took a deep breath, as if trying to steady his voice. "Do you remember the night we met? When I told you I had just gotten out of a bad relationship?"

"Yeah?"

"Well, that relationship was really... *really* bad. Part of the reason it was bad was because the guy I was with was very... how about we call it... aggressive? Especially in bed."

"I don't know what you mean."

Erick blew out a breath. "He was rough, okay? Really rough. I haven't been with anyone since him and I just don't know if I can be yet."

Something here wasn't quite adding up for Bo. "When you say he was rough... he didn't hurt you, did he?"

Erick made a sound that almost sounded amused. "You could say that... yeah." Before Bo could ask anything else, Erick said, "Look, I don't really want to get into all of gory details, okay? The point is, as much as I would love to make love with you, I don't know if I can bring myself to be that vulnerable to anyone yet. To open myself up that way. I thought I could. I've thought about it a lot. But now that I'm here... I know I can't. I'm sorry."

Though the thought made him distinctly uncomfortable, Bo said, "It wouldn't have to be that way, if you're not ready. Me making love to you, that is. If you wanted, we could, you know, go the other way."

One of the tears that had been welling up in Erick's eyes spilled over, but oddly enough, he smiled. "You know... I think that might just be the sweetest thing any guy has ever said to me." He reached out one finger and caressed Bo's cheek. "As much as I appreciate the offer, I'll have to decline. I don't do that."

"Do what?"

"Go the other way. I'm strictly a bottom. Always have been."

Bo couldn't help feeling a twinge of guilt at the relief he felt. "You must know *I* would never hurt you."

"I do know that. I still can't do it. Not yet. I'm sorry."

There was a long moment of silence between them before Erick said, "If you'd rather just take me home now, I'll understand."

Bo had to work to keep the annoyance out of his voice. "Are you trying to pick another fight with me?" When Erick's eyes filled again, Bo couldn't resist anymore and he took Erick in his arms, brushing his hand over Erick's hair as he cradled his head against his shoulder. "Hey, look, it's okay. I'm not disappointed. Or at least not much."

That got a laugh out of Erick. A watery one, but still, a laugh.

"How about you come inside with me, okay?" Bo eased off so he could wipe away Erick's tears. "I promise I won't ask to make love. We don't have to do anything at all. Just sleep beside me. That's all I ask."

"Oh, I think I can manage to deliver something a little more exciting than that."

"It doesn't matter." Bo kissed Erick's forehead, then both his cheeks, then touched his lips to Erick's. "Nothing matters as long as we're together."

"All right. Let's go be together."

Erick opened his door and got out as Bo slid over and got out the other side. When they met on the other side of the truck, Erick accepted the hand Bo held out to him and together they strolled to the front door.

Once they got inside the apartment, they headed straight for the bedroom, and even before Bo turned on the lights, Erick turned to him and, lifting on his toes, put his arms around his neck.

"Thanks for understanding why I need to wait."

Bo wasn't altogether sure he did understand, or at least not fully. He could and did accept it, which, he supposed, would have to be good enough.

CHAPTER
FIFTEEN

DESPITE not having made love the night before, Bo woke the morning of his birthday feeling completely satisfied. So much so that he found himself whistling in the shower. He felt good, strong, and ready to take on the world. When Erick tugged aside the shower curtain and stepped in behind him, he knew his life was complete.

He turned to Erick to slip his arms around him and give him a hug.

"Good morning."

"Morning," Erick replied, and the two exchanged a long, lingering kiss. With his eyes still closed, Erick hummed. "Mmm. Now that's what I call the breakfast of champions."

That got a laugh out of Bo.

"Turn around and I'll wash your back for you," Erick said, and despite the heat of the water, when Bo first felt Erick run his hands, slick with soap, over his back, he shivered.

"You know," he said, "if we're going to make a habit of this—and I sincerely hope we will—I'm going to need to find a place with a bigger shower. "

"Why? Do you object to being close?"

"Not at all," he said huskily as Erick moved his hands downward and rubbed his ass. "Still, a little more room to maneuver might be nice."

"I think we can make do with what we've got." Erick rose on his toes and whispered in Bo's ear, "I have a present for you."

Bo felt the breath back up in his throat at the seductive tone of Erick's voice.

"You already gave me one last night. Remember?"

"I know. But this is something different. Something I save for really special occasions."

"Oh, really?" Bo's heart began to pound. "So what is it?"

"I'm afraid it might lose a little bit in the telling. How about if I just show you instead?"

Seductively, Erick ran his hands up Bo's back again and down his arms. Then, taking Bo's big hands in his, Erick guided them up until they were braced against the front wall of the shower. Gently he nudged Bo's legs back a bit so he was leaning forward slightly.

Kissing his way up Bo's neck, he whispered in his ear again. "Some guys like this. Some guys don't. Just let me know which it is for you, okay?"

Bo managed to squeeze out a husky, "Okay."

Erick ran his nimble tongue down Bo's neck, as he slid his soapy hands down his back.

The water running over Bo was hot, but Erick's tongue was hotter as he licked his way down Bo's spine like a brand, burning along his nerve endings. The feel of Erick massaging and teasing his ass cheeks, then slipping inside to slide hotly over previously uncharted territory, had Bo fighting to draw a deep breath.

Erick knelt down behind him, and Bo's heart stuttered with a combination of nerves and a kind of forbidden excitement. He wasn't at all sure how he felt about what he thought Erick was going to do, but just as he was about to object, Erick reached around and gripped Bo's cock even as he slid his tongue farther down to swirl and lick and tease Bo's untried opening, and the combined pleasure made Bo's eyes roll back in his head. It was the hottest thing he had ever experienced—trapped between the sleek movements of Erick's talented fingers and the wild guilty pleasure of his nimble tongue moving in counterpoint to the relentless stroking of his hand.

Even if he had wanted to, he couldn't have protested, and when he came wildly, he didn't know whether to thank Erick or apologize.

Erick rose to his feet and turned Bo so they could exchange places under the spray. He washed himself off briefly before turning his back to the water spray and then, lifting his arms around Bo's neck, he stretched up to kiss him again.

"Happy birthday," he said.

Bo couldn't think of a better way to celebrate being a quarter of a century old.

AFTER his heart rate had finally dropped back to normal and he had tugged on a pair of faded jeans, then zipped his fly, Bo turned to Erick, who was still drying off.

"I'm going to go start the coffee, but if you're hungry, I think we're going to have to go out to eat. That is, unless I can interest you in a bowl of Cap'n Crunch."

"Thanks, but I think I'll pass."

"It's your loss."

In a great mood, Bo opened the bedroom door and nearly jumped out of his skin. Mac was standing in the middle of the living room with a bottle of Bo's favorite scotch adorned with a Mylar balloon in one hand and a huge grin stretched across his face.

"Hey, happy birthday, dude!"

"For God' sake, Mac, you scared the shit of me," Bo said breathlessly. "What the hell are you doing here?"

"Delivering your birthday present, of course."

Mac gave the bottle a little shake and the obviously delighted smile on his face seriously confused Bo. "I thought you were pissed at me."

"I am. Or at least I was, but... it's your twenty-fifth birthday, for Pete's sake. How could I let that go by unacknowledged?" Mac asked. "Besides, I'm the one who got drafted to come over here and get you and bring you down to Daisy's for the surprise birthday breakfast the guys and I planned. They're all there waiting for us now."

Terrific! How the hell was he going to get out of this one? Sometimes, Bo decided, the only defense is a strong offense.

"So... what? You just waltz in here? Uninvited?"

Obviously taken aback, Mac said, "Well... yeah... I guess."

"How the hell did you get in?"

Mac looked at him strangely. "Ah... the same way I always do. I buzzed Mrs. P, told her I was you, then used the key."

"Haven't you ever heard of knocking?"

"I did knock. In fact, I just about busted the door in, but you didn't answer, so I figured you were in the shower or something."

At that moment, Erick came through the door and practically ran into Bo's back. "Hey, what's going on?"

Mac winced. "Oh, jeez, dude, I'm sorry. I didn't stop to think you might have company." Though Erick was mostly hidden behind Bo's back, Mac must have caught a glimpse of him because his eyes narrowed sharply. "Hang on a minute."

Shit!

Bo put his arm out, as if to shield Erick, but the damage was already done.

"What the hell's going on here?" Mac asked.

Heaving a sigh of resignation, Bo stepped to the side so Erick was now visible.

Unlike Bo, Erick was wearing a shirt as well as a pair of pants, but Bo knew there was no way anyone could mistake his gender. Or the situation.

"Who the hell is this?" Mac demanded, then his eyes went wide with shock. "Wait a minute. I know you. You're that guy from the party. The one Bo thought was a girl." He turned to Bo. "Does this mean he really is a girl? Or a… whatever it is they call those girls that used to be guys?"

"No." Bo was ashamed when he heard his own voice shake a bit. "No, he's not a… ah… ah…."

When Bo just flapped his hands helplessly, Erick said quietly, "I think the word you're looking for is 'transsexual'."

"Thanks, but I'll handle this," Bo said curtly, then looked at Mac directly. "No, Erick's not a girl or a transsexual. He's just a guy."

"And that's this so-called 'mystery girl' you've been seeing all this time? A guy?"

Bo winced at the anger in Mac's voice. "Yeah."

"Since when do you play both sides of the fence?"

"I don't know. Since I met Erick, I guess."

Mac spun away and began pacing the room, letting out a string of curse words that should have had the plaster igniting. It might have been comical, what with the way the shiny balloon bobbed along behind him as he paced, but Bo had never felt less like laughing in his life.

"You lying, sneaky son of a bitch." Mac whirled and pointed one furious finger at his friend. "I ought to knock you into the middle of next week for this, you asshole!"

"Hey!" Bo said, getting annoyed in turn. "What is your problem?"

"What do you mean, what's my problem? This…." He waved his hand up and down as if to encompass the entire scene. "This whole thing is my problem. How could you do something like this without telling me?"

"There's no law that says I have to tell you everything," Bo retorted. "If I want to keep some of my personal life private, that's my business."

"Keeping it private is one thing. Fucking lying to me is something else."

"I haven't lied to you."

"The hell you haven't. You've been lying to everybody. Letting us all think you've been with a girl when all this time you've really been with a guy."

Bo couldn't help the twinge of guilt. Mac did have a point. Sort of.

"I didn't mean to lie about it, exactly. I just didn't want to deal with all the shit the guys would dish out. You know what they're like. If they found out I was dating a man, all hell would have broken loose. Keeping quiet seemed easier, that's all."

"It might be easier, but that doesn't make it right. Besides, I'm not just one of the guys, am I? I'm supposed to be your best friend."

"You are my best friend."

"Doesn't that mean anything to you?"

"Of course it does."

"But it doesn't mean more to you than him."

"I didn't say that."

"You didn't have to. Your silence said it all," Mac said in disgust. "Then again, I guess I can see how something like this could happen." The words might have sounded reasonable but the tone was bitterly sarcastic. "After all, it may not be my first choice but I could see how you might rather bang some willing gay guy than hang out with your friends. At least you get your rocks off that way."

Bo felt his temper beginning to rise and he took a step forward.

"You'd better watch yourself, Mac. You're about to step over the line."

"Fuck you and him too! Although I'm sure you already are."

This time both men took a step toward each other, but suddenly, Erick pushed his way past Bo and stood between them, holding his hands up like a cop directing traffic.

"Stop it! Both of you. Mac, this isn't Bo's fault. It's mine."

"Yeah, right!" Mac scoffed. "You tied him up and forced him to have sex with you. Look at you. You're so small, it's amazing Bo doesn't lose you in the sheets. Don't tell me it's your fault he's turned queer."

Bo growled deep in his throat, but Erick ignored him and directed his words at Mac.

"You're right. Bo's attraction to me is not my fault, but his not telling you about it is. He wanted to but I... *encouraged* him not to. I told him it would be better if he waited."

"Waited for what?" Mac challenged.

Erick seemed to hesitate for a moment. "I was going to say 'for him to be surer of his feelings', but I think we can agree there's been more than enough lies and half-truths going on around here."

"You bet your ass there have. So what's the real story?"

"The real story is: I thought it would be better for Bo if he waited until it was over before deciding whether or not he wanted to tell anyone about having been with another guy."

As Bo appeared to have been struck dumb, he was almost grateful when Mac demanded, "What do you mean, wait until it was over? What were you planning on doing? Screwing him for a while, then dumping him when you got bored?"

"Of course not. But I knew that sooner or later this would end, and I didn't want Bo to risk losing any of his friends over something that was only going to be temporary."

Of all the words that had been hurled back and forth across the room this morning, those were the ones that wounded Bo the deepest. No one seemed to be paying any attention to him anymore.

"You don't know a thing about Bo's friends," Mac said contemptuously. "And temporary or not, he still should have told us the truth." Mac looked beyond Erick to Bo. "Have a nice life with your new boyfriend."

Mac turned to go and then, at the last second, he turned back.

"By the way...." Stepping closer, he slammed the bottle of scotch down on the coffee table so hard Bo was amazed neither it nor the bottle broke. "Happy fucking birthday."

When Mac left, he slammed the door behind him and there was utter silence in the room.

Then Bo asked, "Did you mean that?"

Erick turned to look at him, and his expression was one of bewilderment. "What?"

"Is that really why you didn't want me to tell anyone about us? Because you think this is all temporary?"

Erick shook his head. "Bo, don't you get what happened here? You just lost your best friend. Over me."

Oddly enough, Bo found he didn't care about that right now.

"Just answer the question. Is that why?"

Erick seemed to consider that for a long moment. Then he sighed. "Mostly? Yes. I didn't think... I didn't *expect* we would get as close as we have, and I didn't want you to risk alienating your friends over something that might or might not last."

Once again, Bo felt this temper rise. "Let me tell you something: if being with you is going to alienate my friends, then the way I see it, they aren't really my friends. But that's not the point, is it? The point is, this is not a temporary thing for me. This is real. It's always been real." When Erick didn't say anything, Bo got a very bad feeling in his gut. "Isn't it real for you?"

"Of course it is," Erick said earnestly, but somehow Bo wasn't reassured. And he found he was right when Erick added quietly, "It's just not forever."

Bo didn't know it was possible to ache this badly. "I don't understand."

"Don't you remember the night we met? When I said there must be a reason why we met when we did? Well, ever since then, all you've talked about is how you feel like you need to get your act together, to move on in your life. I think that's why I'm here. To help you do that, because that's what I do. I help people get their acts together. Or as together as anyone's act ever gets."

"But that doesn't mean I have my own act together. In fact, I'm about the least together person anyone's ever met. The last thing you need in your life is someone like me weighing you down, holding you back from reaching your dreams. That's not what I'm here for. I'm just here to help you figure out which fork in the road to choose before we say good-bye."

"I don't believe that," Bo said stubbornly. "I think we're together because we want to be."

Erick took a deep breath and then blew it out slowly, and Bo could tell he was forcing back tears. "For now, we do. But believe me when I say in the long run, you'll be better off without me. Especially in light of what just happened."

"Mac will come around," Bo said but the truth was, he wasn't quite as sure of that as he sounded. "It'll take time."

"Maybe so but, for the moment, I think it would probably be best if I left. That way you can go find Mac, make up with him, then go have your birthday breakfast with your friends."

"So that's it, then?" Bo asked, feeling sick. "This is good-bye?"

The tears Erick had tried to hold suddenly spilled over and Bo could tell it was an effort for him to speak calmly. "It can be. If that's what you want. I hope it isn't. I think there are still ways I can help you if you'll let me. But either way, your making up with Mac is more important than the two of us standing around arguing about how long our relationship will or should last."

Bo stood there, staring, as Erick picked up his shoes and things and walked to the door. He paused, then turned back.

"I know you're not really sure of where you're going right now, but I think we both know, wherever you end up, you're going to want Mac and the others with you. So why don't you go concentrate on them for a while? You know where to find me if you need me, okay?"

Bo didn't answer. He just let him leave.

CHAPTER
SIXTEEN

Bo KNEW it was good advice. Erick always gave good advice.

It was one of his more annoying qualities.

Rather than take it, however, Bo spent the rest of his birthday in the company of the bottle of scotch Mac had brought, drinking himself into forgetfulness.

It wasn't a perfect solution, but it was the best he could come up with.

Between bouts of blissful unconsciousness, he didn't bother to answer the phone, or call anyone, or do much of anything else.

He drank and brooded and felt sorry for himself.

Even the massive hangover he had on Friday morning didn't stop him from arriving at his father's office at nine o'clock sharp. Oh, he'd thought about not going in. He'd thought about it a lot. Why should he care if Mac and the rest of the guys would be out on their asses if he didn't show up? What with the way Mac had treated him, maybe he deserved to get fired.

But for some reason, he did care.

So he showed up.

Though it was probably the closest he'd ever come to actually being in hell, he spent the next few hours working with his father on the bid for the new project and straining to push away any thoughts of Erick. But though his headache eventually abated, by two that afternoon Bo had just about decided he would rather run his neck through a table saw than endure any more of this.

Then his cell phone rang.

Ignoring his father's grumbling against "newfangled technology," Bo snatched it up and checked the caller ID. He'd been hoping it was Erick. Or even Mac.

It wasn't either of them.

Struggling with disappointment, he answered it anyway. "Hey, Ham, what's up?"

"I just got a call from Andrea," Ham said, sounding frantic. "She went to the hospital this morning for some 'nonstress' test or something, and now they think there might be something wrong with her and the baby."

"Where are you?" Bo asked, already getting to his feet.

"I'm in the car on the way to the hospital. Can you come down and bring Pop with you?"

"Yeah, sure, we're on our way." Bo hung up and slid the phone in his pocket.

"Where do you think you're going?" his father asked. "We still got a ton of work to do here."

"The work can wait. Right now we need to get to the hospital."

"What for?"

"There's something wrong with Andrea and the baby."

Without another word, his father lumbered to his feet and they left.

It was a silent drive to the hospital, and it took a while to find a place to park and then to locate the maternity ward on the third floor. Once they got there, despite the Boss Man's blustering, no one would tell them anything except that Andrea was there and they would tell Ham and Andrea their family had arrived.

They were directed to the family waiting room and ordered to wait. So they went to the room and waited.

About fifteen minutes after they got there, Ham came in, looking a little wild. Both Bo and his father got to their feet.

"What the hell's going on?" the old man demanded.

"I've only got a minute," Ham said, the stress on his face clearly evident in his voice. "They're prepping Andi for surgery."

"Surgery?" both men echoed. Then his father said, "What the hell happened?"

"I don't understand it all exactly. They said she's got something called eclampsia, but I'm not sure I know what that means. All I know is the test they did this morning showed the baby wasn't moving very much and Andrea's blood pressure was up. They decided to try to induce her, get her labor started now. Whatever they gave her made her blood pressure go up even higher, and right after I got here, she had a seizure. They're going to take the baby by C-section. They said they can't let me go with her, but I can wait outside, so I gotta go."

"Well, then, go," Bo said, but Ham was already out the door and gone before he got the words out. He and his father looked at each other.

And waited some more.

As far as Bo could tell, time had never passed more slowly.

Every time somebody walked by, his head would jerk up of its own accord. More than anything he hoped to see Ham coming back, telling them everything was fine. But he didn't come for what seemed like forever. Another familiar face did come to the door, and Bo jumped to his feet and walked over to greet his oldest brother.

"What are you doing here?" he asked, exchanging a one-armed hug with him.

"Ham called me at work. How's Andi?" Charlie asked, looking about as stressed as Bo felt.

It was funny. Of the three of them, Charlie had always been the handsomest. The one all the girls were crazy for. With the long, thin face and the lean, lanky build of their mother's side of the family, he had always seemed to Bo like a slender birch tree surrounded by a bunch of solid stumps.

Dressed as he was now in his lawyer's suit and tie, he looked even more out of place than ever.

"She's in surgery," Bo told him.

"What happened? Last time I talked to her, she was fine."

"She's got something Ham called eclampsia?" To his amazement, Charlie nodded. "They're doing a C-section on her right now, but that's all we know."

"What the hell are you doing here?" his father demanded, and when Bo turned to look at him, he had that same look on his face he always had when Charlie was around—as if all the blood in his body was pooling in his cheeks.

Charlie didn't take the bait. "Andrea's my sister-in-law, Ham's my brother, and that baby is my niece," he said quietly. "So like it or not, I'm here and I'm staying."

Maybe it was the air of the place or maybe it was the seriousness of the situation they were in, but rather than respond audibly, Bo's old man just grumbled to himself and retook his seat.

They waited some more.

They waited for what felt like an eternity, but finally Ham came walking into the room. He was obviously shaken and his face was pale and shiny with sweat. The shirt he wore was soaked with sweat as well, but he was smiling.

Wanly. But still smiling.

"It looks like everything's going to be okay," he said, and Bo felt his heart rate finally begin to slow. "The baby's fine and Andi's blood pressure is already starting to come down. They're giving her something, some kind of medicine, to bring it down even more, and once she's out of recovery, they're going to put her in ICU for observation. But she's going to be okay. The baby too. They've got him in the NICU—the neonatal ICU—right now, to keep an eye on him, but they're pretty sure he's okay too. They're both okay."

"Hey, that's great news," Charlie said, but Bo honed in on one word.

"What do you mean '*he's* okay'?"

Ham laughed weakly. "Guess that ultrasound tech needs to go back to sex ed. The baby's not a girl, it's a boy. All eight pounds, twelve ounces of him."

Bo's father let out such a loud whoop, it made Bo jump.

"How do you like that?" he crowed. "I've got me a grandson and Sanford and Sons has got a new crown prince."

"He would care about that," Charlie said dryly, but it didn't seem to dent his father's enthusiasm. In fact, to Bo's surprise, his father walked over to Ham and hugged him tightly. "I'm glad everybody's okay," he said. Backing off, he whooped again. "Well... I think I'll go buy myself a box of cigars and start handing 'em out. Tell that wife of yours I'll see her later, when she's feeling better."

With his chest stuck out so far it was amazing he didn't fall over, Bo's father strutted out of the room.

Bo was still trying to adjust his mental processes. "It's great that everybody's okay, but what are you going to call him? Last I heard you were still trying to decide between Daphne and Stephanie."

Ham laughed again. "Obviously neither one of those is going to work. But since neither of us had a boy's name picked out, we decided to name him after Grandpa. Andrew James Sanford II. We're calling him AJ for short."

Suddenly the nervous energy that had propelled Ham thus far seemed to desert him, and he went across the room and collapsed onto the couch. He leaned forward and dropped his head into his hands. Bo went over as well and sat on the table in front of him.

Ham didn't look up, so Bo reached out and put a hand on his shoulder. "Hey? Are you okay?"

"Yeah," Ham said, but his voice was shaky and he still didn't look up.

Silently, Charlie sat next to Ham and put his hand on his other shoulder so the three men were linked for a moment.

"I swear to God, I've never been so scared in my life," Ham said, and Bo heard the tears in his brother's voice and felt his body shaking under his hand. "For a while there, I thought I was going to lose them both. It was awful. What was worse was what was going on inside my head. The whole time, all I could think was, what if I have to choose? What if they tell me I have to choose between saving one or the other? Which one do I pick?"

Bo found himself blinking back tears of his own so he was thankful when Charlie said calmly, "Nobody would have made you do that. Nobody could ever expect you to make a choice like that."

Ham nodded, but, again, he didn't look up, and they all sat there for another few moments. Charlie got to his feet, and when Bo turned, he saw Charlie's law partner, Robert Cohen, enter the room.

Though Bo had never had the thought before, it suddenly occurred to him that, in some indefinable way, Robert looked quite a bit like Erick. Not in appearance so much as having the same feminine qualities to his bearing and features.

He was startled when Charlie went up to Robert and hugged him.

"Everybody's fine," Charlie said, backing off but keeping his hands on the other man's upper arms. "I'm sorry I didn't call and let you know as soon we heard."

"It's all right. It doesn't matter. As long as everyone is safe, that's all that counts." Robert squeezed Charlie's arms in return. Then he looked over at Bo and Ham. "So… does this mean congratulations are in order?"

Now Ham did look up, and this time, his smile was a little more convincing. "I guess so. I'm a dad."

Ham stood up and Robert crossed the room to exchange a hug with him, but Bo continued to sit there a minute.

Something wasn't quite adding up here—or maybe it was, but Bo couldn't quite believe the answer he was getting. He saw Charlie and Robert turn to one another and smile, and he closed his eyes.

"Oh, for the love of God," he said wearily, then opened his eyes and looked at his brother and the man he now recognized as his brother's lover. "Why didn't anybody tell me?"

For the first time that day, Ham smiled for real. "Well, I see that light has finally dawned on Marblehead." Then he clapped his brother Charlie on the shoulder. "I'm afraid the cat's out of the bag now, boys. Good luck trying to explain the facts of life to that knucklehead. If it's all the same to you, I think I'll skip the question-and-answer period and go visit my wife and son instead. I think I've had enough family drama for one day."

After Ham left, Bo sat there for another minute, watching as Charlie and Robert crossed the room and sat down on the couch in front of him. They weren't touching in any way, but now that his eyes had been opened, Bo could see the connection… the love… between them.

When he looked into his brother's eyes, he recognized the wariness in them. "Why didn't you ever tell me you two were together?" he asked.

Charlie shrugged. "There never seemed to be a good time. It's not exactly something that comes up in casual conversation."

"I know but…." Bo was still having problems processing. "How long have you been…?"

"Gay?" Though he obviously tried, Charlie couldn't quite contain the smile. "Ahh… pretty much always."

Bo blew out a breath. "I meant, how long have you known you were gay?"

"Again. Pretty much always."

"But how can that be? You used to have girls crawling all over you."

"'All over *me*' being the key words. I was never the one doing the crawling, believe me. I've never been attracted to girls." He turned and smiled at Robert. "It's always been boys for me."

"Me too." Robert offered, smiling back. "Especially since I found you."

Bo felt his heart go soft but he still didn't have an answer to his question. "Why didn't you tell me?"

"Bo, you were only thirteen when I left home," Charlie pointed out. "Mom had just died. And somehow I didn't think adding the information that I was gay was going to help you cope with everything else that was going on at the time."

"You could have done it later."

"I know. But like I said, there never seemed like a good time. I almost told you when Robert and I became not just boyfriends but partners. When we made it 'official', I guess you could say. I wasn't sure how you'd react."

"Did you think I'd be like Pop?" Bo asked, hurt at the very idea. "That I'd stop talking to you or something?"

"Of course not."

"Then why tell Ham and not me?" Bo asked. Then he closed his eyes, shook his head, and answered his own question. "Andrea."

Charlie grinned. "Yeah. She figured it out in about two seconds. But even after she filled Ham in and I confirmed it, it took him a little while to accept it. And even more time to be comfortable with it.

Oddly enough, you're reacting much better than he did when he found out. Which is weird, because I thought for sure you wouldn't understand."

"You might be surprised by how much I understand," Bo said dryly, but before his brother could ask him any questions, Bo asked one of his own. "Is that why Pop and you don't talk? Because he knows you're gay?"

Charlie and Robert looked at each other significantly. Then Charlie turned back to Bo. "That's part of it."

"What's the other part?"

Again, Charlie and Robert looked at each other, but this time Bo got annoyed.

"Look, I'm not thirteen anymore. I don't need you to protect me."

"I'm not protecting you," Charlie said. "Or not only you."

"What does that mean?"

"It means there's a lot you don't know, okay? And lot of it is really ugly stuff."

"Like I said, I'm a big boy now. Whatever it is, I can handle it."

"I know that. But once you know something, you can't unknow it, even if you want to. So I don't want to tell you straight out without warning you that you might not like what you hear."

At one time, Bo might have been insulted, but he was a little wiser now.

"I can appreciate that, but as far as I'm concerned, there've been too many secrets in this family for too long. I'm tired of them. Whatever you have to say, just say it. I'll find a way to deal with it in my own way."

Charlie drew in a breath and let it out slowly.

And began.

CHAPTER
SEVENTEEN

"YOU were only twelve when Mom died," Charlie said.

"When she killed herself, you mean," Bo said bluntly, wanting to be done with evasions.

Charlie sighed. "Figured that out too, huh?"

"Yeah. A long time ago."

"Guess I shouldn't be surprised. You're not nearly as slow as you look."

"Thanks. I think."

Charlie smiled slightly. "That was supposed to be a compliment. Anyway, to get back to what I was saying…. You were only twelve when all that was going on, so I don't know how much of it you picked up on. But I was almost eighteen, and I don't know if it was because I was gay or what, I think I saw more than most eighteen-year-olds might have seen. And in the year before she died, I could tell Mom was having an affair."

"What? With who?" Bo asked, shocked despite himself.

"It doesn't matter." As Bo opened his mouth to protest, Charlie put up a single finger, holding him off. "It was a long time ago and he's gone now and it really doesn't matter who he was because he wasn't the problem. Or not really. The problem was, Mom loved him and she wanted to leave Dad to be with him."

"Why didn't she?"

"Because Dad threatened her. He told her if she left, he'd sue her for custody of us and make sure she never saw any of us ever again."

"And she believed him?" Bo was astonished. He couldn't imagine anyone being taken in by such an obvious ploy.

Then again, he supposed she must have been. Otherwise, things might have turned out differently.

"I don't know for sure what she believed or didn't believe, but you remember how it was between them. Pop was the head of the house and that was that. She was never very good at standing up to him. Even under the best of the circumstances. In fact, I would say she was probably a little afraid of him. I think we all were in one way or another."

Bo couldn't exactly argue with that.

"Anyway," Charlie continued, "things finally got to the point where Pop gave her an ultimatum: she could leave this guy and come back to him, or she could have this guy and never see her kids again. It was a horrible thing to do, making her choose. Not just between the two men, which would have been easy seeing as, by that time, Pop had made her life so miserable she couldn't bear the thought of being his wife anymore, but by making her choose between two loves—this guy or us. As much as she loved him, I don't think she could bear the idea of leaving us, of never seeing us again."

"You were almost an adult," Bo cried. "Hell, you left home pretty much right after she died. So how could Pop have stopped her from seeing you? And we'd have all been grown up sooner or later."

"You're arguing from logic and hindsight. And, for the most part, you're right. There were a million things she could have done. Number one being get a good lawyer. Hell, she didn't even need a good one. Any halfway decent one would have told her there was no way he was going to be able to keep her from her kids. But like I said, she was afraid of him and probably feeling guilty and depressed, and so rather than choose between what she saw as two impossible choices, she chose a third route and left all of us."

Bo was having a hard time believing what he was hearing. How could all of this have been going on around him and he hadn't noticed? "Did you ever confront Pop with any of this?"

Charlie laughed but it was a hollow sound. "Have you ever known me not to confront somebody? Especially when I think they're wrong?"

Now Bo laughed too, just as hollowly, remembering the fights they used to have.

"No. I guess not."

"Then the obvious answer to that questions is, yes, I did confront him. Pretty forcefully, I might add. In my self-righteous eighteen-year-old wisdom, I basically called him a murderer. I told him he'd killed her just as if he'd driven that car into the wall for her. I called him a few names too. Like tyrant and bully, and then he beat the crap out of me. Do you remember that paddle he used to have?"

Bo's backside almost winced at the memory. "Yeah. So…?"

"So… didn't you ever wonder what happened to it after I left? Why it suddenly disappeared? Well… it wasn't because I took it with me for old times' sake, believe me. It's because he broke it. On me. After my bruises healed, I left. And that's where we still stand today."

"Not completely," Robert said quietly and put his hand on Charlie's arm.

Charlie patted it gently. "No. Not completely."

"What do you mean?" Bo asked, unexpectedly touched by their interaction.

Charlie smiled. "It means that, that in my now almost-thirty-one-year-old wisdom, I realize none of it was quite as simple as I had made it out to be. Yeah, Pop's a bully and a tyrant and I'm happier than I can tell you to be out from under his thumb. But he didn't kill Mom. She killed herself. Either because she loved us and that other guy too much to choose between us or because she didn't love any of us enough to fight for us. Either way, it was her choice. Not Pop's."

Bo couldn't tell what he was feeling right now. Intellectually, he knew he must be feeling something. How could anyone hear all that and not feel anything? But mostly… he felt numb.

"Thanks for telling me," he said.

"I'm still not sure I should have," Charlie said, but Robert contradicted him.

"No. I think Bo's right. There've been too many secrets."

"Well… then," Bo said with a sigh, "in the spirit of full disclosure, I guess now would be a good time to tell you guys I'm sort of sleeping with a guy at the moment."

Charlie looked stunned. "Wow. That's… unexpected."

"I didn't expect it either, but there it is."

"How long has this been going on?"

"Three months, give or take. It's complicated."

Charlie rose to his feet and pulled his brother up by the arm and gave him a hug.

"Life is complicated. That's why people need lawyers."

"That's funny, I thought lawyers just made life more complicated," Bo teased but he returned the hug.

"That depends on which side of the fence you're on. So to speak," Charlie said and turned to Robert. "Now that we've got all that sorted out, what do you say we go down to the nursery and see if we can bullshit our way into getting in to see our new nephew?"

"Isn't that what lawyers do best?" Robert answered.

Charlie turned to Bo. "Are you coming?"

Bo wasn't sure he was up to visiting the baby right now, or Andrea, for that matter.

"No. I'll see everybody later, I guess."

He waited until his brother and Robert left and then stood there for a long few minutes. He didn't want to be here. He knew that much. But he didn't want to go home either. In fact, he had no idea where he wanted to be.

He only knew with whom.

THE drive over was short enough that Bo didn't have time to rethink his decision, but he almost changed his mind when, after asking, "Who is it?" Erick's green eye peered out at him from the crack in the chained door.

When Erick opened the door to him fully, Bo couldn't think of a single thing to say.

They stared at each other until Erick finally said, "I'm a little surprised to see you. I wasn't sure you were still speaking to me."

"I wasn't sure I was either."

"What are you doing here, then?"

Bo felt the back of his eyes start to sting with tears.

"I'm here because my old man is trying to blackmail me into staying at the company by threatening to fire my crew if I quit. And while I was busy trying to figure out whether it would be better to spend my life working for a son of a bitch who doesn't give a shit who he hurts as long as he gets his way or to let my friends down by putting them out of work, I almost lost my sister-in-law and my brand-new nephew.

"While I was still trying to recover from that I found out my oldest brother is gay and has a partner he never told me about. And that he left home and never came back because my mother was having an affair and my father tried to blackmail her into coming back by threatening to never let her see us again. And that she pretty much came to the same conclusion I was coming to: that she'd rather die than have to make what she considered an impossible choice—only she actually went through with it. And I'm really, really scared that's going to be me if I can't come up with a solution I can live with.

"And as confused and hurt and pissed and everything else that I am right now, the only thing I'm sure about is you're the only person in my life who won't tell me what to do or force me to choose up sides or try to make the decision for me or threaten to leave me if I don't do what you want. You'll just help me figure out what's best for me. Right now, as selfish as it sounds, that's what I need."

"As I said, that's why I'm here." Erick opened his arms. "Why don't you come in and we can talk things out, okay?"

Despite everything that had gone on between them—despite what stood between them even now—Bo found he could only be grateful for the promise of comfort as he walked into Erick's arms and shut the door behind them.

CHAPTER
EIGHTEEN

EARLY the next morning, Bo once again tried to tiptoe out of Erick's apartment. This time it wasn't because he wanted to avoid a confrontation. He was trying to be considerate. Erick had been up most of the night helping Bo sort through his feelings, and when they'd finally gone to bed, despite not having come to any conclusions, Bo had felt better.

He awoke early with at least one thing resolved in his mind, but rather than wake Erick, he left a quick note and let himself out.

There were certain moments in life in which timing is everything.

This was one of them.

Though he was determined in his course, he found he had to take a deep breath before knocking on Mac's mother's front door at eight o'clock on a Saturday morning. He knew *she'd* be awake. Mary Elizabeth MacGuire was always up early.

It was her son he needed to catch off guard.

"Well, look who's up with the sun today," Mary said, opening the door.

Though he hadn't thought of it in quite that way before, just lately Bo had begun to realize that from the time his own mother had died, this plump, homey-looking woman had been almost like a surrogate mother to him, full of wisdom and comfort and advice. Someone who scolded him when he needed it, rejoiced with him when he deserved it, and baked him homemade chocolate chip cookies for just about every other circumstance in between. During all that time, in her own quiet little way, she'd been the perfect soft shoulder to lean on.

And he loved her for it.

"Hey, Mrs. MacG," he said. "How are you doing?"

"I'm just fine. Come in. Come in," she said, shutting the door behind him. "How are you doing?"

"I'm okay, I guess." Feeling awkward now that the moment had come, he held out a bunch of flowers he'd picked up at the market for her. "Here."

"For me?" she asked, laying a capable hand on her ample chest.

"Yeah. I just wanted to say thanks for being there all these years." He handed her the flowers, then cleared his throat. "Is Mac up yet?"

"At eight on a Saturday morning?" she asked with a twinkle in her eye. "What do you think?"

"I think he's probably still in bed snoring like a hibernating bear."

"I think you're probably right. But somehow I get the feeling you're planning on changing that."

He was certain she knew he and Mac were at odds. Even if Mac hadn't told her, she would have known. She was just that way. It wasn't the first time they'd been this way, not by a long shot, so he thought she probably wasn't all that concerned.

Bo only wished he felt the same.

Still, he was determined he needed to do this. And do it now.

"Yeah. Pretty much."

"Good luck to you, then. Try to keep the damage to a minimum, will you? I just replaced the carpet in that room."

As she moved off toward the kitchen, Bo made his way down the hall to Mac's bedroom. Though the door was closed, he didn't bother to knock. He just opened it and found Mac right where he had expected him to be, sprawled on his back on the bottom bunk of the set of bunk beds he'd had as long as Bo had known him.

Erick probably would have told him it wasn't the best way to open a delicate discussion, but Bo went with his gut, and grabbing the handles on the mattress, jerked it up and dumped Mac on the floor.

"Get up. We need to talk."

"What the…? For Christ's sake, Ma! I'm sleeping here," Mac sputtered. Then he got a look at his attacker. "What the hell are you doing here?"

"Like I said, we need to talk."

"I'm not talking to you, remember?" Mac scowled as he sat up and ran his hands through his rumpled hair. "So shove off and don't let the door hit you in the ass on the way out."

"I'm not leaving. Not 'til we talk."

Mac looked up at him and narrowed his eyes. "Didn't you hear what I said? I'm not talking to you."

"Fine, then you can just listen. I'm sorry I didn't tell you about Erick from the beginning. I should have told you right from the start that he was a guy."

At that, Mac bounced up off the floor and glared at Bo. "Let's get something straight right here. I don't care if Erick is a guy or a girl or a prize-winning poodle. That's not the point. The point is, you fucking lied to me about the whole thing. About him. About your relationship. All of it."

"I know. I'm sorry."

There was a short pause; then Mac demanded, "That's it? You're sorry? What kind of lame-ass apology is that?"

"What do you want me to say?"

"An explanation would be nice. Like *why* you lied to me. And don't give me that bullshit about it being 'temporary'."

Bo's stomach roiled but he forced it back down. "It wasn't because it was 'temporary', at least not for me. It's that I didn't think of what I was doing as lying. I thought of it as keeping things private, but I can see now I was wrong."

"You bet your ass you were wrong."

"I know. And I'm sorry." When Mac didn't respond, Bo asked, "What more do you want me to say, Mac?"

"I don't know," Mac cried, sounding almost frustrated. "All I know is, I can't blow this off because you come over here and say I'm sorry. I deserve better than that. We've been friends for fifteen friggin' years, Bo. That's got to be worth more than an 'I'm sorry'."

"You're right. I owe you big-time for being such a jerk. So here." Bo pointed to his chin. "Take your best shot."

"What?"

"Hit me. Give me one good punch. Right here. We'll call it even."

The tightness around Bo's heart eased a bit when he saw the slightest twitch of a smile on Mac's lips. "You're friggin' crazy, you know that?"

"What's the matter? Too much of a wuss to take a shot at me?"

"Take a shot at you? I'd like to beat the crap out of you," Mac said, but he was definitely loosening up.

"Go ahead. I promise. I won't even hit back."

"Yeah, right, like I'm scared of that," Mac scoffed. "I'm more scared that Ma will kill me for getting blood on the carpet."

Bo grinned at that, but when Mac didn't return the smile, he went serious again. "I really am sorry I lied to you. To everyone, really. But especially you. I didn't do it intentionally. I guess I didn't want to get razzed to death."

"I wouldn't have razzed you," Mac said, equally seriously. "Not if I knew it was important enough."

"I know that. But the other guys would have."

"So…? I would have kept it quiet if you asked me to."

"Uh-huh. Like you kept it quiet that I used to have sex dreams about Geraldine LaRusso even though she weighed about 250 and had a face full of zits and had a headful of stringy hair?"

"That was back in eighth grade," Mac defended. "I've improved since then."

"Oh, really? Well, then, how about the time I finally talked Maria Sweeney into the back of my old pickup and my race car crossed the finish line before the starting gun went off? Or the time I had to go to the clinic downtown because I thought I had picked up some unwanted livestock from that girl over at the university? Or the time I got my dick stuck in—"

"All right. All right. I get the point." Mac rubbed his hands over his unshaven cheeks. "I don't have the greatest track record at keeping secrets. Or of not razzing people about stuff. Even important stuff."

"No, you don't," Bo admitted. "But if I had known how much my *not* telling you about Erick would hurt you, I would have told you and put up with the razzing."

"You did hurt me," Mac said quietly.

"I know I did. You have every right to be pissed at me." Bo had to swallow a lump in his throat. "But please don't stay pissed forever, Mac. I don't want to lose my best friend. Not like this."

Mac seemed to consider that for a minute. "I'm going to ask you a question and I want a straight answer. No dodging. No bullshit. No matter what the answer is, you tell me the truth because if you won't be honest with me about something as important as this, I swear to God, I don't want to be friends with you anymore."

Bo blew out a short, nervous breath. "Okay. What is it?"

"Did you not tell me because you thought I'd be a jerk about it? That I wouldn't want to be friends with you anymore because you were queer or something?"

"No! Not for a single minute. The thought never even entered my mind. I always knew you'd be my friend. Gay, straight, or... dating prize-winning poodles." Bo sat down on the edge of the bed. "Believe me, Mac, I wanted to tell you. I just didn't know how. Not in a way that would make sense, anyway. Come on, you know me almost as well as I know myself. Does any of this make sense to you?"

Mac gave a half laugh and sat down next to him. "Are you kidding? I couldn't understand how gone you were over him when I thought he was a girl. But a guy? Forget it. Even after seeing him come walking out of your bedroom, I'm still not sure I believe it."

"Yeah, well, half the time, neither do I," Bo admitted. "So how was I supposed to explain it to you when I couldn't even explain it to myself? I guess I was partly waiting until some of it made sense but... it still doesn't. I don't know if it ever will. All I know is, I've never felt this way before. About anyone. A girl or a guy. I'm so in love with him it's scary. And the sex...." Bo blew out a breath. "The sex is mind-blowing."

Mac winced. "All right. You don't have to draw me a diagram. I get the picture."

"Don't worry. That's one part of this I'm still planning on keeping to myself. But the rest of it... I really was planning on telling you. Eventually. I just didn't get around to it before you found out on your own. And I'm sorry for that too. Not for you finding out, but for the way you found out."

"Yeah, well. Part of that was my own fault," Mac admitted.

"How so?"

"Oh, come on, Bo. Like I wouldn't have known 'mystery girl' would be there the morning of your birthday."

"You knew?"

"Well, duh! The whole I reason I went over there to surprise you was because it seemed like the only way I was ever going to meet her. So I guess it's not your fault I didn't like what I found when I got there."

There had been a lot of that going on lately, Bo decided.

But now wasn't the time.

"Like I said, if I had known how much it was going to hurt you, I would have told you sooner." Bo put out his hand. "Still friends?"

Mac looked down at his hand, then smacked it away. "Screw that sideways!"

Then he pulled Bo into a bone-crushing hug. "Of course we're friends."

Bo hugged him back, feeling a sense of relief so intense he was a little dizzy.

He was thankful when Mac backed off, saying, "But since you did haul me out of bed at the crack of dawn, the least you could do is buy me breakfast."

Bo wasn't sure he wanted to hear the answer to this question but he forced himself to ask, "Speaking of breakfast, what did you tell the guys about why I didn't show up at the diner the other day?"

When Mac winced, Bo's worst fears were confirmed. "Great! Thanks."

"Yeah, I know," Mac said mournfully. "Me and my big fat mouth. Maybe you ought to be the one hitting me, huh?"

"Like your mom wouldn't kill *me* for getting blood on the carpet."

Wanting to get the worst over with, Bo stood up and crossed the room to lean against the dresser.

"How'd they take it?"

"To be perfectly honest, it was kind of a mixed bag." Mac scratched the back of his head. "Some of the guys didn't think it was any of their business who you're banging as long as it's not them. A couple of them were jerks about it, making noise about not wanting to work with a faggot and all that other kind of narrow-minded crap. Pretty much everybody agreed you should have told us the truth instead of letting us all think you had a girlfriend when you really had a boyfriend."

"They're right. I should have told the truth. About a lot of things. And I will. First thing Monday morning. For the moment, there are still some things I need to tell you."

"Ahh, shit!" Mac moaned. "You mean there's more?"

"Yeah, there's more." Bo opened one of the drawers, pulled out a T-shirt, and threw it in Mac's direction. "Why don't you get dressed and I'll tell you about it over breakfast?"

THOUGH he fought against it, Bo couldn't help feeling a pang of sadness when they ended up at the same diner where he and Erick had spent that first night talking. It felt like years had passed since that night, but the sights, the smells… even the waitress … were all the same. For the moment, he put it aside.

There were other things he had to deal with right now.

Knowing Mac's tendency to be grouchy when he was hungry, he waited until they were both almost finished with their hash and eggs before laying it all out for him. When he did, Mac didn't react quite as he'd expected. Bo had expected irritation. What he got was outrage.

"You mean he's going to fire the whole friggin' crew?"

"That's what he said," Bo answered. "And one thing you can say for the Boss Man—he may be a bastard but he's not a liar. He doesn't make empty threats either. If I don't stay on, I think he really will fire everybody, out of spite, if nothing else, even if it does put him behind on the rehab."

"What are you going to do?"

This, Bo knew, was going to be the hard part—where the hammer hit the nail head, as his Grandpa used to say.

"I'm going to quit anyway. As bad as I feel for the crew, I can't keep working for my old man anymore. I've had it. I'm done."

Mac pointed his fork at him. "You've said that before, you know."

"I know. But this time I mean it." Bo glanced away for a minute, gathering his thoughts. Then he looked his friend in the eye. "All my life, Mac, I've always taken the easy road. Kept the peace. Didn't make waves. Oh, I might have put up a fight now and then, but whenever things really got really tough, rather than hang in there and keep fighting, I would just give in. Hell, I've even quit quitting, like you said. I'm done with that now. I have a chance at doing something I really want to do with my life and I'm taking it." Bo took a deep breath. "I want you to come with me."

"Come with you where?"

"I want you to come to work for me. Flipping houses. To start with." When Mac didn't say anything, Bo rushed on. "I know I won't be able to pay you much at first. But after a while, after we sell the first house, I think I could probably pay you enough to get by. If things go right, eventually we could make some decent money."

"You really want me to work for you?"

"Well, yeah. We've been doing it all these years, right? I think we make a pretty good team. Besides, at least that way, I'll know I didn't put everybody I care about out of work."

"You're not the one putting them out of work, Bo, your Pop is," Mac said, surprising Bo. "Besides, even if you don't quit, as soon as the crew finds out Sparks is going to be coming on as foreman—even temporarily—some of the guys will probably quit anyway."

Bo shook his head. "What are you talking about?"

"Dude, half those guys only work there because you're there. They hate working for your old man. If you want the truth, I hate working for him, no offense."

"None taken. Do you mind if I ask why?"

"You mean besides the fact he's a cheap, grouchy, nitpicky son of a bitch who'll do anything to avoid paying overtime, even if it means cutting corners on a job?"

"Point taken."

Mac went on. "And everybody who worked this last project knows the only reason it turned out so good is because, unlike your Pop, you *refuse* to cut corners. Hell, you'd rather do the work yourself and not put in for it rather than accept sloppy work. The only reason it came in on time is because you do whatever you can to keep the Boss Man off our backs so we can get things done. You think Sparks is going to do that? Run interference for us? Hell, no. He'll be too busy throwing his weight around and kissing your old man's ass to care about helping us out."

While that may not be a visual Bo wanted stuck in his head, he appreciated the sentiment. "What are they going to do?"

"Ahh… get jobs somewhere else." Mac shook his head at the look on Bo's face. "Contrary to what your pop's been telling you all these years, there are other construction companies out there. Most of which are a lot better to work for than that cheap, penny-pinching outfit he runs."

"Like who?"

"Well, I heard Arnot's hiring. So is Shay's. There're probably others. Even in this economy, somebody's always hiring, and if you ask me, it's not going to be hard for any of the guys *you've* trained to get a job. Everybody knows your rep for demanding good work and getting it. Meanwhile, it's going to take your old man ages to put together a crew half as good as the one you've got because he'd rather hire kids who don't know anything than anyone with any experience, because they're the only ones who are too dumb to know they're overworked and underpaid. Trust me, anybody with half a brain is going to steer clear of Sanford and Sons unless he's desperate or new in town or just plain stupid."

Bo wasn't exactly sure how he felt about that. Despite his anger with his father, he found himself feeling bad about the mess he'd be leaving behind.

Resolving to put that on the back burner for consideration later, he decided to go back to their discussion about his new enterprise.

"So what about you? Are you desperate or new or stupid enough to come to work for me, knowing there's a good chance I'll fall flat on my face?"

"Actually, after I found all that stuff you put together, I started thinking about it and I've been kind of thinking about doing something a little different myself." Bo felt his heart sink; then he saw Mac's smile. "Like go into business *with* you instead of working *for* you."

For a minute Bo just stared at him. "You mean be partners?"

"Yeah."

"Where the hell are you going to get the money to do something like that?"

"I've got some money put away."

"Where? Stuffed in your sock drawer?"

"If it was up to me, probably. But unlike me, Ma believes in banks." Bo's confusion must have shown on his face because Mac grinned. "You don't think she'd have let me live at home rent-free all these years, do you? No way. She started charging me $600 a month the day I graduated high school. Only she didn't keep it all as rent. She kept $100 of it for food and stuff and made me put the rest in the bank. Not that I never managed to slip a couple bucks out here or there, but most of it's still there. And I figure I could use it to put up half the money we'd need to do the first place and see how it goes. If it works out with us being partners, great! If not, you give me my investment back, plus my share of the profit, and I go back to working for someone else on the weekdays and helping you out on the weekends. Which I was gonna end up doing anyway, even if I didn't end up working for you. Right?"

"Right."

"This way, I don't have to work for someone else. I can be my own boss. More or less. I mean, even if we start out fifty-fifty, it's not like you aren't going to end up being the senior partner. But that's okay with me. I'd rather leave all the details to someone else while I do what I do best."

"What's that? Drink beer and pick up girls?"

"Well, yeah, that. And use my charm and good looks to schmooze the real estate agents into giving us better purchase prices and then poor-mouth my way into getting the subcontractors to give us heavy discounts because I'm just a dumb schmuck trying to make a go out of this whole building stuff."

Somehow Bo could see him doing exactly that, and it made him smile.

"And you're sure you're ready to do this?"

"Are you kidding? I've been ready for ages. I've just been waiting for you to get up the guts to actually go for it."

Bo felt a shock through his system. "Well, then, why didn't you ever say so?"

"Because I know you, and if I'd have said that's what I wanted to do, it would have been just one more thing you felt like you had to do so you didn't let anyone down. That's your biggest problem, Bo. You've always been so afraid of letting anyone else down that you've been letting yourself down. But something's changed lately. I don't know what exactly… maybe it's Erick or turning the big two-five or something else altogether but either way, it's obvious you're finally ready to put yourself first and to hell with what everyone else wants you to do or be. And that's a good thing."

"I'm glad you think so."

"I know so." Mac stuck out his hand. "So what do you say? Partners?"

Bo wanted to accept. He did. But, still, he hesitated for a moment.

"I know Erick said he doesn't intend to be a permanent fixture in my life, but the truth is, I'm planning on doing everything I can to change that. So before we agree to do this, I need to know if that's going to be a problem for you. For us."

"Nah. Like I said, I don't care if you're with a girl or a guy or a pet poodle as long as it makes you happy." Then Mac grimaced a bit. "Just promise me I'm not going to be walking in on you guys making out or anything, because while I'm okay with it in theory—the reality of it is still a little freaky."

"For you and me both," Bo admitted. "You don't have to worry. I kind of like keeping that part of my life to myself. I mean, it was fun for a while—bragging to the guys about how many girls you could bag in a weekend—but it's different with Erick. Special. Private. I like it that way. Still, you might want to avoid using the spare key from now on, just in case."

Mac smiled. "I guess I can live with that."

Bo smiled as well, then stuck out his hand.

"Well, then, yeah… partners."

CHAPTER
NINETEEN

BECAUSE he didn't want to wait a minute longer to start his new career, Bo spent that afternoon and early evening at Charlie and Robert's house, hammering out a partnership agreement with Mac.

Mac insisted they didn't need one, but Bo wanted to make things official.

He wasn't risking their friendship because they'd been too naïve or too cheap to put things in writing.

Unfortunately, by the time they were done, Erick was already at work so Bo couldn't sneak in a visit, or even a phone call. So filling him in would have to wait.

But when he got up the next morning, the first thing he did was check his messages. There was one from Erick from late last night, saying he was sorry they'd missed one another. Then another from very early this morning telling him he had just picked up an extra shift and wouldn't be available until after lunch.

Bo tried calling him back but his phone just went to voice mail, telling him Erick was still at work.

He left a message of his own to the effect that he would talk to him later and then headed over to the hospital to see Andrea and admire his new nephew. Both mother and baby had been moved to the regular maternity floor and were scheduled to go home the next day.

Though he didn't confide in her—or the new daddy when he arrived—about his plans for the future, Bo did promise to stop by later in the week, once they had settled in.

But that still didn't save him from having to hold the baby.

When the obviously deranged new mother simply picked the poor kid up and plopped him into Bo's big, clumsy hands, Bo found he could scarcely take a deep breath. He'd never held a baby before and he was terrified he might break the little guy. But in the way of all small creatures, by the time Bo handed AJ back to his mother, the kid had wormed his way into his heart so deeply Bo would never get him out again.

As he headed back to the parking garage, he was already imagining the swing set he and Mac would build for AJ in the backyard at Ham's house. In the meantime, he vowed to open a college savings account for him right after he sold his first house.

This newest little Sanford son would have a choice if it was the last thing Bo did.

As soon he got in the truck, he took out his phone, then realized he didn't have any service. Crap! Erick might have been trying to call him all this time and he wouldn't have known it.

Sure enough, as he left the parking lot, his phone beeped, telling him he had a message. At the first red light he hit, he took out his phone and dialed his voice mail.

"Hey, Bo, it's me, Erick," the voice said. "I'm sorry I seem to have missed you again. Unfortunately, I'm heading to the library now to work on my research study so I'll have to turn my phone off for a while. I'll try calling you as soon as I'm done, okay? I miss you."

Just hearing his voice made Bo smile and, even though he knew Erick wouldn't get the message until later, he sent him a text saying, "I ms u 2."

Feeling at loose ends, Bo decided to run a few errands—including spending some time with a real estate agent gathering more information about several houses in the area he and Mac were considering for their first flip. He was still meeting with her when he felt his phone vibrate in his pocket. He knew it was probably Erick and a part of him was tempted to take the phone out, but he forced himself to wait. If he was going to be a professional, he was going to have to learn to act like one… right?

As soon as he was out on the street, he pulled it out and listened to Erick's voice teasing him.

"This is getting pathetic. I feel like we're playing telephone tag here. Anyway, I guess this means you're 'it'. So call me."

Immediately, Bo did and was frustrated when it went directly to voice mail.

"Now who's 'it'?" he teased back. "Call me when you get this and I promise I'll pick up, no matter where I am or what I'm doing, okay?"

Putting the phone away, he told himself to be patient, and with paperwork from the Realtor in hand, he drove to Mac's house.

The two of them spent a couple of hours discussing the pros and cons of each house on the list, and by the time they were done, it was well past dinnertime. Bo still hadn't heard back from Erick, and when he tried to call, not only didn't Erick answer, but it didn't go to voice mail, either. It just rang and rang.

And rang.

He knew it was ridiculous to worry. Obviously, Erick had either turned his phone off again or the battery had run out. Probably from all those messages they had exchanged. But rather than go home, he decided to swing by Erick's apartment.

Just in case.

To his relief, when he turned onto Erick's street, he saw the lights were on in his apartment, and he began to smile even as he jogged up the stairs.

When he got to the door, he knocked and said, "Hey, Erick. It's me. Bo."

As usual, Erick peeked out through the crack, but this time, rather than undo the chain and open the door, he said, "Hey. I'm sorry I didn't answer your last message."

"It's okay," Bo said, a little confused when Erick continued to stand there. "Can I come in?"

"I don't think that would be a good idea right now."

Bo shook his head. "Why not?"

"Because I'm busy, that's why."

Funny… he didn't sound busy. He sounded perfectly relaxed. He was even smiling, but there was something in his eyes that reminded Bo of an animal in a cage. A kind of restrained terror.

"Is there something wrong?" he asked.

"Of course not," Erick said, still sounding perfectly calm. "There's just something I need to… deal with right now. I'll see you later, okay?"

"Okay." Bo couldn't help feeling a little put out by his cool dismissal. "I'm sorry I bothered you."

Again, something flickered in Erick's eyes, something like desperation, and then it was gone.

"It's not a problem," he said, but then he hesitated for a second.

"What?" Bo asked.

Erick had scarcely opened his mouth to respond before he winced as though in pain, which concerned Bo even more. Then his face went blank again and his voice was cool and even. "Nothing. Everything's fine. Good-bye."

With that, he closed the door in Bo's face.

For a few more seconds, Bo stood there, puzzled. Then he turned and made his way back to his truck. But even as he put the key in the ignition, he couldn't seem to shake his uneasiness. There had been something odd about the way Erick had reacted to his visit. He'd been so cold, so… aloof. Almost distracted.

Even if he had been busy, it wasn't like Erick to be that unwelcoming.

He scolded himself. What did he expect? That Erick would be delighted to see him each and every time he happened to show up on his doorstep? How stupid was that? Not to mention egocentric. It was only natural Erick would have his own things to do, his own life to live. Everybody did. So why not Erick?

In fact, what with all of the problems Bo had been having, he had been taking up a lot of Erick's time lately. He was bound to be behind in his work. So rather than being upset about not getting to see him now, Bo should be grateful Erick had made as much time for him as he had. And he was. He was grateful.

Grateful enough to leave the guy in peace to do whatever it was he had to do.

Then again, there was this nagging feeling inside him that something wasn't quite right. And sometimes you just had to go with your gut!

Bo got out of the truck and went back upstairs. This time, when he knocked, Erick didn't answer at all, which concerned him even more. Then he heard a muffled crash—like the sound of a dish breaking—coming from inside, and he didn't bother to knock a third time.

He lifted his foot and kicked the door in.

He might have been sorry about the mess it made, but at the moment, it scarcely mattered. The whole apartment looked like a horde of marauding pirates had pillaged the place. Broken glassware and plates littered the kitchen floor, books had been thrown everywhere, the bedclothes had been torn off the bed and lay in a crumpled heap on the floor. It looked like a war zone.

"What the hell...?"

Bo only got half the question out before he saw Erick go flying backward, tumbling over the edge of the couch before hitting the floor and rolling to a stop almost at Bo's feet. His T-shirt was torn at the neck, as if someone had tried to rip it off him, and there was a red mark on his cheek that was already beginning to turn purple in the center.

Standing in the middle of the whole mess was a man almost as big as Bo. But unlike Bo, this guy was obviously drunk and was glaring at Erick with something akin to hatred, his fists clenched and a savage look on his face.

"I don't ever want you to talk to that guy again, do you hear me?" the man said, ignoring Bo as if he were nothing more significant than a fly that had happened to buzz in the window. "Never again."

"I'll talk to whomever I want to, Scott," Erick spat back, but the words didn't have the assurance Bo was used to hearing in Erick's voice. They trembled and shook even as his hand did when he lifted his wrist and wiped at the rivulet of blood just beginning to ooze down the side of his mouth. "And if you don't like it, you know exactly where you can go. Right straight to hell!"

Bo wasn't exactly sure what was going on, much less what he should do about it, but when he saw the man advance toward Erick, he didn't stop to think. He reacted. With a roar, he charged the guy, hitting him midbody and taking him down like a defensive tackle sacking a quarterback, and the momentum of their two big bodies colliding sent both men flying across the room, where they crashed into one of the homemade book shelves, knocking it askew before landing in a tangled mass of arms and legs on the floor.

There wasn't a whole lot of room to maneuver in the small space, but the man tried to put up a fight. He even managed to get in a few punches, but they barely registered in Bo's consciousness. He was too intent on doing some damage of his own. Bo took one good hit to the shoulder and another to the chin as the two rolled across the floor until Bo's back slammed solidly into the box spring of the bed.

He had just enough time to turn his hip in order to deflect the knee the guy had aimed at his balls. The cowardly move only increased Bo's anger as the two rolled again, with Bo delivering a solid uppercut to the guy's chin with his elbow before they both knocked into Erick's desk chair, sending it skidding across the room.

This time, Bo ended up on top. And though he thought he heard Erick's voice calling his name, he was too busy pummeling the guy beneath him to pay much attention, and though the guy did manage to get in a few more halfhearted licks, in the end, he was no match for Bo's muscle.

Or his rage.

Even Bo was helpless against the fury of it as it poured through his blood and roared in his ears. In fact, the sound of it was so loud, at first he didn't hear Erick calling to him.

"Stop it, Bo! Stop it! You're going to kill him."

"You're goddamn right I'm going to kill him!"

"No, I mean it. You're really going to kill him. You have to stop."

This time something of Erick's panic got through and Bo was distracted enough to realize he'd wrapped his fingers around the man's neck so tightly his face had been rapidly changing from a choleric red to a sickly shade of purple.

With enormous effort of will, Bo managed to loosen his grip and let Erick tug his hands away. He waited for a moment, body tensed, ready for reprisal, but rather than reengage, the man simply rolled to his side, coughing weakly.

"It's okay now," Erick said to Bo, helping him to his feet. "It's okay."

"The hell it is. That guy hit you," he said as if Erick wouldn't already have known that, but Erick didn't seem to mind.

"I know, but it's all right now. He's leaving."

From what Bo could see, the guy wasn't in much shape to go anywhere, which, frankly, was right where he wanted him to be.

"What the hell is going on here?" he asked. "Who is this asshole?"

"I'll explain later." Oddly enough, now that the crisis was under control, Erick sounded perfectly calm again. "But first we've got to get him out of here."

"Screw that!" Bo told him. "We're calling the cops."

"No, we're not."

"Yeah, we are."

While the two men were arguing, the other man tried to get up. Bo made a move toward him, intent on putting him back down. Permanently. But again Erick held him back.

"No. Let him go. He's not worth it. You hear that, Scott?" he said, his voice sounding firmer now. "You're not worth another second of my time. If you don't get out of here right now, I'll let Bo finish what he started and you'll be out of my life for good. Take this as your one 'get out of jail free' card and leave me the hell alone."

The man nodded weakly, and with one hand still held to his throat, got up as best he could and all but stumbled his way out the door. Bo had to force himself to stand there until the sound of the man's footsteps faded. Then he whirled on Erick.

"What'd you let him go for?"

"I told you. He's not worth getting yourself charged with assault over."

"Fuck that, it was self-defense."

"It was defense of *me*," Erick corrected. "And while *I* appreciate it, Scott could use it to make trouble for you. Claim 'excessive force' or say you attacked him out of jealousy or something. Believe me, he's capable of it. Especially if he knows it would hurt me. This way, I can call the cops tomorrow and put them on notice that he broke the restraining order and hopefully keep you out of it."

Bo didn't care if he was in it or not; he had other things on his mind right now.

"Broke the restraining order? What restraining order? Who the hell was that guy anyway?"

"That guy—" Erick blew out a very shaky breath. "—was my very charming ex-boyfriend, Scott."

"Judas fucking Priest," Bo breathed. He'd known Erick had been in a bad relationship but this? This was something else entirely. "Is that why you didn't want to call the cops?" he demanded. "Because you still care about that asshole?"

"I hate that asshole with everything I have in me." Though the words were harsh, there was no heat in Erick's voice. Instead, he sounded eerily calm. "But if I call the cops, they're going to want me to go to the hospital, and frankly I can't afford any more medical treatment. I'm still trying to pay off my debt from the last time this happened."

Bo would have offered to pay for it—to pay for anything—but there was a deeper issue at stake. "You mean stuff like this has happened before?"

"Of course it's happened before, you idiot. Why do you think I needed the restraining order?" Before Bo could take offense at his tone, Erick drew in a breath, blew it out slowly and went on more calmly. "I'm sorry. Obviously, I'm still a little upset. The truth is, getting the restraining order wasn't all that difficult, under the circumstances. But since I had failed to report any of his previous... we'll call them 'indiscretions'... I knew I'd need hard evidence. So, like it or not, the last time this happened, I had to let the cops take me to the hospital. Thus the medical bills. After paying the fees to the court and moving into this place and buying a stronger lock for the door, at this point, I can barely afford the gas to get to work every day. Not to mention, if the landlord found out the cops had been here, I'd probably get evicted, which is something else I can't afford right now."

Bo had a few thoughts on that subject, as well, but now wasn't the time.

"Why would he evict you for that?"

"Because he can't risk having the building inspector find out about this place. It's not a real apartment, remember?" Erick blew out another breath. "And anyway, it doesn't matter anymore. The important thing is, he's gone. With the scare you just gave him, I doubt he'll ever bother me again. So, for what it's worth, thanks."

Then, to Bo's absolute amazement, Erick closed his eyes and began pacing back and forth across the room, his thumb and index finger pressed to his forehead.

"ZYXWVUTSRQPONMLKJIHGFEDCBA," he muttered under his breath. "ZYXWVUTSRQPONMLKJIHGFEDCBA... ZYX...."

"What the hell are you doing?" Bo asked, mystified.

"I'm reciting the alphabet backwards," Erick replied, still pacing.

No shit! Bo could hear that for himself. "What the hell for?"

"Because I need to think, and in order to do that, I need to calm down. This is how I calm down. So do you mind giving me a minute here?"

"Calm down?" Bo threw up his hands in sheer frustration. "How the hell can you calm down? You're so friggin' calm right now, it's creepy. Frankly, you're scaring the hell out of me."

When Erick stopped and turned to look at him, Bo got a good look at his eyes.

The emotions in them—the pain, the anger, and the fear—were anything but calm, but somehow, the wildness he saw there made Bo's own jangled emotions begin to settle. Right now, Erick didn't need his anger. He needed his help.

"All right. For now, we'll just let things ride. In the meantime, what can I do?"

Strangely enough, the gentle tone in his voice did something that nothing else had seemed to do thus far. It brought tears to Erick's eyes.

"You could start by getting me some ice."

When the tears spilled over, Bo had just managed to get his arms around Erick before he broke down completely.

CHAPTER
TWENTY

IT DIDN'T take long for Erick to cry himself out, but when he did, he was limp with exhaustion. Bo decided it was just as well. Had Erick been more himself, Bo would never have been able to talk him into leaving. As it was, he'd had to promise to pack up Erick's laptop which was, thankfully, undamaged, as well as the few other things that remained unbroken, before Erick would agree to go.

He also had to rig up some way of blocking off the doorway. Not that it mattered much. To his mind, most of Erick's stuff had been junk anyway, and now, it was broken junk. What mattered more was getting Erick away from there. Not that Erick agreed, as he insisted it would be a cold day in hell before Scott gathered up the courage to come back, but Bo wasn't taking any chances.

In his experience, cowards were often more dangerous than bullies, and the last thing he wanted was another confrontation, especially if, this time, Scott chose to bring reinforcements. They did make one stop along the way, however, to pick up a bag of ice, but Bo didn't really breathe a sigh of relief until they were in his apartment, spare key in hand and the door locked firmly behind them.

When he got to the living room, he found Erick standing there, swaying slightly as if every ounce of energy had been drained out of him, and it tore Bo's heart to see how listless he was.

"Why don't you go lie down?" he said, giving Erick a gentle push toward the bedroom. "I'll be in in a minute."

Erick nodded and slowly began to move off.

Damning Scott to the depths of everlasting hell, Bo went to the kitchen and filled a baggie with ice and put the rest in the freezer. Then he went to the bedroom and found Erick lying on his right side on the bed. Gently, he laid the bag of ice against Erick's bruised cheek, wincing himself when Erick hissed in a breath.

"Sorry," he said, feeling helpless.

"It's okay."

Bo's first thought was to leave Erick alone for a bit, but when he began to move off, Erick reached back and grabbed for his hand.

"Don't go. Please?" Bo stepped back and took his hand. Erick gave it a little tug. "Would you lie down with me for a little while?"

"I don't want to hurt you," Bo protested.

"Please?"

Though terrified of causing Erick pain, Bo did as asked, moving as slowly and carefully as he could, trying not to touch any part of Erick that might be bruised, until he lay behind him, one arm above his head, the other arm lying down by his own side.

Of his own accord, Erick scooted back until he was cuddled in the shelter of Bo's big body and closed his eyes with a sigh.

Bo wasn't sure how long they lay there. They could have dozed off for a while for all he knew, and then Erick's quiet voice spoke out of the darkness.

"I'm sorry I didn't tell you about Scott."

"It's okay."

"No, it's not. I should have warned you about him from the very beginning."

The bag of ice had long since melted and been set aside. Even so, Bo was careful as he lifted his hand and very gently ran his fingers down the side of Erick's cheek, along the hairline and around his ear.

"To be honest, I'm glad you didn't," he admitted. "There's no way I would have understood something like this. Not back then, anyway."

"And now you do?"

Ignoring the disbelief in Erick's voice, he again ran his fingers along Erick's hairline, avoiding the area that was swollen and blue.

"Not completely. But I know if you'd told me before how bad things had been between you two, I would have run full speed in the other direction. Not because of what he did but because I would have assumed you were weak or wimpy for letting him get away with it."

"I am. Or at least I was."

"Oh, really now," Bo drawled. "Is that what you're planning on telling your patients someday? That the reason someone abused them is because they're weak or wimpy?" When Erick didn't answer, Bo lightly kissed the back of his head. "I didn't think so."

Erick sighed. "I know you're right. I shouldn't blame myself for what happened, but I can't help feeling I should have seen what he was from the very beginning."

"So... what? Now you're supposed to be a mind reader? Able to predict the future?"

"No, but I should be able to see something as obvious as this when it's staring me straight in the face. I am educated about this kind of thing. Or at least I should be. I could probably sit down right now and write you out a fifty-page thesis on the subject of 'Domestic Violence and the Abuse Cycle', and yet I still managed to get myself caught up in it. I mean... how stupid is that?"

"You're not stupid," Bo snapped, irritated by Erick self-denigration. "You just care about people, that's all. I'll bet when you first met Scott, he didn't seem abusive. Or crazy. He probably seemed like a normal guy who had a few issues, including a little bit of a problem controlling his temper. Am I right?"

"Yeah." Erick sounded a little surprised. "How did you know that?"

"Because, number one, I knew a guy like him once. He worked on my crew for a little while a couple years back. Not such a bad guy, all in all. A little hotheaded, maybe, but basically normal. Or so we thought. Until one day he got arrested and we found out that every night, after working all day with us, he'd stop off for a few drinks at a local bar, then go home and beat his wife and kids. It's not something I understand, but I know it happens. Even more important, I know you. You try to help everyone you meet. You can't seem to help yourself. You're a complete sucker for people who need a little help straightening out their lives. Just look at me."

"You're nothing like Scott."

"That's not true," Bo corrected. It was something that had struck him from the second he'd laid eyes on Scott. "I'm a lot like him. Same height. Same general build. Hell, we even have the same haircut. Now that I think about it, he looks more like me than my own brothers do. Which is why I'm amazed you're not the one who ran in the opposite direction the first time you saw me."

"Actually, I'm kind of amazed too," Erick admitted. "I did see the resemblance and it was a little… disturbing. At first. But there was just something about you. A… gentleness I guess you could call it… that told me that you would never do to anyone what Scott did to me."

"I'm not so sure about that, either. I mean, obviously I would never treat you that way."

"Why not? Because you don't hit girls?" Erick asked sarcastically. "As comfortable as it may be for you to think of me that way, I'm not a girl, Bo. I'm a guy. Just like you."

"I know you're a guy," Bo said, forcing back another wave of irritation. "But in my book, you shouldn't pick on people who are smaller than you. Girls or guys. You certainly don't go around abusing the people you love. Which—whether you're comfortable with it or not—is who you are to me. But while I might not do it on a regular basis, I have hit people before. Hell, Mac and I punch each other regularly. Or at least we used to. So, to go back to my original point, what makes me different from Scott?"

"Like you said, you don't abuse people you claim to love. Hitting Mac is different. In a strange way, I think it's how you two show each other affection. And while the two of you might exchange a punch once in a while, I don't think either one of you would ever really try to hurt the other. Not like this, anyway."

Erick touched his cheek, and Bo had to acknowledge he was right. Neither he nor Mac would ever hit the other hard enough to do so much damage.

But still....

"Maybe I wouldn't hurt Mac that way, but you saw what I almost did to Scott. If you hadn't been there to stop me, I think I might really have killed him. I wanted to."

"If I wasn't there, he wouldn't have hit me and you wouldn't have gotten mad enough to kill him," Erick countered. "Which just goes to show that you like to help people too—people who might be good at advocating for others but aren't all that good at standing up for themselves. Like me."

They were both quiet for a moment before Erick said, "I guess I don't understand why I didn't leave the first time this happened."

Bo didn't understand it either. He couldn't imagine staying with someone who hurt you, but that didn't really matter right now.

"The important thing is, you did leave him."

"Yeah, I did. Do you know what it took for me to finally get up the guts to do it?"

Bo closed his eyes against the emotion welling up inside him. He was pretty sure he did know. He'd been thinking about it for days. Though he thought he had come to terms with what he was sure had happened, that didn't mean it was going to be easy for him to hear it confirmed.

"I think maybe I do. I think you tried to tell me that night in my truck when you said you weren't ready to make love with me." Bo felt a shudder run through Erick's body and his heart gave a painful squeeze. "It's okay if you don't want to talk about it. I think I get the general idea."

"I don't want to talk about it," Erick said. "I don't want to think about it. But I think it would be better if we got the truth out in the open, if that's okay with you?"

As much as he would have liked to avoid it, Bo knew Erick was probably right and so he drew in a breath and then let it out slowly. "Okay. Go ahead."

As if he needed something to hold on to, Erick reached back and took Bo's hand, pulling it around himself as he began. "You were right when you said I knew Scott had issues when I met him. Which I suppose isn't surprising since I met him at an Alcoholics Anonymous meeting."

"You went to AA?" Bo asked, surprised.

"Not as a participant. I was observing for a class I was taking."

"They let you do that?"

"At some types of meetings they do. They have what they call open meetings, where pretty much anyone is welcome as long as they announce themselves as nonparticipants and no one objects to their being there. But Scott was there as a participant. He'd been sober for three months and seemed to be doing okay with it. Or so he said. After the meeting was over, he came up to me and asked if I had any questions I wanted to ask. I didn't, really, but I thought he was cute and I was pretty sure he was gay, so I lied and said I did and he suggested we go out for coffee and talk. So we did. We talked for hours that night."

"Oh, great. Yet another thing we have in common," Bo teased, but the truth was he wasn't sure how he felt about the similarity to his own experience with Erick.

Obviously, Erick sensed the direction of his thoughts, because he said, "It might sound the same but it wasn't, not at all. You and I?

We talked about each other. We shared our lives. But Scott? He didn't want to talk about himself. At all! He was completely, totally, and utterly fixated on me, like he was drinking in every word I said, desperate to know every little detail of my life."

Erick gave a little laugh.

"I know that sounds really creepy—and, in hindsight, I can see it was, but at the time, I was flattered. I'd just been through a series of what basically amounted to one-night stands and my ego had taken a real beating. Now here was this person who actually seemed to care about me, who wanted to know everything about me. It was pretty heady stuff. And even though it wasn't something I did on a regular basis, I ended up having sex with him that night. I know that's probably not easy for you to hear, and I'm sorry."

No, it wasn't easy to hear. But it wasn't altogether unexpected, either.

"It's okay," Bo said, feeling a little awkward. "It's not like I never did the same thing. Or not exactly the same because they were girls, but... what I meant was, it's not like either one of us were virgins when we met. Or I guess in a way we were... or we still are... just not the same way. I mean, it's the same thing, only different. Or not completely different but...."

By this time, Bo could only be thankful for the darkness that hid his wild blush, but he felt better when Erick chuckled.

"It's okay, Bo. I know what you're trying to say. And you're right. The fact that we both have a past is a reality. Since I don't like dwelling on you being in bed with anyone but me—even if they were girls—I'll spare you the details of my being with Scott except to say not only was he really lousy in bed, but by letting things move as fast as they did that night, I made a huge mistake."

"How so?"

"Because it made everything else move too fast too. He was like this force of nature that slammed into my life and swept me away. Literally. One minute we were strangers and two weeks later I was moving out of my dorm room and into his apartment. It was crazy. I knew in my head it wasn't healthy, somehow the two of us got so completely wrapped up in each other we basically ignored everyone and everything around us. Nothing mattered but the two of us being together, and the longer it went on, the worse it got. My friends tried to warn me about how possessive Scott was getting, but I guess I thought of it as the honeymoon period and eventually things would level off.

"Then he started to get more demanding. He stopped wanting me to see any of my friends, at all. He said all we needed was each other. He started questioning me about where I'd been and what I'd been doing whenever we weren't together. Which, of course, should have been a major red flag, but somehow I didn't see it as him trying to control me. I thought he was insecure and that, after a while, when he saw he could trust me, that would get better too. But it didn't. It got worse. I had become his drug of choice, and he needed more and more of me just to stay level."

Erick was silent for a long moment; then, suddenly he turned over and wrapped his arms around Bo, resting his sore cheek against Bo's shoulder. Bo wasn't sure why, exactly—maybe he needed something to hold on to—but he responded to the need he felt in Erick and put his arms around him as well, holding him close.

"The first time he hit me was when I was late getting home from school one night." Erick's voice was husky with tears. "I'd run into a friend on campus and got talking, and I guess I lost track of time. Not to mention I forgot to turn my cell phone back on. When I finally did get home, Scott was furious—and drunk. I couldn't believe it. He'd been doing so well with his recovery and now this? All because I was late? I tried explaining it had all been perfectly innocent, but he was stomping around, screaming and yelling, and I knew I wasn't getting through to him. I kept trying and he kept yelling, and at some point, he spun around to say something and the back of his hand connected with my cheek. I was shocked. Nothing like that had ever happened to me before. And for a minute, I didn't know what to do. How to react. And do you know what he did next?"

"What?"

"He cried. Just broke down and sobbed like a baby. He said it had been an accident. That he hadn't meant to hurt me—I just got in his way. And when I asked about the alcohol, he said he'd been so worried about what might have happened to me that he couldn't resist taking a drink and, somehow, I think I really came to believe it was entirely my fault. That somehow I had made him do it. But he swore it would never happen again. He promised he'd stop drinking. He'd go back to the AA meetings he'd been slacking off of. And he'd never, ever hit me again."

"And you believed him?" Bo asked, almost wincing at the disbelief in his own tone.

Erick didn't seem to take offense. "Yeah, I believed him and I kept on believing him. Every time it happened, every time he said it would never happen again, I believed him. I even forgave him. Still the same thing would happen. He'd go on the wagon for a while and things would be okay. Then something would go wrong and he'd fall off again. Not in a major way—just a drink or two here and there—nothing serious. But sooner or later, something would set him off and he'd get really drunk and then he'd hit me. Then would come the tears and the remorse and the promises and the makeup sex that always left me feeling used and empty. He'd get back on the wagon again and the whole cycle would start again. It was like a nightmare I could never wake up from."

By now Bo could feel Erick shaking and the wetness from his tears had soaked into Bo's shirt, and everything in him longed to comfort him. He was still afraid to hold him too tightly, so he ran a gentle hand over his hair instead.

That seemed to help a little and, slowly, Erick stopped shaking. It was still several minutes before he could continue.

"The final straw happened one night after we'd been to a party to celebrate a friend's engagement. He'd started drinking again the week before, and I knew something was going to happen. It was just a matter of time. By then, I swear I was almost used to it, like I expected it, even longed for it in a way, because at least then the horrible anticipation would be over. When we got home, it started like always, with him accusing me of having flirted with some guy at the party.

"The weird thing is this time, he was right. I had been flirting with the guy, just a little. Not because I was interested, necessarily, but because by then my ego was so far down the toilet it felt good to see the attraction in someone else's eyes. I don't know if it was that added boost to my self-esteem or if I'd finally had enough but this time, when he hit me, I hit him back. It was the first time I'd ever done that. The first time I'd ever hit anyone, actually. The look on his face—the shock and the fear—made me feel powerful. For the first time since he'd first hit me, I felt strong. Like I could hold my own with him. So I told him I was tired of this and I was leaving.

"And I did. I didn't even take any of my stuff. I just said good-bye and walked out the door. I didn't even know where I was going. I was determined to get away from him for good."

"What happened?"

"I got about a third of the way down the stairs before he caught up with me, but instead of grabbing me back, like I expected him to, he shoved me and I tumbled down the rest of the stairs. When I finally hit the bottom, for a minute, I was too stunned to even feel any pain." Erick drew in a shaky breath and blew it out. "Then suddenly he was on top of me, hitting me in the face. It was the first time he had done that since the first time he'd hit me. Most of the time he'd hit me places it wouldn't show. This time he was too far gone to care, and while I was still seeing stars, he raped me. Right there on the landing."

This time, when Erick burrowed closer, like a wounded animal cowering in its den, Bo didn't think about Erick's bruises. He wrapped himself around him and held him tight.

"After it was over, he went back upstairs like nothing had ever happened," Erick continued in a dull monotone. "And I lay there for a long time. I knew I had a choice to make. I could go back upstairs and let him keep doing this to me or I could get out. It was the hardest decision I've ever had to make."

"Why?" Bo asked. "Why was it so hard?"

"Because when you've been beaten down that far, you start to feel like you don't deserve any better. Or that by letting the other person get away with it for so long, you've essentially given him permission to do it. And refusing to keep letting him do it feels like going back on your word. I know it sounds strange but... that's how it feels."

Bo wasn't sure he would ever fully understand that, but frankly, that wasn't the point. "What made you get up?"

"In a way, I guess it's like you said earlier. I thought, what would I tell one of my patients to do in this situation? Would I tell him he deserved to be beaten and raped just because he'd flirted a little bit at a party? Or would I tell him to get up off the floor, get himself out of this sick, twisted relationship, and get on with his life?"

"So you got up, got out, and got on with your life."

"Well, two out of three, anyway," Erick said, and now that the worst seemed over, he sounded calmer. "I got up. I called the cops. They were the ones who got me out and called the ambulance to take me to the hospital. The X-rays showed I had two cracked ribs and a hairline fracture in my collarbone, all of which probably resulted from the fall. And even though it was the most humiliating thing I've ever had to do, I let them do a rape kit on me. Scott hadn't used a condom, so there was plenty of evidence, but it was still a hard thing to do."

Bo couldn't even imagine it, nor did he want to. "If you did all that, then why the hell is this guy still walking around free?"

"Because while the exam confirmed we'd had sex, when the cops questioned him, Scott claimed it had been consensual. He freely admitted to hitting me, but he claimed I'd thrown the first punch and then fallen down the stairs all by myself. I think the cops probably knew what really happened, but what could they do? There were no witnesses. I hadn't even told my friends the things that had been going on, never mind reported him to the police. It was my word against his.

"But whatever they believed or didn't believe, my injuries alone were severe enough to warrant a temporary restraining order, and the cops kept him away from me while I packed up my stuff. I didn't have much since—as you saw earlier—Scott has a habit of breaking things when he's pissed. I took what I could salvage and left. I lived in my car for about a week until I found the place I live in now."

"Is tonight the first time he's come around?" When Erick hesitated, Bo felt his stomach begin to churn. "Don't tell me he's been there before?"

"Well… yes and no."

"What the hell does that mean?" Bo demanded.

"It means yes, I've seen him hanging around a couple of times—either on campus or at the coffee shop—but no, he's never gotten close enough to violate the terms of the restraining order. So there was nothing much I could do about it. I do have a record of it… somewhere… but like I said, he didn't get close enough to actually break the law, so I couldn't do anything."

"You could have told me," Bo said, feeling resentful in spite of himself.

"I know. I was afraid if I did, you'd go after him."

"You're right. I would have."

"I know. And after seeing you in action tonight, I guess I didn't need to worry so much that he'd hurt you. At the time, I was worried. And I guess in a strange way, I was embarrassed. Like you said, I didn't want you to think I was weak."

Bo didn't have to like it but could, and did, understand it.

"Okay. I guess I can't blame you for feeling that way. But what about tonight? How did he get in? Did you let him in?"

"Are you kidding? Even I'm not that stupid. He was there when I got home. To tell you the truth, I'm not really sure how he got in, but I was up on the terrace earlier, and even though I'm usually good about locking the place up when I leave, things have been so good lately—with you and me—I guess I could have gotten careless. Either way, when I got home, he was there."

Bo had to force himself to ask the question he'd been dreading. "Do you think my coming by made things worse?"

Erick shook his head. "No. Scott always thinks I'm seeing someone else, whether I am or not."

"Why didn't you let me in when I knocked? I could have helped you."

"Maybe. Or maybe you'd have gotten hurt. I couldn't be sure which it would be and I didn't want to risk it being the second. Besides, Scott didn't give me much of a chance to say anything at all."

"How so?"

"When I answered the door that first time, he was standing right next to me, holding on to my arm. He wanted to be sure I didn't say anything that would let on that anyone was in there with me."

"Is that why you winced when we were talking? Because he was hurting you?"

"You saw that?" Erick asked, surprised, and Bo nodded. "Wow! You see more than I give you credit for. Yeah, he was squeezing my arm." Erick sat up a bit and when he lifted his arm, there was a very definite purple handprint there. "It's one of his tactics for keeping me in line—painful, but easy to hide."

Bo leaned in and kissed the blue marks there. "I'm sorry. Sorry if my being there made things worse. I know he was pissed about you talking to me."

"If it hadn't been you, it would have been something else. He was drunk and irrational, and whether you showed up or not, something was going to happen. I can tell you this: I'm glad you came back. I'm not sure why you did but, I'm glad."

"So am I. Although to tell you the truth, I'm not altogether sure why I did, either. Something just didn't feel right. Now that I think about it, it scares me to death to think of what he might have done to you if I hadn't followed my gut."

"The important thing is… you did," Erick said. "And now it's over."

"What makes you so sure?"

"Because if there's one thing I've learned about Scott, it's that deep down, he's a coward. That's why he bullies people who are smaller than he is. You gave him a taste of his own medicine tonight, and I don't think he's going to stop running until he hits Canada."

Bo wasn't completely convinced of that, but for the moment, it didn't really matter. "I just want to keep you safe, that's all."

"You did. And you always will. No matter what happens between us."

"How so?"

"Because you care about me," Erick said, and the wonder in his voice made Bo feel sad somehow. "Despite everything you know about me, you still care. And if someone as wonderful as you can feel that way about me, then there must be something inside me that makes me worth caring about. Worth being treated like someone special. So no matter what happens with us, I can promise you I'll never settle for being treated as anything less than that ever again. Maybe that's what you're here to teach me: to respect myself enough to demand being respected. Or maybe it was simply to put the fear of Bo into Scott. Either way… thanks."

Despite knowing Erick's mouth was bruised, when Erick looked up at him with love in his eyes, Bo couldn't fight the urge to kiss him. Trying to be careful, he barely brushed Erick's lips and was gratified when, rather than pull away, Erick returned the gentle caress.

They kissed that way for long moments, exchanging light kisses that tantalized even as they soothed, and Erick threw one of his legs over Bo's, wrapping it around him, pulling him closer, so they were twined together like vines.

Despite the circumstances, Bo could feel himself getting aroused.

"Look… I know this is probably the completely wrong thing to say right now," he said between kisses. "And I know it's not gonna happen. Especially tonight, but for some reason, I feel like I have to say I'd give anything to make love to you right now. I want to show you how good it can be when two people care about each other." Bo blew out a breath. "Which, when you think about it, is really stupid, because I don't have the first clue how to actually go about doing that with you, never mind doing it as gently and tenderly as I want to, but… somehow I just thought you should know."

Once again, Erick had tears in his eyes. "Actually, that was probably the most perfect thing you could have said to me."

"It was?" Bo asked in disbelief.

"Yeah. Sometimes rape survivors feel like damaged goods. Like they're dirty or used up. They wonder: What if someone finds out what happened? Is anyone ever going to want me again? Knowing what I've been through?"

"I want you," Bo said huskily, kissing Erick again. "I'm always going to want you."

"I want you too. But I think I'm a little too sore to do much about it right now."

"I know. Like I said, I just wanted you to know."

Because he needed a little distance to help him cool off, Bo gave Erick a careful hug then let him go and sat up.

"Now, on a more practical note…," he said. "I think we should probably get changed and try to get some sleep."

"You're probably right," Erick said, sitting up as well. "Seeing as we both have to be at work tomorrow morning."

There was no way Bo was letting Erick out the door tomorrow morning, but he didn't see the point in arguing over it now. Instead, they went about the business of getting ready for bed, including Bo checking that the door was, indeed, still locked.

A first for him.

Finally, they both ended up in Bo's bed, snuggled up like two spoons in a drawer.

Erick must have been exhausted because his response to Bo's whispered "Good night" was slow and slurred, and Bo felt his heart turn over when Erick's hand suddenly went limp in his.

"I love you," he whispered and brushed his lips along Erick's bruised cheekbone.

And let himself follow.

CHAPTER
TWENTY-ONE

DESPITE Bo's best efforts at persuasion—and a near heated argument—Erick still insisted on going to work the next day. It wouldn't be the first time he'd gone in with bruises, he said, but since it would be the last, he could go with a smile on his face.

Besides, he couldn't afford to miss any more work.

Bo didn't like it but even he had to acknowledge it was just as well. He, too, had things he had to do. So he gave in to the inevitable and agreed to meet up at Erick's place at the end of the day to assess the damage and see what could be salvaged.

In the meantime, rather than go directly to his father's downtown office, Bo stopped by the Second Street work site to talk to the crew. It took a little longer than he thought it would and it was close to ten thirty by the time he made it into the office.

"Where the hell have you been?" his old man barked as he walked in the door. "You were supposed to be here hours ago. We've got work to do."

"The work's going to have to wait. We need to talk."

His old man leaned back in his chair, making it squeal, and Bo suddenly realized just how much he hated that sound.

"If this is about that crazy-ass notion of you quitting the company, you can forget about it," his pop said. "You're staying right here where you belong."

"No. I'm not."

From the rear pocket of his jeans, Bo pulled out a white, legal-sized envelope and tossed it on the desk in front of his father.

"That's my official letter of resignation. It says I'm leaving as of June 17. That is, if you want me to stay on for the two-week notice I promised you. Otherwise, you can fire me now and I'll leave today. It's your choice."

While his father's mouth was still hanging open, Bo pulled two lists out of his other pocket. He held one up in his hand. "This? This is a list of all of my crew members who are also giving their two-week notice as of today."

Now the old man narrowed his eyes sharply. "What the fuck did you do?"

"I did something that doesn't get done very often around here. I told the truth," Bo said with no small sense of satisfaction. "I went out to the job site this morning before your temporary foreman—who was forty-five minutes late for his first day on the job, by the way— showed up, and I told my crew I told you I wanted to quit and you threatened to fire them all if I did. I told them that while I feel bad about that, I wasn't going to let it change my mind. I've had it with this place. And you. I've had it with you trying to control my life. So I'm moving on. These are the guys who said if I go, they're going too."

Bo held up the other list for a second, then set it down on the desk in front of his father. "This, on the other hand, is a list of all the guys on my crew who agree with you. They think I'm an ungrateful, unappreciative, snot-nosed punk who doesn't know a good thing when he's got one, and if I go through with this crazy-ass notion of mine, I'm going to end up crawling back here on my hands and knees begging you to take me back, and when I do, they're all going to get together and have a party to celebrate you kicking my ass back out the door.

"They also said they like working for you and they want to keep doing it. I didn't promise you would keep them on, but I did promise to do what I could to convince you to because each and every one of them is a good worker, and as evidenced by what they said this morning, they think you're right and I'm an idiot. Personal differences aside, I think we can both agree that kind of loyalty should be rewarded. But it's your choice what to do about them. I've done all I can."

His father barely glanced at the list on his desk.

"What about all those other idiots? Those so-called 'friends' of yours," he asked. "How do you think they're going to feel when their bills start coming due and there's no money to pay them? How many of them do you think will be loyal to you then?"

"They won't have to be loyal to me because they won't be working for me. They'll be working for someone else. Because, again, I told them the truth. I told them while I couldn't afford to hire them, I could and would do whatever I could to help them find other jobs. In fact, I've already called Arnot's and Shay's and put in a good word for a couple of them, and they got hired straight away. I don't think it'll be long before the rest of them get hired too. The ones that don't? Well, I can only do what I can. The rest is up to them."

There was a long moment of silence during which Bo could all but hear the beating of his own heart.

"You really think you've got me over a barrel, don't you, boy?"

There was an odd sort of tone in his father's voice, a hint of grudging respect that at any other time might have made Bo smile.

They were past that now.

"No, I don't. I think you overplayed your hand. If you had been willing to listen to me, to talk about what I wanted instead of always focusing on what you wanted, we probably could have worked something out. I could have stayed on here and still done what I really wanted to do—use my hands. Build things. But you wouldn't listen. You never listen. And I'm tired of trying to make myself heard."

"So that's it, then?" his father demanded. "After everything this company—this family—has done for you, you don't give a shit about what happens to it as long as you're happy?"

"No. I still care about the company, and if it ever runs into trouble, I'll be happy to lend a hand. It's my family I really care about, which means I'll do anything I need to do to keep them. So if Ham and Andrea ever want or need my help—with AJ or the company or anything else for that matter—I'll be there for them. No questions asked. That goes for Charlie and Robert too. I'd even be willing to give you a hand now and then, if you need it, but I guess I've finally come to accept that after everything I've done for the company and the family, you don't give a shit about whether or not I'm happy. That's no way to run a business. Or a family, for that matter. I think Grandpa would agree with me."

"You don't know anything about what Grandpa would or wouldn't do. As far as I'm concerned, you can kiss my ass. Now get out of my office. You're fired. You can tell all those ingrates on that little list of yours they're fired too. You're all fired. As of right this minute."

"And the others?" Bo couldn't resist asking.

"That's not your problem anymore," was as far as he would go, and Bo had to content himself with that.

Bo nodded and crossed to the door, but then he turned back.

"Oh... and since this is probably the last time you're ever planning on talking to me again, I have something else I want to say. I want you to know I never blamed you for Mom dying the way she did. Or her, for that matter. I never blamed either one of you. Ever. I have come to the realization that, on some level, I did blame myself. I thought I had done something to upset her or make her mad and that's why she had that accident.

"So I guess that's part of why it's taken me so long to do this. Because as stupid as it sounds, I was afraid if I made you mad enough, something might happen to you too. I'm older now and I know that sometimes you have to do what you have to do and let the chips fall where they may. All of which is to say, while I don't like the idea of being at odds with you, I have to do what I think is right for me. To live my life my way. And part of that is telling you the truth, even if I know you're not going to like it. So even though I can't think of a worse time to tell you this, you might as well know… I'm bisexual and I have a boyfriend. I don't ever expect you to be happy about that, I do hope someday you can at least accept it. There isn't anything I can do about that either. I guess I'll just have to find a way to deal with whatever happens next."

"The only thing that's going to happen next," his father growled, "is that I'm going to call the cops and have you hauled out of here if you don't get the hell out of my office."

Because he'd known it could happen, and because he had made his choice regardless of the consequences, Bo didn't argue.

He just left.

LATER that afternoon, Bo was standing on a ladder in the middle of the apartment when Erick walked through the brand-new door Bo had just finished installing. It was a proper entry door this time, with a high-end lockset and a sturdy dead bolt. The place was still littered with debris from the night before, but in the center of the room was a tarp covered in sawdust and bits of roofing material, and above Bo's head was a giant hole in the ceiling through which clear blue sky could be seen.

"What hell are you doing?" Erick asked.

"I'm putting in a skylight."

Erick looked up at him in shock, and Bo couldn't help but smile.

"Don't worry, I already cleared it with the landlord. He promised that, despite the noise complaints he got last night, he won't evict you—if I agreed to repair the damage to the door, which, as you can see, I already did. And if I installed this window for free. Unfortunately, I couldn't talk him into actually paying for the window, but he did agree to drop your rent by fifty dollars a month for three months. So we called it even."

He nodded toward a cardboard box that sat on what was left of the shelf next to the refrigerator. "I also brought you some boxes and a couple of heavy-duty trash bags so we can start cleaning this place up, but try to stay out from under the ladder until I get this thing secured, will you? It'll be bad for business if anyone finds out I dropped a window on some guy's head while installing it in an illegal apartment with a nonexistent building permit. Besides, I don't have time to take you to the hospital right now. I want to get all of this over and done with. Today!"

"I see." It was said quietly, and without another word, Erick moved off toward the kitchen to start the cleanup.

Bo went back to work.

CHAPTER
TWENTY-TWO

THE two men worked in silence until well past dinnertime, but by the time Bo finished sealing the window, Erick seemed to have disappeared. The place was certainly brighter with the skylight in, and now that all the broken bits and pieces of Erick's former life had been picked up, it was at least livable again.

But there really wasn't much left, and Bo found himself feeling mildly depressed.

He was certain Erick felt the same way, so he was pretty sure he knew where to find him. He went out the window and climbed up onto the roof, where he found Erick just where he'd expected to find him, sitting on the "terrace." It was late enough the sun was starting to go down behind them, and after Bo sat down, the two just looked out at the slowly darkening horizon in silence.

Once the sun had gone down completely, Erick said, "You were right about the skylight. It does brighten the place up." The words might have been cheerful but his voice was flat and lifeless. "Thanks for putting it in for me, and for the new door."

Uncomfortable with Erick's gratitude, Bo sat forward and pulled up his legs, wrapping his arms around his knees. "It was no problem. Besides, I was the one who broke the door in the first place, so it was the least I could do."

They were silent for a few more minutes before Bo offered, "I quit my job today." Finally, there were signs of life from Erick as he sat up, and when Bo turned his head, he found himself looking into a pair of very surprised eyes.

"You did?"

"Yeah. Well… technically, I got fired, but since I gave my two-week notice knowing it would get me fired, I suppose it amounts to the same thing."

"Wow! How'd your father take it? Aside from firing you, that is?"

"Better than I thought he would, actually. He did threaten to call the cops and have me hauled out of his office, but at least he didn't take off his belt and start to beat me with it, which was his usual MO when I was a kid."

"You never told me he did that," Erick said, sounding almost sad.

"Yeah, well, it's not something I like to think about, so… I guess I don't talk about it much. You know how that is… right?"

Erick bumped him with his shoulder. "Yeah, I know how that is."

"All things considered, I came out on top of the whole deal, so I guess I can't complain." Bo waited a beat. "I also met with a real estate agent and put in an offer on a duplex down on Oak Street. The inside's a mess, but the structure's sound and the foundation's good. If all goes well and the owners accept the offer, once the paperwork goes through, Mac and I are going to start fixing it up."

"I see," Erick said. "I take it that means you and Mac have made up."

It wasn't really a question, but Bo answered it anyway.

"Yeah, on Saturday. We hammered out a few things, so to speak, and ended up agreeing to go into business together. We had Charlie draw up the paperwork for the partnership and he's got a friend who does real estate who can help us with all the rest—

purchase and sales agreements, title runs, the whole works." Bo shifted a bit, trying to get more comfortable. "We figure once the repairs are done, we can turn the building into a condo and sell it off as two separate units. It should be worth about twice what we put into it if everything goes well."

"Wow!" Erick said again. "You've been busy."

"Yeah, I guess I have. I would have told you sooner but...."

"Certain extenuating circumstances got in the way."

Bo couldn't help but smile at the understatement. "Yeah, I guess they did."

"It's okay. As long as you're happy with the way everything turned out, it doesn't matter that you didn't tell me."

"I am happy, for the first time in a long time."

The two men were silent for another long stretch, long enough that the first stars were starting to come out when Erick again broke the silence.

"You know, Bo, if you're here to say good-bye, it's okay. You can just say it."

"Why would you think I'm here to say good-bye?"

Bo had a few ideas of his own on that subject but he was curious how Erick would answer.

"I don't know. I just figured now that you've quit your job and bought this new house, you're going to be starting a whole new life. I thought you might want to start with a clean slate, that's all."

"I do want to start with a clean slate," Bo admitted. "Which is why I do have some things I need to say to you."

"All right. Go ahead."

Though Erick leaned back so he was reclining against the roof again, Bo stayed where he was, looking out over the city.

"Do you remember the morning of my birthday? How you told Mac you didn't encourage me to tell anyone about us because you never expected what we had to last?"

"Yeah."

"Well, you need to know when you said that, it hurt me. A lot."

"I know it did. I'm sorry."

"I know you are. Just like I know you didn't mean to hurt me as much as you did. In fact, it's not even your fault it hurt as much as it did. Part of it was my fault too."

"How so?"

"Because after I thought about it for a while, I realized the reason it hurt so much was because I had it all backwards."

Erick sat forward again, and when Bo turned to look at him, he could see the confusion on his face. "I don't understand what you mean."

"When you said you thought it was only going to be temporary, I thought you meant you wanted it to be temporary, that you didn't want me to be a permanent part of your life. Now that I've thought about it for a while, I realized that's not what you meant at all. You meant you thought I was only going to want *you* on a temporary basis. You thought that after you'd helped me figure out my life, I wouldn't need you anymore. Or I would decide being with a guy wasn't really what I wanted for my life, and I'd say that good-bye I promised you and it would be over. I think on some level, you've been waiting for that ever since the first time we kissed. I didn't understand it before, now—I think I know why."

"Oh, you do, huh?" Erick said doubtfully.

"Yeah, I do."

"Okay. So what's your theory, doc?"

"I think you expected to be temporary to me because that's all you've ever been to anyone else in your life. Temporary."

When Erick turned his head away, Bo reached out and gently took Erick's chin in his hand, guiding him back so they were eye to eye.

"You've never been permanent to anyone, have you? You've always been just temporary. A temporary burden to your mother, until she finished paying for her 'mistake'. A temporary nuisance to your stepfather until you were old enough to leave home. A temporary entertainment to Steven. A temporary experiment to those guys on campus. In your whole life, nobody's ever wanted you permanently."

"Scott did," Erick said bitterly. "He pretty much wanted to own me, body, mind, and soul."

"I know he did. That is, until he managed to kill you. Or had beaten you so far down you wouldn't have been a challenge to him anymore. In which case, he would most likely have dumped you and found someone else whose life he could make miserable. Either way, I think deep down you always knew that relationship was doomed from the first time he hit you. So when you got involved with me, I think you naturally expected it wouldn't last either. You thought I would only want you until whatever it was you were here to help me with was finished and it would be over. Unfortunately, there was something you didn't know about me when you agreed to take our friendship to a higher level."

The tears in Erick's eyes made his voice hoarse. "And what's that?"

"It's that, when it comes to stuff like this, I don't do temporary. I do—or at least I have done—one-night stands or short-term flings. And I admit, I've done them better than I should have because they were easy. That's what I wanted... easy.

"But nothing about you and me has ever been easy. When I agreed to take our friendship up a level, I went into it intending to put everything I had into making it last, to making it permanent. Because when I set out to build something, I build it to last. That's just the way I am. But you didn't know that. So I guess I can't hold it against you that you thought I wouldn't want you permanently."

Erick reached up and gently pushed Bo's arm away so they were no longer touching. "It's not so much that I didn't think you'd *want* me permanently as much as it is that I know, on a permanent basis, I'm no good for you."

Bo had to force back a surge of irritation. "That's funny. I thought you were the one who was always telling me *I'm* the one who should decide what is and isn't good for me."

"I am."

"So… what? Now suddenly I'm too stupid to know what's good for me?"

"Of course not," Erick said wearily. "It's just… you're not seeing the whole picture. You're only looking at the here and now. You're not looking toward the future."

"You're wrong. For the first time in my life, I am looking toward the future. It's never looked better or brighter."

"Exactly! That's why you need to say good-bye to me. Now. Before I get a chance to mess that up."

"How are you going to do that?"

"Just by being me. I mean, I know when we first met, you thought I was someone who had his act together, but by now, even you must know my life is a fucked-up mess."

"You're wrong. I don't know that."

"Oh, come on, Bo. Open your eyes," Erick cried. "I'm such a mess it's amazing I can still put one foot in front of the other."

"How?" Bo demanded. "How exactly are you a mess?"

"Well, for one thing, I'm so deep in debt right now, I'm not sure if I'm ever going to be able to dig my way out. Especially seeing as I now have to replace pretty much everything I used to own. What makes it worse is, I'm not even done yet. I still have another semester's worth of classes I have to pay for before I can even start doing my internship. After that, there'll still be the clinical hours I'll have to put in and licensing exams I'll have to take before I can actually start practicing. It will be even longer than that before I start earning any real money."

"So… money will be tight for a while," Bo said. "So what?"

"It's not just that. It's the way I am. You said it yourself. I'm a sucker for people who need my help. I'm always on the lookout for someone I can rescue. And just about every one of my professors has told me the same thing: I get way too involved with my patients' problems. I'm working on it but… I know myself too well to think I'll ever be completely able to do it. So when I do start practicing, I can guarantee I'm not going to be able to leave my problems at the office when I go home at night.

"None of that can even begin to compare to the aircraft carrier's worth of emotional baggage I'm carrying around. Between what Scott did to me and my screwed-up family, face it, I'm a walking advertisement for the necessity of my own profession. Do you honestly want to be permanently hooked up with someone like that?"

"Oh, I don't know," Bo said airily. "It's not like I'm any kind of prize at the moment either."

"What are you talking about?"

"Well, as of today, I have no job, no income, and a father who will probably never speak to me again. I've just signed a partnership agreement with a guy who thinks 'overhead' is when you let the girl be on top. I'm about to sink every dime I have plus a couple hundred thousand more I don't have into buying a complete dump, a dump I'm actually going to be living in while I fix it up. Only to turn around and sell it so I can immediately go out and use the profit to buy another dump which I will also probably be living in.

"And while I may have a little less emotional baggage than you do, I still have my share. Including a mother who quit on me as much as she did on herself, and some good people who I used to consider friends who will probably never speak to me again seeing as my best friend—who can't keep a secret to save his soul—went out and told them all that I've been… how did he put it? Doing the naked pretzel with a guy. Which," he said sternly when Erick opened his mouth, "is not your fault because you didn't make me this way. You might have brought it to the surface but it was always there. It had to have been, because people don't change like that because of other people. Besides, I was attracted to you even before I spoke to you. So you can't even say we ended up together because you put me under your 'gay spell'.

"The way I see it, we ended up together because I love you and I admire you and because you turn me on so much that ever since I met you, I spend half my time with my hands in my pockets trying to disguise a semipermanent woody."

For a minute Erick looked like he might continue to argue, then it seemed his sense of humor got the best of him. "Oh, you do, huh? And are you sure it's not because I put you under my 'gay spell'?"

"Actually, I think it was your excellent taste in beer that really got to me, but that's beside the point."

"Then what is the point?" Erick asked, suddenly serious again.

"The point is, for the next little while at least, my life is going to be just as much a mess as yours. So maybe you're the one who should be saying good-bye."

"Is that what you want?"

"No. I want to be with you. I want to build something that lasts with you. Or at least give it a damn good try. But if for some reason you can't or won't work with me on that... like maybe I was wrong and you really *don't* want me to be a permanent part of your life..." Bo had to swallow, hard, before he could finish. "... then I think we probably should say good-bye. Now. Before either one of us gets any deeper into this."

There was a short pause before Erick said, "I do want you to be a permanent part of my life."

Feeling a flood of relief, Bo let out the breath he'd been unconsciously holding.

But then Erick went on, saying, "I just don't know if I'm capable of building anything permanent. As you said, I never have before."

"Are you kidding?" Bo asked. "You're an expert at 'permanent', you just don't think of it as 'building'. You think of it as 'sticking'."

"I don't know what you mean."

"Just look at what you've managed to accomplish in your life with no help from anyone."

"What? Accruing a massive pile of debt and conducting a dysfunctional relationship with an abusive drunk?"

"How about earning a bachelor's degree and most of a master's degree all on your own? Or taking care of yourself when no one else would? Or finding the courage to get involved with me after being raped by that bastard? Face it, Erick. No matter what comes your way, you never quit. You just hang in there and keep going."

"That's not called 'sticking', that's called 'pigheaded stubbornness'," Erick said, but underneath the words there was a note of teasing, and Bo felt the tightness in his gut ease.

"Well, whatever it's called, it's worked for you so far. Why not stick with it? So to speak." When Erick didn't answer, Bo said, "I'm not asking you to promise me 'forever'. Even I know it's way too soon for that. Just don't quit on me. On us. Not yet, anyway. Let's keep going and see where we end up."

"Oh... I think we both know where we're going to end up," Erick said dryly, and for the first time, Bo felt hopeful. But before that hope grew too big, Erick said, "Before we get there, I think I'd like to clarify a couple of things. The first one being... what exactly are you asking me for?"

Because he'd been ruminating on it for a while, Bo didn't have to think about the answer he would give. "Well, the way I see it, you have a couple of choices here. Number one, we could keep going on the way we have been. Seeing each other when we can, enjoying spending time together, seeing where it goes. Or...."

"Or what?"

Bo took a secret deep breath. "Or we could make a little bit of a firmer commitment to each other and you could move out of *this* dump and move into *my* dump. With me."

When Erick didn't say anything, Bo rushed on. "I know it's kind of sudden, but like you said, things happen for a reason. And even though I'm not sure I fully agree with that whole master-plan thing of yours, in this case, even *I* think the timing is too good to be a coincidence. Why go out and buy anything new when I already have everything we need? Including a few things we don't need and won't be able to take with us anyway. Like my king-sized bed and my leather sofa." Bo gave a huge sigh. "And my big-screen TV."

"You're selling your TV?" Erick sounded shocked.

"I have to. The sucker's too big to fit on any of the walls in the new place. And I doubt I'm going to have a whole lot of time to sit around watching it, anyway." He sighed again. "Besides, I think the transmission on my truck has about had it, and since I need it more than the TV, guess which one wins?"

Erick let a long, low whistle. "Wow. You really are committed to this, aren't you?"

"Yeah, I am. Like you said—I'm starting a whole new life and I want you to be a part of it. If not on a *permanent* permanent basis yet, then at least on a temporarily permanent basis with the option to upgrade at some later date if we both decide that's what we want. So what do you say?"

"Okay," Erick said simply, and for a second, Bo just stared at him.

"That's it? Just 'okay'?"

"Well… I think there are still a few details we should… how did you put it before? Hammer out? I think we can probably discuss those over the pizza I'm going to let you buy me later. Right now, I think we should go back to talking about that semipermanent woody you've been carrying around. I don't know about you, but I think somebody should really do something about that. Soon! We wouldn't want there to be any kind of permanent damage down there, now would we?"

When Bo leaned in and kissed Erick's smile, it was the sweetest thing he'd ever tasted. "I think you're probably right."

Bo thought he heard Erick murmur, "I think *we're* right," against his lips.

But he couldn't be sure.

CHAPTER
TWENTY-THREE

ODDLY enough, once the decision was made, all of it worked out more easily than Bo could ever have dreamed.

Erick's landlord was not only willing to let him move out on short notice, he was obviously thrilled to do so. If Erick left, he reasoned, he wouldn't have to lower the rent at all and thus had essentially gotten the skylight for free. In fact, he thought he could probably charge the next tenant a little bit extra because of it.

As Erick had little left beyond his clothes, his books, and his laptop, packing up took less than an hour, and by the end of the day, he was living in Bo's apartment.

With Bo.

The rest took a little longer to organize itself, but not by much. The owner of the duplex Bo and Mac bid on snapped at the offer so quickly it gave Bo a few moments of worry. What if they had missed some major problem and that was why he was so eager to unload it? After he'd calmed down again, he remembered that, as they had "low-balled" the offer in the first place, fully intending to go higher if necessary, they could probably cover any unforeseen problems with the additional money. So in the long run, it would probably work out.

Two weeks later, he and Mac signed the papers, and Bo and Erick moved into the slightly less awful side of the duplex.

It was the first test of his and Erick's ability to live together. While Bo would have been happy just to chuck things in boxes, Erick insisted on labeling everything—what the box contained, where it should go. It drove Bo nuts. They were only going five miles across town, for Pete's sake! Just toss everything in the truck and be done with it.

However, when they arrived at the new place, the shoe was on the other foot. Bo's complete lack of interest in where everything should go drove Erick to distraction. No matter how hard he tried to elicit one, Bo had absolutely no opinion as to where to put the furniture or even which bedroom they should use. Forget about decorating!

They were only going to be here for long enough to fix up the other side of the duplex and then they would be moving again, Bo reasoned. Who cared whether the towels matched the bath mat? Both problems were easily fixed. They each worked to their strengths and kept out of the other's way. And by Fourth of July weekend, they were all settled.

Rather than begin demolition on the other half of the duplex that day, Erick insisted Bo attend Ham and Andrea's annual Fourth of July barbeque.

"The work could wait," he told him.

Family couldn't.

Even as they turned the corner onto Ham's street, Bo was still grumbling.

"You know… we really do need to get started on the kitchen," he said. "The plumbers are due in at the end of the week."

"It'll be fine," Erick soothed. "The demo isn't going to take more than two days, you said so yourself. Besides, it's not the demo or the plumber you're worried about, it's the party."

Sometimes, Bo decided, it just didn't pay to be living with a psychology major.

"I just don't want to risk ruining Andi and Ham's day with an ugly scene. If my pop is there—which he will be because he never misses a party—he's bound to cause one."

"Oh, I think Andrea can handle him," Erick said easily as they pulled up in front of Ham's house. "See? What did I tell you?"

When Bo followed where Erick was pointing, he saw a huge flag flying out in front of the house. A natural thing on the Fourth of July, he supposed.

Except… it wasn't "Old Glory" waving in the breeze.

"What the hell is that?" he asked.

"It's the flag of Switzerland," Erick said with a grin.

"Okay," Bo said, baffled. "What's it supposed to mean?"

"It means that someone around here has a sense of humor." Erick opened the passenger door and got out. "Come on. Let's get this over with so you can relax."

As Erick reached into the back to pick up the bowl of potato salad he and Bo had put together that morning, Bo got out the other side, then reached into the back of the truck and picked up the cooler full of beer he'd been requested to bring along.

As they made their way around to the backyard, they could already hear the sound of a party going on. Though the house was in the city, it did have a fairly large yard—perfect for kids—with space for the set of swings Bo was planning, a sandbox that had already been provided by Uncle Charlie and Uncle Robert, and ample room left over to host parties in.

Like the one today.

When they got around back, they saw Ham manning a huge grill that was belching out the smell of grilling steaks. Charlie and Robert were there, too, standing under a tree, talking to some of Bo's cousins. And there were several dozen more family and friends who were milling around, drinking beer and talking.

In the middle of it all—seated on a chaise lounge with her feet up like a queen surround by her minions—was Andrea, AJ held securely in the crook of one arm while she directed traffic with the other.

The two men walked up to her and Bo put down the cooler, leaned down, and kissed her cheek. "Hey, Happy Fourth."

"Happy Fourth to you too."

"How are you feeling?"

"Wonderful," she said with a serene smile. "A little sore, a lot tired, but still wonderful. How about you? How's the new place?"

"A dump," Bo said with a smile.

"Speak for yourself," Erick said taking his turn greeting Andrea by leaning down and kissing her cheek as well. "For me, it's a major step up."

"That's a sad statement," Andrea said. "Good luck with fixing it up."

"Thanks," Bo said. "We'll need it."

"One of us will, anyway," Erick said. "Me? I'm just there for moral support. Speaking of moral support, thanks for the invitation today. I know it might make things a little awkward having me here."

"Maybe a little," Andrea admitted. "But you're family now, so like it or not, you have to deal with this insanity the same as the rest of us. Ham, tell your nephew if he doesn't put down that stick right now, I'm going to come over there and beat him to death with it! God! Why do I do this to myself every year?"

"Maybe because you're crazy?" Bo offered, but he wasn't paying all that much attention. His gaze was following Erick, who had suddenly turned and walked toward the edge of the yard. Without Erick having to say a word, Bo knew it was because what Andrea had said had touched him. He had never had a real family before, and it was obvious to Bo he was having a little trouble adjusting to the fact that he had one now. Something similar had happened the first time they'd had dinner with Charlie and Robert. The four men had gotten on famously, and Bo was enjoying the new sense of closeness he had with his older brother after all these years.

Feeling a surge of affection for Erick, Bo pulled two beers out of the cooler, popped the tops, and walked over to where he was standing, facing the fence that was covered in climbing roses.

After handing him one of the beers, he reached up and swiped his thumb under Erick's eye, brushing away the tears that lay there. "You okay?" he asked quietly.

"Yeah, I'm okay," Erick said, still sounding a little husky. "Just took me by surprise, you know?"

"Yeah, I know." Bo slipped one hand around the back of Erick's neck and pulled him closer so he could kiss his forehead. "I love you."

"I love you too."

Bo rested his cheek on top of Erick's head for a moment, but when he lifted it again, he saw his father glowering at them from across the backyard. When he began stalking toward them, Bo automatically braced himself. Erick must have sensed something was wrong as he turned as well, until they were standing side by side facing the old man, who was bearing down on them like a heat-seeking missile.

"What the hell are you doing here?" his old man demanded.

"This is still my family," Bo said more calmly than he was actually feeling. "So like it or not, I'm here and I'm staying."

"I wasn't talking to you, I was talking to your little girlfriend here."

Bo opened his mouth to retort, but Erick said easily, "Actually, I'm Bo's little boyfriend, not his girlfriend. But since better men than you have made the same mistake, I'll let it go. This time. And as for why I'm here, I'm here because Andrea and Ham invited me."

"That's because they're a couple of soft touches. Some of us are a whole lot smarter than that."

"You mean some of you are more narrow-minded and bigoted than that," Bo said heatedly.

"You watch your mouth, boy."

Bo might have said something really nasty at that point. He was certainly thinking it, but it was obvious Andrea was not as tired or sore as he'd thought because suddenly she was there, holding the baby in one arm, holding the other with her hand up like a traffic cop.

"Hold it right there. Both of you!" she ordered, and reaching out, she plopped her son into his grandfather's arms.

At first Bo thought she must be crazy, giving his father the baby that way, but he was astonished at how suddenly the old man's demeanor changed. In the blink of an eye, his expression softened and he got almost a dreamy look on his face.

"Now... let's all get something straight right here and now!" Andrea went on, loud enough for the whole party to hear, and Bo realized his exchange with his father had not gone unnoticed.

Everyone, it seemed, had been watching the show.

"As far as anyone standing in this backyard right now is concerned, this place—this whole house, in fact—is neutral territory," she told them. "Everyone is welcome here, at any time, and everyone who comes here will be expected to conduct themselves in a civilized manner.

"The only exception to this rule will be AJ, because he's a baby and doesn't know any better. Everybody else, however, ought to know better, and thus, will be expected to behave like the adults they're supposed to be. This means there will be no fighting, no name-calling, and no hashing over old business, no nothing! Everyone gets along with everyone else—or at least puts up a good front when necessary and otherwise stays as far away from the other as logistically possible—or I will personally kick that person's ass from here to kingdom come! Now. Have I made myself clear?"

"Yes, ma'am," Bo said meekly but he couldn't help smiling.

Leave it to Andrea to put everybody in their place.

"Pop?" Andrea said pointedly.

"Fine," he grumbled, but there was little heat in it, and he moved off with the baby.

"How do you do that?" Bo marveled as he watched him walk away. "Nobody handles the old man the way you do."

"That's because none of you have ever taken the time to understand him."

"Understand what? That he's a bully?"

"No name-calling, Beauregard," Andrea said sternly. "And, yes, he can be a bully. But that's just because he's scared."

Bo was shocked. "Scared" wasn't exactly a word he would ever have associated with his father. "Scared of what?"

"Of losing you. The same way he lost your mother. And for the most part, Charlie, as well, although he'd never admit that."

When she said that, Bo felt the shock all the way down to his toes.

"Why else do you think he holds on to you and Ham so tightly?" she went on. "He's terrified that if he lets you go, even for a minute, you'll be gone forever."

"But that's nuts," Bo said. "Doesn't he know the tighter he holds on, the more determined we are to get away from him?"

"Probably he does," Erick put in. "On some level, anyway. But when rationality and fear go to war, guess which one usually wins?"

"Erick's right. Fear almost always overcomes good sense," Andrea said. "Especially when you're someone who has a hard time admitting any kind of weakness. All your father really wants is what's best for you. Unfortunately, he has a tendency to assume he's the only one who knows what that is. But he's not. You are. Even Ham figured that out. A long time ago."

"Then how come Ham's still busting his ass at the company?"

"Because it just so happens Ham likes working for the company. He loves what he does. The continuity of it, one generation to the next. It satisfies him. But not you. You want to make your own way. So the best thing you can do is to go out there and do it, and hopefully someday Pop'll come around.

"In the meantime, the steaks are ready. And we've got potato salad and pasta salad and corn on the cob and a mountain of watermelon to eat. Not to mention three different kinds of pie for dessert. So we'd all better get to it before Huey, Dewey, and Louie get to the table, in which case there'll be nothing left for the rest of us."

When she walked off, Erick and Bo exchanged looks.

"I'm almost afraid to ask, but… who the hell are Huey, Dewey, and Louie?" Erick asked quietly.

"My Aunt Theresa's triplets. They're sixteen. She's a Disney fan. Don't ask."

"Don't worry, I won't." Instead, he took Bo's arm and tugged him toward the picnic table. "Come on. Let's eat."

SURPRISINGLY, the rest of the afternoon went peacefully. They ate and talked and ate again, until even Bo couldn't force down another slice of pie. But he had to admit, he was enjoying himself. Due in part, he thought, to the fact that Andrea had obviously filled everyone in on his and Erick's relationship. She must have, because no one so much as raised an eyebrow when Bo forgot himself and caught a dribble of watermelon juice that had escaped down Erick's chin with his finger and a quick kiss.

After eating, they played boccie and horseshoes and even a little bit of touch football, from which Erick excused himself after witnessing the Sanford's men's definition of "touch," which appeared to be synonymous with "annihilate."

Bo even talked Erick into taking a turn holding the baby, expertly putting him in Erick's arms as if he'd been handling babies all his life. He felt an odd stirring in his heart when his Aunt Clara snapped a picture of the three of them together.

With all that going on, it was past sundown when the two men finally got home. And though it was too late to do any work, Bo couldn't resist the urge to go next door and review the plan again in his head. Maybe it would be better to start by tearing out the wall between the kitchen and dining room rather than by ripping out the cabinets. It would give them a better sense of what the place would look like when they were done.

Then again, removing the cabinets first would give them more room to maneuver. He couldn't seem to make up his mind and he was beginning to discover being the boss—the one ultimately responsible for making all the decisions—wasn't as easy as he'd thought it would be.

But he supposed all he could do was to forge ahead and hope it worked out.

Somehow.

When he got back to his and Erick's side of the house, he didn't see Erick anywhere on the first floor so he followed the sound of soft, mellow music to the second floor and into the room they had decided to use as the master bedroom.

There he found Erick lighting the last of a dozen or so candles that had been placed around the room.

Erick had taken off the T-shirt and socks he'd worn to the party and was just in his jeans, and though he knew it was ridiculous to be so turned on by a pair of naked feet, Bo felt his heart rate begin to pick up.

"What's all this?" he asked.

Erick turned toward the sound of his voice and the way the candlelight made his eyes glow had Bo's throat going tight.

"Oh… you know… I just figured since we decided to skip out on watching the fireworks tonight, it might be nice to try to make some of our own." He moved toward Bo and when he got close, he lifted his arms and put them around Bo's neck. "By making love. If you're not too tired, that is."

Bo had to swallow hard before any sound would come out. "I'm not tired. But are you sure you're ready?"

"As sure as I'm ever going to be."

"How come?" Bo shook his head. "I mean, what changed your mind?"

"I didn't change my mind," Erick corrected. "I've always wanted this. I just wasn't sure I would be able to do it, that's all."

"And now you are?"

"As much as I can be, yeah."

"How come?"

"For one thing, I took your advice. I went downtown to the rape counseling center and spoke to one of their counselors."

"You did?" Bo asked, surprised. "When?"

"While you and Mac were busy signing all the paperwork for the house. At first, I only did it to make you happy, but in the end, it turned out you were right. It did help to talk to someone who's been there and knows what it feels like. Plus, once I told him about you and me, he was able to fill me in on a little bit of what I might expect to feel this first time and gave me some pointers on how to make things easier."

"Like what?"

"Like suggesting we make love face to face so I can see that it's you and not Scott. Stuff like that."

"Okay. So what was the second thing?"

Erick shook his head. "I don't know what you mean."

"You said 'for one thing' you went to the counselor. What was the other thing?"

Erick smiled and, as always, Bo felt something move inside him. But now he knew what that something was.

It was love.

"It was seeing you hold the baby that really decided things for me."

Now it was Bo's turn to be confused. "Why would that change anything? It's not like we're gonna end up making one of our own, you know?"

Erick laughed. "I know, and believe me, I'm more grateful than I can say for the fact we can't. As much fun as it was to hold AJ, somehow I don't think either of us is ready to be a father... yet. It's just... you were so gentle with him. This big tough guy holding this tiny little baby—it was cute. Really cute. And *incredibly* sexy."

Erick reached up and kissed Bo, a long, tender kiss that went on and on until both men were feeling the heat. "It made me realize, again, that you're nothing like Scott. You're a gentleman, in the truest sense of the word. So there's no way you would ever hurt me."

"I hope I won't," Bo said sincerely. "But seeing as I've never done this before, I can't promise anything."

"Don't worry. I'll be there to talk you through it. Okay?"

"Okay."

"Good." Erick reached up to kiss him again.

IT REALLY wasn't all that different, Bo discovered.

Except he'd never wanted anyone—man or woman—the way he wanted Erick. But the steps and stages were pretty much the same. The deep, drugging kisses that made his heart feel too big for his chest, the sweeping caresses that made the blood pound in his head, and the feel of Erick's skin, so smooth and sleek against his own, was like a fever burning him alive.

When he found himself sitting back on his haunches between Erick's thighs, rolling on a condom, he realized he was no longer nervous. His whole life had been leading him to this point, and when he looked into Erick's eyes, he could see the love shining in them. When he applied some lube to ease their way, he saw the pleasure turn those sparkling eyes a deep and sultry forest green.

Even as he set the tube aside, he asked huskily, "Are you sure this is what you want?"

"Shouldn't I be asking you that question?" Erick teased. "After all, you're the virgin here, remember?"

Rather than answer, Bo slipped his arms under Erick's knees and leaned forward, pushing Erick's legs back as, with one smooth motion, he entered him. He had a moment of worry when Erick arched his back, his mouth open as if in a silent scream, but almost immediately, Erick relaxed again. Taking that as a good sign, Bo slowly pressed deeper, keeping up a firm yet gentle pressure until he was fully seated.

When Erick finally opened his eyes, they were dazed with pleasure.

And surprise.

"Wow! Where did you learn to do that?" he asked breathlessly.

Bo grinned and experimentally pulled out a bit and pushed in again, making Erick's eyelids flutter closed.

"They have this amazing new invention nowadays called the Internet."

Again, Bo pulled out and pushed back in, pleased when his actions forced a moan out of his lover's mouth. "And you would be shocked at the stuff that you can google."

When Erick reached for him, drawing him close, Bo let the hold he'd kept on his own need slip away. Gracefully, powerfully, they moved together, pleasure building upon pleasure until the peak came and they were once again satiated and calm.

"I love you," Erick said, nestled against Bo's chest.

"I love you too," Bo returned holding him close.

Those were the last words either of them spoke for a very long time.

EPILOGUE

BY 11:00 A.M. the next morning, the temperature inside the unit where Bo was working was already well into the nineties. Just that morning, the weatherman had predicted the beginning of a heat wave that was going to blanket the city for the next several days, with highs promising to hit a hundred degrees with near 100 percent humidity.

Stripped to the waist, covered in sweat and Sheetrock dust, Bo found himself swinging a sledgehammer in the half-demolished kitchen. Already, he had cut the back of his hand on a nail he'd missed when pulling down a two-by-four, found a rat's nest hiding in the back of one the cupboards, and discovered the plumbing in this place must have been installed by a demented four-year-old. And the wiring had been done by his younger yet equally demented brother.

Taking a break to guzzle water and wipe his brow, he found his mind drumming the same terrifying thought over and over again in his head: *The first mortgage payment on this dump is due in three weeks, and I have no idea where the money is going to come from.*

Not only that, but before his best friend and business partner had finally arrived—nursing a hangover and waxing poetical over a girl he'd had the pleasure of banging the night before—Bo's live-in boyfriend had stopped by to tell him he was on his own for lunch as he, Erick, was going to the library because he couldn't stand the noise anymore.

In other words, just about everything that could possibly be going wrong… was!

And it was pretty much the best day of Bo's life.

FOR the curious among us:

"I want you naked and in bed" = "Volo uidere nudos in lecto"

K.L. BELANGER has always had a love affair with words, so it just seemed natural she would grow up to use those words to paint a portrait of a love affair; of romance and passion and the struggle of the heart to overcome all the obstacles the world throws in the path of those who—by choice or design—dare to walk a different path. To choose to love, despite the obstacles, is the highest form of courage, and to give oneself without restraint, the most beautiful picture of sacrifice. To change the world, we must first choose to change ourselves.

Until It's
Time To Go

Connie Bailey

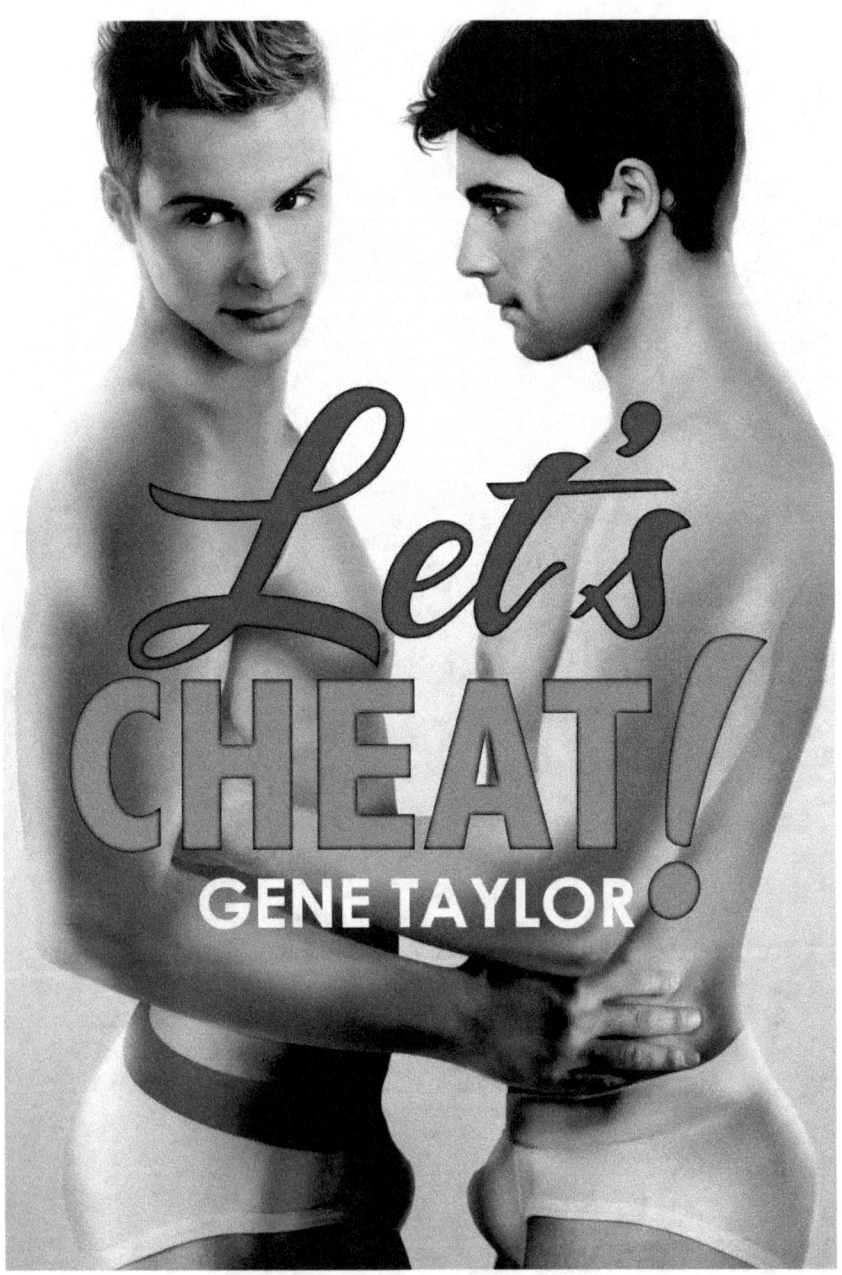

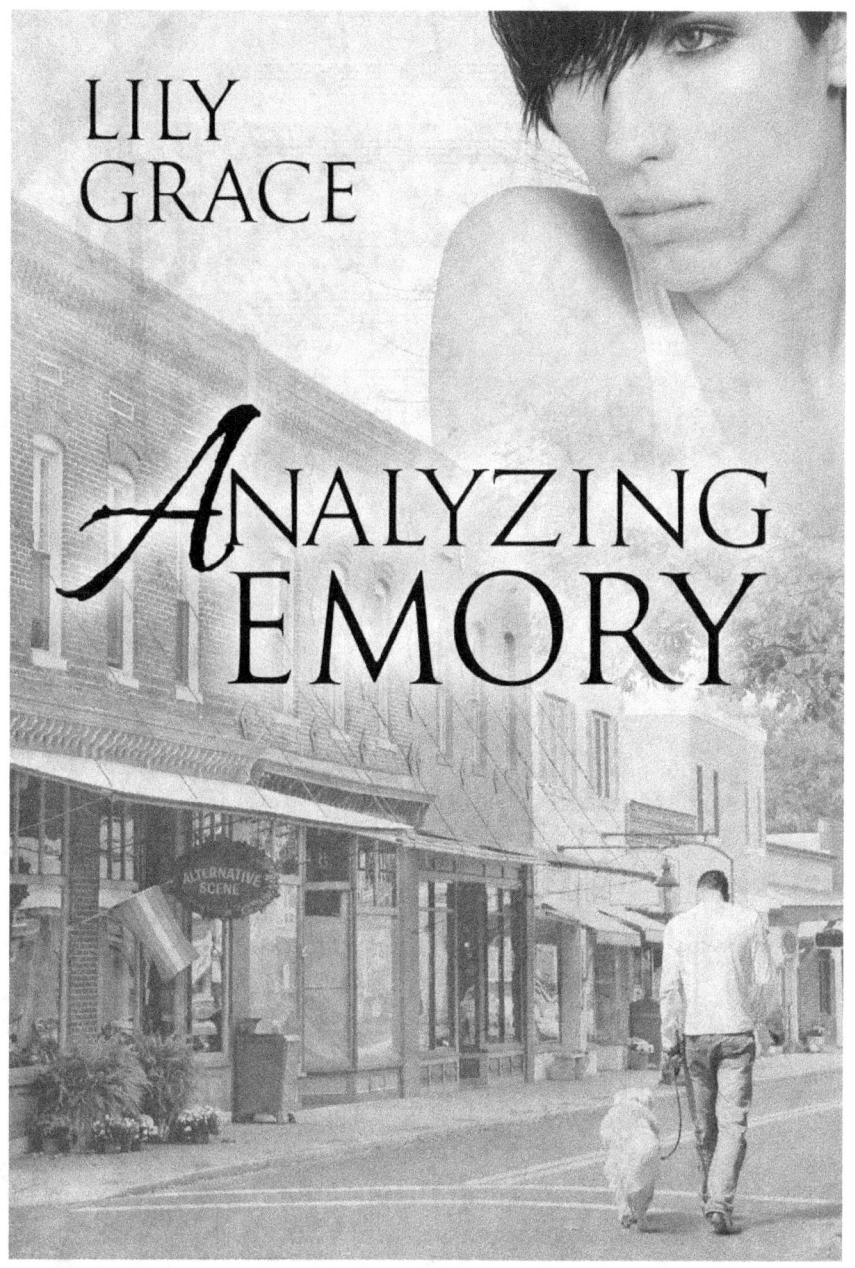

LILY
GRACE

ANALYZING
EMORY

www.ingramcontent.com/pod-product-compliance
Lightning Source LLC
Chambersburg PA
CBHW051633260626
47170CB00004B/1158